T0129866

AMERICAN BLOODLINE

THE RIGHTFUL HEIR RECLAIMS EUROPE

BOB NIENABER

AMERICAN BLOODLINE
THE RIGHTFUL HEIR RECLAIMS EUROPE

iUniverse books may be ordered through booksellers or by contacting:

iUniverse
1663 Liberty Drive
Bloomington, IN 47403
www.iuniverse.com
1-800-Authors (1-800-288-4677)

ISBN: 978-1-5320-6862-1 (sc)
ISBN: 978-1-5320-6863-8 (hc)
ISBN: 978-1-5320-6864-5 (e)

Library of Congress Control Number: 2019902273

Print information available on the last page.

iUniverse rev. date: 03/01/2019

To my wife and daughter for their zest in life, dedication
to finding happiness, and constant desire to make
the world a better place for everyone

Preface

This story was written using actual historical facts paralleled with a modern story about Charlie, who, unbeknownst to him, possess powers from his bloodline and claims to wealth beyond anyone's wildest imagination. As the historical details of Charlie's lineage and powers slowly present themselves, the young man quickly learns why these family secrets were kept secret from him to begin with. As Charlie records the newfound facts, which he converts into a storyboard of events, the circumstances that began thousands of years ago start to make more and more sense and ultimately affect many aspects of the world today.

False stories with altered facts that have been repeated throughout the centuries in books and through stories passed from generation to generation are without one major fact: the truth.

This story adds the main character who stumbles into the truth and forever changes history and the future.

Contents

Prologue

Shadows of Lineage

The night air was stale and eerie as an unusual midnight storm made its way across the city of Chicago in early June 1964. Storms in Chicago were not uncommon on warm, muggy evenings, but this one seemed different. An individual could feel an unusual energy from the storm, which lifted their spirits and exuberance but also caused them to feel anguished to the very pit of their stomach. They would be left to feel excited and sick at the same time. One could compare it to a kid with the stomach flu on Christmas morning, excited for the presents but nauseous as they were being opened.

The city seemed wide awake as a result of the lightning and strong, muggy winds, yet no one dared to step out of the building that currently separated them from this evening's elements.

It was 1964, a simpler time. No cell phones, few streetlights, and hardly any stoplights, and on this night, very few other cars were out. The car had a radio by definition, as there were knobs and speakers, but the reception, or lack thereof, was the result of good or bad luck. On this night, the radio reception suffered bad luck, as the man was not able to dial in a clear station and instead focused on the task at hand. He continued to speed aggressively to the nearest hospital, running stoplights and swerving through the sparse traffic that made its way down the boulevard. The father, Henry Benjamin—or Bud, as everyone called him—felt out of control yet comfortable in his mission to get his wife, Josephine, to the hospital where she would soon deliver their son. She was currently lying down in the back seat of the family station wagon.

Bud cared dearly for his wife, as he genuinely cared for others, but right now he was thinking only about himself and how much he did not want to have to play delivery doctor for his new son, so he sped frantically along.

Josephine, on the other hand, couldn't care less about who would deliver this child, as she was just ready for the pains of labor to be over. She was in advanced labor and felt the pains associated, but she seemed content with everything going on. She wasn't screaming or crying or gasping out for help. She was merely wanting to finish the delivery and be done with it.

Don't be mistaken. She was in pain, and it felt to her like Bud was able to find every pothole along the way, which caused her to grimace as they continued their journey together, but she was able to manage her pain like that of a professional athlete. Bud knew she was being a champ while she staved off the pain, but he didn't want to start a dialogue or turn around to see how she was doing for fear he may see or hear something that could scar him for life.

The lightning and gusts of wind didn't slow the couple down in their progress. The weather only added excitement to the ride. The brief flashes of light from bolts that descended from the sky caused a warm, almost supernatural, glow.

Although Josephine, who should have been in a considerably greater amount of pain because of her advanced situation, presented herself to her husband as being comfortable, inside her mind was a different reality altogether. She was frightened and curious at the same time. She loved her husband and had always been faithful and believed fully in the sacrament of marriage, but she also felt something was unusual about this pregnancy. Her gaze through the car's rain-glistened window into the city's night lights told a different story as she was in deep thought.

Her other children had been conceived and delivered without incident, and there was no question who the father was, as she would never stray outside of her marriage. But this pregnancy had been different from the beginning. She felt a different energy, which added humor, excitement, and relaxation to her inner person. She knew this was a result of the pregnancy, but she was confused because the baby she was carrying gave her unusual glimpses into her future, as well as details into a past life. The past life she saw was not her past life but rather the unborn baby's. She was worried, as none of this made any sense to her.

For nine months she wondered, *Is Bud the father?* She hadn't drifted at all or been with another man, but this pregnancy just felt different and gave off an indescribable energy. Could she ever see a time when it would make sense to talk with Bud about these visions or feelings? Would he believe her or just think she was nuts? She would often think to herself that she may be going a little nuts. Bud would think it was the only way she could ever explain the events and feelings she was going through with this pregnancy. She was afraid.

Instead, Josephine would keep quiet to keep the peace. She would just enjoy the feelings that this baby's presence was creating and see what life would bring her. The funniest thing that she would learn over time was that the oddities of this child were actually related to a long history of odd, magical powers that pulsed through her husband's veins. Many in Bud's lineage had the very attributes of this child. These oddities had been secretly recorded in Bud's lineage by others over the centuries and had never been disclosed to the relatives, in order to protect them from their own family secrets.

These traits generally only revealed themselves to outsiders about every fifth or sixth generation, so inconsistency generally eliminated unwanted attention, which could mean death to the family members who possessed the oddities—by burning them during the witchcraft days or by crucifixion during religious uprisings. In the end, prior to the birth of this child, Bud's family secrets had remained a secret to Josephine and Bud himself, so neither was aware any of these traits existed. Because Bud himself never possessed any of these family traits, there was never any reason to know about them. Bud had heard rumors, some vague past stories, from some of his family members when he was a kid, but nothing ever direct or earth-shattering. He thought they were all simply made-up stories. His own reality and upbringing were normal, so to him, there wasn't anything to think about related to these stories.

The lineage traits that showed up as odd to past relatives usually showed up in only one of the children every five or six generations. An infrequency such as this created a shortage of consistent data to be presented to future offspring or their immediate family members. This ultimately created a lack of successful preparation from people from the past or those around them now. People from the past who'd witnessed some of the freakiest events would report the oddities during that individual's lifetime, but if it wasn't repeated for several generations to come, then the stories would simply be forgotten over time, disappear, and not be associated with the lineage. So when new events showed themselves, even though these events were part of something connected with the past, they were thought of as just part of the current person's oddities.

From Josephine's first days of discovering she was with child, she couldn't remember a dull moment, almost as though her body and very soul were full of a happiness and energy she had never before experienced. With these delightful and invigorating feelings, she privately reviewed in her mind questions around the timing of the conception itself. After the baby was born, Josephine would be relieved that the baby looked so much like his father that it had to be Bud's, and her concerns about not remembering the conception would soon fade. However, she would never escape the feelings of intense energy or the hundreds of visions she'd had during her pregnancy. This made no sense, but she believed this child was a shared body carrying many souls. She learned to dismiss these inner thoughts as crazy imaginings of a busy mind, even though her instincts told an entirely different story that would reveal the truth in the years to come.

The storm intensified outside the car. Bud and Josephine kept the windows rolled up as the rain pounded the windows and lighting continued to light up the sky, occasionally turning night into day.

Finally, the couple reached the hospital—none too soon for Bud. He ran inside, returning only moments later with a doctor, a couple of nurses, and a gurney in tow. They gingerly raised Josephine onto the prepared gurney and quickly escorted her into the birthing room.

One of the nurses held Bud back and directed him toward the waiting room and then provided him with a cup of hot black coffee. He thought to himself and quietly giggled in relief, *Damn, they didn't even give me any cream.*

Amazed by the intensity of the storm outside contrasted with the comfort of the warm, dry waiting room and the fact that he had successfully completed his task of delivering his wife into the safe arms of the hospital staff, Bud started to relax, unwind, and regain his normal identity as a quiet and thoughtful man.

Bud thought about how only a couple of rooms away his wife was probably now writhing and screaming in pain as she delivered this child. He felt a little guilty for not being in the room with her, but he was also comforted by the thought of her being in good care with the doctors. Bud was just happy he didn't have to watch all the details of the delivery. Normally he hated coffee, especially without cream. Tonight, however, he loved his black coffee, quiet surroundings, and the lightning show outside as it started to fade away.

As the doctors worked with Josephine and the soon-to-be-delivered new son, they were in awe of how peaceful the event was going. No pain shots were needed, no emergency procedures, no anything … just *poof*, and there was the new son, Charlie, for everyone to see. The doctor and nurses cleaned the boy up and wrapped him in a little blue blanket and presented him to Josephine for the very first time. She was delighted to see him but was very much looking forward to enjoying a peaceful nap.

Out in the waiting room, Bud swirled his coffee in a counterclockwise direction to help cool off the dark liquid while he continued to stare out the window in a semiconscious state of mind. Suddenly, a soft touch on his arm broke his momentary gaze and brought his mind back to tonight's events.

The nurse said, "Would you like to see your new son? Your wife is fine and would love to give you a hug and a kiss. They are both doing fine. There were no complications, but your wife is exhausted and wants to see you before she goes to sleep."

With that, Bud followed the nurse toward Josephine and their new son, Charlie. Turning back to look over his shoulder at the intense storm one last time, he saw that the storm had completely and instantly disappeared and was replacing itself with an intense orange-and-purple glow in the sky.

Bud would meet and hold his son Charlie for the first time and would feel the power of this child's love immediately. Josephine would continue to believe the boy was Bud's son even though she always knew something was odd about the child. She loved them both, though, and over time as the boy grew, the mother and father never stopped loving the boy even when Charlie started displaying some strange behavior. When they looked at some of the child's odd appearances, such as his webbed toes or unusual stretchy skin, they would become perplexed. But as loved ones usually do, they looked past the quirks and focused on how much they loved little Charlie.

Charlie and his immediate family consisted of just his parents, one older brother, William, and one old sister, Lynn. Charlie was always a very happy kid and loved his family. Similar to Josephine, Charlie's father often wondered whether he was the boy's true father. It seemed the boy's appearance resembled Bud's, but he thought, *What a personality and crazy amounts of raw energy!* Inside, though, Charlie's father knew this boy was his flesh and blood, just with some obvious oddities. Charlie and his family would continue to strengthen their bonds in life, and Charlie would always feel their love.

From Charlie's earliest memories he'd always had a vivid understanding of who everyone truly was around him. Without talking to people or spending time with individuals, Charlie was always been able to see through the images people were trying to convey outwardly and see who they really were inside—what they were really feeling and thinking—by catching a brief glimpse of them.

Comments later in life from people who were very close friends of Charlie indicated they always knew that he was different from other people. Many friends and family members have always felt he had psychic abilities or a sort of supernatural intuition. If you asked Charlie this, he would laugh it off and tell you he had neither. If someone was close enough to him and he trusted the person, he would respond by simply explaining how a slight difference in his vision from birth made his life somewhat different from others' because it caused him to see things a little differently. People close to him would often discuss with one another that "Charlie must be downplaying just how unusual his life has been as a result of his visual differences."

When Charlie was born, he shared the same senses that all children are born with—the senses of touch, smell, hearing, taste, and sight. Charlie also experienced the sense of laughter, joy, and even pain the same as everyone else. Taking a brief look at Charlie, you would think he was just like everyone else. However, having a close relationship with Charlie would start to give a person strong clues pointing to differences, and really knowing the child and his unusual traits would simply amaze people.

Although the child had oddities, one could look past those as just "one of those things"—small deformities that people could dismiss as being caused by his mom having stood too close to the microwave oven or under an electrical line for too long. One very unique thing about this child that no one could deny was his unusual eyesight.

In the beginning, even his parents didn't perceive the difference; however, as Charlie grew older and especially once he started to talk and describe things, they knew something was quite different. Other children have the ability to see only what is right in front of them, but Charlie could see deeper. When he looked at things, he could see with depth and understanding. If he looked at a flower, he was able to see its sugars and know what its smells would be long before he put his nose up to it. If he looked at people, he could see their happiness or sorrows. He could smell their perspiration and feel old injury pains in their bodies. He could see their souls and know who they really were. If they were good people, he knew this from his first glimpse. If they were bad or evil, he could see this as well.

Charlie's sight would sometimes cause him problems due to his inexperience in life. When the young child saw things, he naturally thought everyone saw them in the same way, so he would report what he saw. But others couldn't see in this way, so they always thought Charlie was just making things up or talking nonsense.

As one would expect, his unique visual abilities presented him with some challenges growing up. His unusual abilities often caused him to be outcast as a young child. People made fun of Charlie because of his oddities and tossed him away from their groups for being weird or touched in the head. They would make fun of Charlie and his ways, and he became alienated from many of the other children.

As Charlie grew older and started to understand that he saw things that others did not, he learned to simply not say anything. He knew what he was seeing was real, but because others couldn't see the same things, there simply was no way to report events without being scrutinized unfairly. These challenges were short-lived when Charlie was young, as the family moved several times due to Bud's job. This gave Charlie the opportunity to start over with new kids. The family ultimately ended up in the small country town of Danville, California.

As he grew up, Charlie's closest friends, and there were few, came to realize that Charlie really did see things that others simply could not. He would say things like, "John really likes Susan in a romantic way." His friends would ask how he knew, and he would describe an energy attraction the couple was showing. Then, over time, they would see that what Charlie had reported long before would hold true as John and Susan would become a couple.

As Charlie would learn years later following some very thorough tests, all babies are born with his sight abilities. Seeing what he would later find out were called auras are how babies can tell good energy from bad energy or pure auras from cloudy auras. This is a protective trait for babies. If you notice, though, babies have only one defense when they're first born, and that is the ability to cry in hopes of being protected by a kind adult. If you carefully watch these children, you'll notice they watch the adults who make them nervous to the point of crying if they get too close. Babies seemingly pick out the individuals who cause them fear well before their vision develops to full clarity.

While watching babies armed with this information, people are surprised to witness babies' reactions when a discomforting individual comes into their line of vision and they start crying. The babies are simply saying through crying, "Hey, get me away from this person. He is dangerous." You'll see the mother instinctively grab the baby away from the person, and then everyone kind of just laughs it off as a baby acting up. However, the mom knows there is something wrong, and so does the baby. As a baby grows, the ability to see auras generally disappears as other defense mechanisms, such as talking, renders the aura abilities unnecessary. From that point on, a child's regular vision fully develops.

What makes Charlie's situation unique is that his ability to see auras stayed with him long after it should have been replaced by the development of his normal eyesight. Charlie's ability to see auras stayed so strong that he came to rely more on his auras than his regular eyesight when looking at things. Because the young boy's ability to see auras never disappeared, he just figured it was that way for everyone else too. It was for this reason that Charlie always felt his development was normal and didn't even start to notice until years later that there was even a difference between himself and others. It took years of noticing that people were identifying things differently than what he was seeing before he even had a hunch that something was amiss. Because the differences were so slight at first, he never said anything, was never too concerned, and just let things slide.

As Charlie became older, the differences were actually more noticeable, and concerns were prompted not from him but by others around him. Charlie noticed the tiniest differences, which would lead to significant outcomes. He would see something that no one else could and just stare and try to figure out why no one else was reacting to such an important thing.

For example, Charlie would see a loving mother hand her child to someone else to hold, which would sometimes result in the baby smiling and giggling and sometimes result in uncontrollable crying. To the unsuspecting adults, this happened for no reason. The adults would say things such as, "The baby must have gas," or a jokester in the crowd would say something like, "Oh no, the baby just learned who his daddy is." However, Charlie started understanding why the babies were crying, as he saw the same auras.

Some children are born with a great sense of smell. Some are born with a great sense of intuition. Some are born with a great sense of hearing. Others are born with a great sense of understanding because of an intense combination of all of them.

What Charlie came to understand many years later was that because others did not retain the extra visual sense, they would be interested working with someone who had retained that ability. This would prove to be an advantage to Charlie in life, but to others it would be viewed as a valuable tool or special power. And to still others, it was an unacceptable ability that should come under the control of the government or be destroyed if control could not be acquired. In short, Charlie could not have survived growing up anywhere else other than in the crazy, mixed-up world of California, where craziness and different people were the norm. But he had to play within the rules, even though he didn't know certain rules existed, or he wouldn't be allowed to play anymore … and this is where his story begins.

The Lost Tribe of Benjamin

Charlie suddenly woke up and sat up in his bed as intense screams echoed in his head. *What the hell is going on?* he wondered. His mind raced, and his nerves were ready to spring into action. He kept seeing flashes of images as they wisped across his vision and heard conversations of languages he didn't understand. *Is this real?* he thought. *Am I going insane?*

"What the ..." he quietly said to himself as he made sure he was awake. He glanced around his bedroom as though he were taking inventory of where he was. *Was I asleep or dreaming?* he wondered.

The feelings and visions Charlie had just seen were so real that he felt he had really witnessed everything in real life. Nothing was making any sense at all. His heart was racing with adrenalin, and he felt as though his jugular veins would rupture at any moment as they pulsed intensely. His sheets, pillow, and pj's were completely soaked. He wasn't scared, but he knew something was seriously wrong. He tried closing his eyes several times, hoping to blink away what he was seeing, but the visions only intensified. Then the visions started flickering with flashes of light, going from current reality to old visions of times when he wasn't yet alive. There were visions of people in ancient times, then visions of fighting someone hand-to-hand in the ocean, and then visions of peacefully looking over a large crowd from a king's perch. The images just would not disappear.

"Damn it!" he shouted, his words echoing throughout his normally sterile room. "I'm going out of my mind."

He tried to steady himself on a small end table next to his bed only to break the table as he struggled to balance. He fell back several times before finally gaining enough strength and balance to steady himself as he stomped his way to his bathroom, trying desperately to compose himself and gain an understanding as to what was happening. Finally, he was able to curl his strong fingers along the vanity edge just long enough to direct his image into the mirror's reflection. As he lifted his head and looked up, he couldn't believe what he was seeing. Was it what he was reflecting or what he was dreaming?

Brief flashes of people were projecting images back at him through the mirror. He had known many of these faces, felt these dreams and visions of these people his whole life, but he had never seen them in person. His body convulsed uncontrollably. He was scared to keep looking, yet his curiosity forced him to hold his gaze into the mirror. His young, smooth skin stretched, becoming weatherworn like an old leather sack until it started bleeding out of control in spots. Soon Charlie realized what he was seeing and experiencing was no dream but, in fact, reality. Then everything stopped.

Charlie was frozen in time as he stared seemingly for hours, but really it was only moments that he looked into the vacant mirror. All the images disappeared. He was unable to move, unable to comprehend what had just happened. He was lost in his mind and probably would have stayed that way for hours if his own pissing on himself hadn't jolted back into reality.

What the hell? he thought as he grabbed a towel off the countertop to control the eruption.

Charlie never required much from churches as he had attended many for long periods of time on and off over the years only to find most of the preachers' messages fueled with hypocrisy and self-dealing. However, Charlie was extremely spiritual and felt he had an amazingly strong relationship with God, which could only be interrupted or misinterpreted if some self-proclaimed holy man or woman started controlling the messages.

Charlie did enjoy some of the teachings he learned and really enjoyed the people he would meet at the churches. Plus, he really liked going to the holiday events because of all of the goodies and gifts that were exchanged. One of the lessons that seemed to always catch Charlie's attention was that of the twelfth Tribe of Benjamins. Whenever he heard it, his mind would travel to that part of the world, and he would see history and current events in full clarity. He always just felt this must be caused by some kind of pure inspiration. Sometimes when he had some quiet time to himself, he would pick up the Bible to specifically read about the Benjamin Tribe, as it would always give him great clarity and energy and make his soul feel full. He couldn't explain the feelings. He just knew he felt right.

It had always been taught and understood by Charlie that the twelfth tribe of Israel, known as the Benjamins, had disappeared. Charlie knew through inspiration and intuition that the truth, however, was that the twelfth tribe never disappeared. Just as people don't just disappear, they sometimes leave to find a better life for themselves or their families. If they fail to document their travels, as was often the case two thousand years ago, then it may seem as though they simply disappeared, but reality dictates the facts. For the Benjamins, leaving Jerusalem was necessary to escape the harsh conditions of being the youngest tribe, or last tribe of Jacob. Being the youngest tribe is no different than a child growing up today with older siblings and aging parents who can't provide them with the same amount of attention the earlier children received. As the younger family members, they would be picked on, disrespected, and maybe receive less love from parents too old to show their worn-out emotions.

In the case of the Benjamins, love would come not from the parents but from a God who was all-seeing, and knowing what was happening to this youngest group, God was full of timeless energy to make sure his love for this group carried on. Covenants could always be challenged but never broken from a patient God to this group. The youngest tribe had a rough, wild start and were being forced to move on and establish themselves in new lands.

Charlie always felt he understood why it was important for him to understand about the Benjamins being treated poorly, as it forced him to clearly appreciate the true relationship between God and his chosen people. A tough relationship isn't without hard work and perseverance.

In the Old Testament and the book of Samuel, God asks the Prophet Samuel to find a leader for his Chosen People. Samuel recommends God anoint King Saul, but Saul proves unworthy. As a result, God's love turned to David, who took the Ark of the Covenant, which carried the tablets bearing the Ten Commandments, to Jerusalem. As a result of God's covenant with the Benjamins in 2 Samuel 7:14, God entered into an eternal covenant with David and his line and promised divine protection of the dynasty and Jerusalem throughout time.

Charlie understood the clarity and conflict that the Old Testament created as it states all Jewish people are not equal as God's Chosen People and, as Samuel clarifies even further, that only the twelfth Tribe of Benjamin and their descendants are the Chosen People. How would that make the other eleven tribes feel? How would it make Christians feel centuries later? Charlie intuitively understood the struggles all this would create and admittedly didn't really give it a second thought until he started to receive these odd visions.

As Charlie grew up and received these visions, he started to understand how the Chosen People would change the world for the better, but first the Benjamins would need to have some serious motivation to leave familiar lands. The eleven tribes who had no covenant with God provided the Benjamins with the motivation they needed. How would anyone respond to the news that God was no longer on your team? How would they respond? They responded the way you would imagine. They humiliated the Benjamins by raping their women to impregnate them to mix the bloodlines. They placed them into bondage, killing the men and constantly treating them as poorly as could be imagined. Even though all twelve tribes were fathered by Jacob, due to the betrayal of Saul resulting in God ending his covenant with these eleven tribes, the Bible tells us the other tribes were left very angry and extremely hostile. The Benjamins were ostracized at every opportunity. The Benjamins had to escape, and escape they did.

With Charlie's visions answering the questions about the Benjamins' disappearance, he now understood what he was seeing but still had no idea why he was seeing these things. Time would give Charlie the answers he was looking for, as little to no material proof existed because a trail of trinkets was not the main proof of the Benjamins' migration.

It's important to remember that during the time of the tribe's removal, these people were poor and lived off the land. Possessions were extremely minimal. They subsisted on nuts, fruits, vegetables, goat's milk, eggs, fish, and flowers. Moving was primarily a slow process due to moving livestock and the need to find rivers and agricultural areas that would support their nomadic process.

Nomads don't carry vast possessions or any material things; they only carry their values as they move across the land. As migration continued over the next several hundred years, we find little recorded history, as the history of the Benjamins seems to simply disappear. Yet, many scholars and historians have provided ample recorded facts from values that transitioned people to the Benjamins' ways of life over their direct paths of migration. Many people would ask, "How would God do this to his Chosen People? Would God really simply allow them to disappear?" People educated in these historical facts understand that the Benjamins never disappeared at all; instead, God protected them during their multicentury travels to a more abundant future.

Charlie's visions gave him complete clarity as to the past travels of the Benjamins, along with clairvoyance into their future. A person would have to understand that God's plan may be longer than mortal man's lifetime. It could take centuries to fully execute and completely understand the history of the Benjamins. Let's face it. Changing the world would take more than a generation if change were to become meaningful and permanent.

The Benjamins would have been considered odd to the world in their day, as they favored one God and delivered and followed the Ten Commandments. They also showed respect to everyone, believing in a system of values, honesty, and equality in the treatment of women and men. They celebrated family and rewarded good deeds. So why would God simply allow these people to seemingly vanish? Maybe he didn't. In fact, as long as a solid foundation was built, man, including the Benjamins, could and would flourish throughout eternity, which would make these early years of struggle while they built the first layers of a strong foundation worthwhile for the entire future of mankind.

Not knowing their future but believing in their God made the Benjamins' plight tolerable. During the Benjamins' exodus, when the Benjamin Tribe was forced to leave their homeland, now under Babylonian rule, it was unusually warm in Judea in the year of 586 BCE. Most would leave for lands far away, while others would travel shorter distances, and some would even return to closer water banks of the area. This pattern left a spotty trail that would ensure tracings of their footprints from their travels by following their impacts, which changed the world forever where they lived into gentler lands.

As they traveled, the Jewish tribal people were sweaty, the air was still and stale from the humidity that wafted over the desert from the recent summer rains. The travelers' mouths were dry and full of dust, stirred up by the droves of people and their animals as they made their way to the waiting boats along the coast to take the tribe members to the new lands that awaited their arrival. They had hopes that these new lands and opportunities would propel them to freedom and away from oppression. Many people felt sick, and some of the elderly and very young who were unable to complete the journey died as the group forged the trail away from their homelands where they had been born and lived their whole lives until now. Family members struggled with the grief of not only losing beloved family members but also having to use their bare hands to dig into the rocky earth to bury those who had perished along their journey. The lands they were leaving were the only lands they had ever known. Families scurried along like a trail of ants in search of a meal. From an outsider's view, the perception would have falsely given the impression that things were chaotic, stressful, disheartening, or even melancholy, but everything was, in fact, very orderly.

It's important before going on to know what had led to these crossroads in the first place. Why had their people and their families turned on them? Why did they suffer so? Would they survive? Would they come to understand why they had to leave? After centuries of tolerating abuse and public humility, rapes, slavery, and murder at the hands, not of invaders, but rather their own half-brothers and half-sisters from the other eleven tribes, the Benjamins would spread a new message of love and loyalty with one God. Today, one can only imagine how they felt—lost, scared, and desperate—but they knew it was their only choice, and they had the comfort of the covenant.

Unfortunately for young Charlie, he saw the visions of these events in detail. His visions and strong feelings enabled him to feel the beatings and to be present at these rapes as an eyewitness of the past. Oftentimes,

Charlie would come out of these trances doubled over, getting sick to his stomach and then lying in shock for several hours while trying to mentally shake off the feelings and disgust.

Charlie knew there was a strong message behind what he was seeing and feeling, so he trusted his intuition to work with the information he was seeing. He knew he had to stick with it in order to get through it properly. He would no longer try to fight the visions but would instead allow them to flow through him so he could record everything.

As Charlie's visions resumed, in the distance he could hear and feel what the travelers were hearing and feeling as they were being laughed at and mocked during their departure. Drums played, people danced along the way, but no one wanted them to stay. These onlookers were family. They were cousins. They were the tormenters from the other tribes of Jacob. These people would not be happy until the Benjamin Tribe was gone, dead, and forgotten. During this time, he wondered why the Benjamins didn't fight back against the other tribes. They had been skilled at fighting and could have easily mounted a strong resistance as they had proven their warrior skills many times over history, so why back down now? Even when harassed, tormented, or outright beaten, the Benjamins would show no pain and would not fight back or cry out against their God, regardless of the tortures they endured. They possessed an inner strength that could not be measured by human experience. Could this strength have been the strength provided to them by God as they were being delivered through exile? Could a human armed only with the strength of man survive the beatings or pain of seeing their loved ones publicly desecrated, raped, tortured, or murdered for no other reason than being the Chosen People unless they were being protected by the hand of God? A difficult question in order to put this into prospective would be, "If this was happening to your child or spouse, could you simply ignore the pain and anger?"

The Benjamin Tribe was on the move. Staying back to fight the oppressors would only result in their possible destruction and torture. Why would family do this to them? Why were these other tribes not able to see God's wrath as they pushed these people, these brothers and sisters out to an almost certain demise?

Thousands of the Benjamin Tribe moved across the desert to an area where the Mediterranean Sea rolls up onto the hot, sandy shores. It is here where they would board their awaiting makeshift rafts and wooden boats that would take them in darkness to protective new lands where they could restart and rebuild their kingdom. As was written through history, these travels were very dangerous, and many would not survive. They had no long-term provisions or weapons and no real plans. All they had were each other, the power of the lineage of David, the king of the Jews, and their trust in their God anointing them as the Chosen People.

Charlie's visions witnessed the ancient travels that had been noted in many situations in the Old Testament where God expresses his covenant with the Jews through Abraham, Isaac, and Jacob. Christians also claim to be one with God due to Jesus's salvations in the New Testament. As being in the same lineage of David, Jesus was also of the same lineage of Jacob, making him one of God's Chosen People when the world would later be introduced to Christianity following Jesus's teachings.

After witnessing many of the historical people and events in his visions, Charlie often struggled with his own teachings. He often started questioning his past teachers, as there were many conflicting points. He would wonder about some of the deeper messages. Was all of this simply a result of there being one God instead of the many gods that existed years prior? As God assisted the Benjamins with their travels, protecting the members both publicly and privately, one can trace their travels by the patterns of change in the culture of the places through which they migrated. But Charlie was still quite confused, as he still wondered why he saw these visions and wondered what they had to do with him.

Charlie's visions would later become more important as researchers who track the Benjamins' movement through patterns of change during the dark historical periods when little written history was recorded could use testimony from Charlie to fill in some of the blanks. Without these patterns of changes recorded by the historians, it would be impossible to track the tribe's movement through time, as many names related to the land they occupied at the time were adopted by tribal members. As the Benjamins traveled through time, their trails offer historical evidence that would better relate the story of how the Benjamin Tribe conquered man's ideology and became the leader of the Franks, ended Roman rule, led most of western Europe as monarchs, evaded destruction by the Roman Catholics, and traveled as unknown kings, not to save the monarchies and their wealth and power but to save the lineage with whom God made the covenant. This bloodline would forever change Europe and ultimately travel to the New World and be instrumental in the creation and maintenance of the most powerful free lands ever before known to the world.

All of this historical research was very interesting, but Charlie never seemed to get answers to his primary questions: *Why am I seeing these visions?* and *What does it have to do with me?* So, in the meantime, he would witness things through his visions, share some of what he saw with the historians, and continue learning from them. He liked history, so he enjoyed learning from these historians the most.

From the start, there was consensus that the other tribes feared the Benjamins because of their covenant with God. Because the other tribes no longer had a covenant of their own, many scholars cite Satan or the lack of a god as being their leader that created this hell on earth that caused the upheaval. This period not only demonstrated intertribal warfare but also drove the world's most powerful army, the Romans, to advance against the Jews. Was this fear, anger, or simply animosity? We may never fully understand, but at the time, one fact stood clear: the Chosen People had to leave or be killed.

During Rome's powerful heyday, it is a vast record of their abuse and atrocities. This is not simply true of the Romans but can be used to describe the many world leaders who went on to abuse the minorities of their times. To blame this on one group or another would be a waste of time, as it is nothing more than class bullying. Historically, leaders of all great nations build their nations on the backs of those in lower classes or minority groups. Once the building is complete, then the lower class must be blamed for their bad behavior and need to be squashed out of existence. The problem is everyone likes to root for the underdog, so eventually, during the squashing periods of history, outside influences rise up to help and ultimately save the underdogs before they are completely wiped out.

So, during the Roman period, people were preaching to many gods, women were outcast once babies were grown, and wild sex was the focus. People were being starved in the streets and finally captured and used as entertainment for wealthier citizens in colosseums, their bodies torn apart by wild animals as onlookers cheered the death of their so-called evil fellow citizens. On and on it went.

You see, many refer to the Bible's Old Testament as being the period of the first God and the New Testament as the second God. The two books are often called the bad or angry God (old) and the good God (new). You can associate different gods with different time periods in the Bible, or you can assume it was one God who in older times was dealing with some archaic people (sacrificing their own children) and had to act severely to correct this behavior. In the New Testament, the same angry God may have been able to act more civilized toward man because man was simply acting better and didn't require such harsh treatment.

Either way, bad treatment is met with opposite results. During the Benjamin period, this twelfth tribe was treated horribly. Within the family, it can be compared historically to religious wars of today. Benjamin was Jewish. He was born Jewish, and he remained Jewish. He was different even though he was from the same family. He was the only child born in Palestine, whereas the others were all born in Mesopotamia in an area associated with Babylonia (current day Iraq). Benjamin was the last-born child of Jacob who was over one hundred years old at the time of Benjamin's birth, so no father-son teachings ever took place. Also, during Benjamin's birth, his mother, Rachel, died during the hard birth, so Benjamin had no mother-son teachings. In fact, even though the boy had been born into this world by the normal way of father and mother, he was, in fact, an orphan. Being raised without parents can lead to a child acting like a wild animal, as was the case with the young Benjamin even to the point of raping a young concubine to death as is told in the Old Testament in the book of Judges. This young, nonparent-led tribe teaches the world many lessons, as, according to Moses, God will protect the young Benjamin and his tribe purely so they can have enough time to mature and redeem their evil ways. God gave the Benjamin Tribe their first king: Saul. King Saul did great things for Israel and was a great leader who pleased God. Further reading in the Old Testament teaches us that the Benjamin lineage also created the Jewish King David. According to Deuteronomy and Psalms, David expanded the Benjamin territories because God (YHWH) will live in the land of the Benjamins.

So, from the beginning you, can see you can't simply be Jewish to be one of God's Chosen People. But you have to be a Benjamin, right? Well, not so fast. What about Jesus's covenants in the New Testament? Jesus was a Benjamin, so wouldn't it make simple sense that if by believing in Jesus, people have to be acting in their best behavior? If people believe in the Bible's teachings that humans are born in the likeness of God, then wouldn't it make sense that God protects those people who are good and follow the teachings of Jesus, a person actually tied to the covenant given to the Benjamins? Is it not obvious that God rewards only good behavior? It is not written anywhere that God rewards bad behavior. The Ten Commandments are clear, and nowhere does it outline any one religion. Jesus taught that believing in him would lead to the forgiveness for your sins and you would go to heaven.

So, when the Benjamins are finally run out of their homeland for the last time, isn't it safe to say they would have been considered the underdogs of their time? Wouldn't you feel sorry for them and want to help? When people want to help, they become more apt to listen to them and their ways.

The Benjamins may have been wild from the start, but over time, they had made changes to their actions while at the same time learning how to treat people fairly and rule lands properly. This is all evident as they migrated across northern Europe. During this period, the people of northern Europe changed in many ways as their beliefs in things like monotheism, fair treatment of women, and a focus on education was introduced.

From the time of their departure from Babylonia in 586 BCE until roughly AD 330, the Benjamins would capture many small towns and add the men to their arsenal of warriors. The women would give birth and march through the countryside with their husbands. The villagers' children were being taught by their parents to follow the new customs, as they were more civilized than the old.

These people the Benjamins captured were peaceful people, simple farmers following the rivers and wildlife as hunters and gatherers. Most were uneducated and preached of many gods. The Benjamins taught them to read and write, how to farm, how to respect each other, and how to fight as a team and for a right cause.

The tribe was so successful in conquering the small villages along the Mediterranean and through eastern Europe that they became known as the Barbarians. The Romans created this label because the Benjamins were feared, they were growing, and they were formally indoctrinating all of the people they encountered. It was never discussed by the Romans among their people that these Barbarians were actually peaceful and were simply merging villages throughout this part of the world as a means for survival. Discussions such as this in the Roman Empire could cause dissention, especially among the women who under Roman rule were often discarded as thoughtlessly as a piece of trash once their necessity of baring and raising children had passed. Under Roman rule, women had no rights, no way to complain, and no way to survive once discarded under Roman authority. So, hearing of the respect the Barbarians provided for all of their people would have caused a threat to the very Roman existence.

The Romans understood this and tried pressing on and destroying the Barbarians in their outreaches to prevent a disaster. One of these conflicts arose in AD 388 along the Aisne River. Merovech was the king of the Benjamins during this time, and the Romans, intent on destroying the Benjamins, would carry the greatest of weapons, lead the best trained army in history, and carry the knowledge that the Romans had never lost a war into their wars with the Barbarians. On the other hand, the Benjamins would carry the strength of the belief in the family who gave them their heart to push through and their belief in one God that gave them their focus and soul to push through. The Benjamins' inner strength was pure and unmatched by the Romans. From AD 388, nothing would ever be the same for the Romans, Europe, or the world as the Benjamin way of life was now in full motion, and history would forever change.

It was very easy for the Benjamin ways to be accepted throughout this migration, as their teachings were simple to follow and understand. The results enjoyed by the natives were immense, as they no longer had to roam the country for food as they learned how to manage crops. They also learned how a relationship with one God was stronger than smaller relationships with many gods. Lastly, the natives learned how making women an integral part of their tribes actually strengthened them by 100 percent.

Life for the European natives was large, and the number of tribes following the Benjamins kept growing. In fact, this group was growing so much that an enemy from Rome was starting to take notice and started to push back against this force. Rome constantly tried to stand in the path of the Benjamin Tribe's success and would threaten to fight to control them. Rome would not be an easy foe to defeat, as they were a powerful force and were described as the most powerful military ever before seen in the world. To defeat Rome, the Benjamins would need a miracle—a hand from God.

The mere thought that a god, any god, would recognize one group over another made no sense to the Romans. They thought it odd and nonsense, which led to many of the unwanted attacks against the tribal members.

The Benjamins were not deported because they were different but because God treated them differently. This single difference created the torturous effects of a constant reminder to outsiders that they could never be from the Chosen People. So, the non-Chosen People were simply doing what was right in their minds by removing the unwanted pressures that existed because of this fact. Their primary migration route carried them through modern-day Turkey and then northwest along the Aegean Sea, over to the eastern shores of the Adriatic Sea, through current Romania, past Czechia, and finally through Germany until they reached the shores of the Northern Sea. This migration lasted almost one thousand years until we see the tribal traits of this Jewish tribe being fully demonstrated by the Merovingians.

Sometimes people are so taken back by some of the sparsely recorded miracles of the time that they question their authenticity. Many scholars have debated where the Benjamin Tribe went, as there is very little written evidence supporting their migration. However, there has been historical evidence supporting changes in behavior by the people of northern Europe that match personal traits that would have existed only upon the melding of Benjamin traits.

Prior to the influx of the migration, the natives of northern Europe were dualist, believed in multiple gods, held women with very little regard, and were thought of as barbarians primarily because they had little knowledge of current civil living teachings that were advanced for the period. If you tracked areas where these natives transitioned to a monotheistic relationship with God, love and respect of women, a focus on family, and an advanced understanding how to live as a civilized population, you could map a direct line over the next several hundred years directly to northern Europe. However, historical and scientific evidence completes the unwritten records as religious activities, dietary findings,

DNA discoveries, and cultural changes recorded today in the migration lines going from today's Israel to northern Germany makes it difficult if not impossible to ignore the fact that this twelfth tribe of Jacob, the Benjamins, became the Frankish Barbarians.

There are no greater accounts historically that pinpoint their probable relocation to northern Saxony where they would eventually become known as the Merovingians, or true kingdom, of Europe, and the story continues from there.

Charlie's conclusion was simple. The Benjamins were never lost. They simply had nothing from the beginning other than God's protection, so they had to leave, which they did. They left with the clothing on their backs and the strength of God in their hearts and made a new beginning that eventually brought them and their ways initially to western Europe, where their ways and learnings would go on to change the world forever. Charlie's main question, wondering what any of this had to do with him was still unanswered. After all, he was a Christian kid living in California with no Jewish connections and limited church affiliations.

2

Meet Young Charlie

Imagine waking up one morning just to find out that everything people had learned about history was wrong, a lie, a pure distortion that if unchanged would continue to give future false results. Upon learning the truth about God himself, would a person keep his same old thoughts? Would that person still love his family in the same way? Would people make adjustments to their lives based on the new information? After learning that past knowledge and beliefs were, in fact, incorrect and that new facts proved history was incorrect and actually purposefully manipulated in order to control a whole society, how much stress would that create? Would people be angry or scared or relieved? Would this create chaos in society as people adjusted, or would it potentially restore order and calmness and confidence? If these false histories had created negative results for your family or children or even yourself, what would you do?

This was exactly what Charlie was faced with as his intense visions led him on a feverish quest of searching for the truth about historical information he had been told and taught about who he was, who his family really was, and the real history of the world around him. Charlie's views and understanding of the world were about to change forever as Charlie combined his God-given oddities with deep research and study in search of his answers.

Charlie's research of history and his family's lineage led him through many different stories about people with unusual oddities. Charlie was often left bewildered and confused by the information he uncovered. Charlie was amazed to find so much information about his own ancestry being so closely aligned with important world historical events. He was also left paralyzed as he learned many of these ancestors had features that Charlie also possessed.

Up until this time, Charlie had always thought he was the same as everyone else. Charlie's studies shattered his old knowledge with his newfound understanding that the oddities he possessed were far from normal. Article after article sighted many eyewitness testimonies from the periods of time with historical documentation from people who had witnessed his ancestors' physical and metaphysical differences.

Charlie's world now started to quickly unravel as he thought back through events when his differences had changed the outcomes. He was embarrassed, scared, and angry all at the same time. He sat shaking as events flashed through his mind. With this newfound information, how would Charlie ever face his friends again? His immediate family shared none of these oddities, so how would he face them? Should he tell them or just run away and hide in the forest?

Understanding how Charlie's differences played pivotal and important roles during his lifetime allows us to understand how if his ancestors possessed these same odd powers during their lifetimes, they would have put them smack in the middle of important events and created significant changes through history. These powers could create animosity in others, as their normal skills lacked these added abilities.

For Charlie, the process of learning through life, growing, and coming to terms with his differences, made him realize his reality being so different than other people would make life a challenge. There were no rule books for Charlie to read from his forefathers telling him that he would uncover many historical facts in life that were wrong. He was never taught how angry some people would become after the new truths were proven. Charlie would also learn, primarily through his own visual differences, how much people exaggerated or flat-out lied when talking to other people.

Charlie Benjamin was faced with this reality as a young man and would spend much of his early life trying to understand the facts versus fiction that surrounded him. As the truth started to unfold, Charlie would try to defend himself against the lies he was taught his entire life. These untruths were not taught to him by malicious or evil parents or teachers, but rather these lessons and stories had been passed down through many individuals for many centuries. It proved that if a lie is repeated often enough, it will eventually become truth. As a result, Charlie found it difficult to discuss events and stories about his ancestors with others or even most family members. If they lacked the gifts Charlie possessed and believed what they had been taught over time, then Charlie's newfound facts would challenge their core beliefs of incorrect data that sat currently and firmly ingrained.

Growing up in a white, Anglo-Saxon, suburban area as a Christian as his baptism papers stated in a small country town with a country club, café, ice cream store, drug store, bicycle shop, some parks, a creek that ran through town, and a couple of schools, Charlie had no idea about other people who existed in the world other than what he would occasionally see on television. Charlie was naïve as he would hear people talking about other religions or beliefs but never thought these basic beliefs or understandings could be much different than his own.

Charlie's abilities required his understanding as he grew. Left unchecked, Charlie could really cause embarrassment for his family and others. As an example, one day when Charlie was four or five years old, he and his mother were at the post office when their neighbor Mrs. Alcorn came in. Charlie noticed how the colors surrounding Mrs. Alcorn intensified when she spoke to the man behind the counter. He tugged on his mother's skirt and said loud enough for everyone to hear, "Mrs. Alcorn is in love with that mailman."

Mrs. Alcorn blushed angrily, and the man laughed in embarrassment. His mother gave him a stern look and said, "Hush, Charlie. That's not so." She turned to Mrs. Alcorn and said, "I'm sorry, Tilly. You know how kids are."

But Charlie couldn't let it go. "It *is* so," he said.

His mother bent down to look him in the eye and said, "That is so rude. Apologize right this minute, or you're going to get a spanking when you get home."

Charlie apologized just to keep the situation from escalating.

In the car on the way home, his mother said, "Charlie, I know you see things others can't see, but telling a lady's secrets out in public is despicable. If you do that again, I'll have your father give you a spanking."

Charlie's remarks would often cause the young boy to be looked at as odd or even a little delusional. Most of the time, others around him would simply shrug him off as just a child being goofy. His parents tried to hide their embarrassment by telling others that many children see imaginary things, so Charlie's behavior was normal and he would simply grow out of it.

As Charlie grew, though, he didn't grow out of it. In fact, his actions only became much more pronounced and descriptive, detailing only what could have been formed from an incredibly detailed imagination. The boy would impeccably describe the smells, sights, and sounds of extraordinary events and visions.

Charlie's father staved off comments from others by jokingly blaming his wife's side of the family by exclaiming, "They drank too much and were a little off." Bud really didn't like to talk about his son in these terms, but he always felt Charlie would simply grow out of things and the talk would quiet down.

Charlie's mother, on the other hand, was a little more pragmatic and truly wanted to either believe her son or get the proper mental health care for him. The boy's charisma and the powerful feeling of love he emitted, which went all the way back to when he was still in her womb, told her everyone was wrong about the young boy.

Charlie, of course, thought both of his parents were nuts, blind, or stupid for not tuning in to everything he dealt with daily. After seeing specific events unfold in front of his parents, he would often ask things like, "Didn't you see the man dressed in ancient clothing?" After all, he had just walked directly past all of them. He thought, *Did they not smell the stench of the man in dirty battle garb?* His parents would look around, trying to spot a dirty hippie or homeless guy to blame the smell on but couldn't see anyone.

The boy would oddly walk around blood he saw flowing down the sidewalk and making small puddles, but his parents would walk right through everything. He would yell out, "Mom, Dad, watch where you're walking. Can't you see all the blood you're stomping through on the sidewalk?"

He wondered if they really couldn't hear the screams of the women whose children were being killed by invaders. They could feel the wind, smell some smells, and hear some things like birds and crickets, but they could not sense all of the things Charlie experienced. Charlie, as one could imagine, was often confused.

Charlie never stopped noticing these things, but as he grew, he learned to stop reporting them as often, as it only led to anger and hateful gossip among his friends and family. He would spend hours trying to understand how he could prove these things existed but to no avail. He would ask himself how people believed in God without ever seeing him, how they had allergies and believed in invisible irritants, and how they believed in love at first sight. But, heaven forbid, he saw something others couldn't see. Then he was marked as a loon or the devil child himself. He would laugh as animals could see and smell what Charlie witnessed. They would even often become aggressive toward the unseen figment, and people wouldn't look twice, but if Charlie reacted, he was thought to be a nut or a fraud.

Another oddity that Charlie possessed that made him stand out from the other boys in town was his long, shiny hair. Charlie's long hair was a real embarrassment to Charlie's father, so Bud was going to get this situation resolved.

As a child of five years old, Charlie refused negotiations with his father to have his hair cut by Ken, the local barber. After the failed negotiation, Charlie's father said enough is enough, concluded all discussions were over, and dragged the young boy to the barber chair. Ken, being an experienced and confident barber in the small town where Charlie was growing up, had cut everyone's hair in town multiple times, each without error. He knew kids, and Charlie would be no different. Ken was not to be trifled with in these situations. He assured Charlie's father that everything would be fine and the haircut would make Charlie once again like a well-kept boy. Ken then made Charlie aware of the risks related to poor barbershop etiquette. It would be wise for Charlie to toe the line. After all, Ken owned sharp scissors and other tactical weapons, such as clippers and even nose hair trimmers. One wrong move, and Ken would have a young child believing that his life would be ended.

Charlie never quite figured how barber Ken was related to the family because he only saw Ken very occasionally when his father and brother went in for their haircuts. Yet, Ken seemed to know everything about Charlie and his family. Also, he had those damn weapons, so Charlie generally kept his feelings to himself and simply did as his father asked. This time, however, would be different, as Charlie's father had requested a crew cut for the young boy.

Charlie had been seated on his booster seat in one of barber Ken's fancy, old-fashioned leather chairs with an apron tied tightly around his little neck, while the butcher stood behind young Charlie with his sharpened tools, preparing to make him his next victim. Charlie, though, had other ideas. As soon as he heard the hum of the clippers, he scooched forward in the chair until he was far enough forward to slip over his booster seat. As he did this, Ken tried to grab Charlie and wrestle him back on to his seat, but he missed the boy fully and was only able to catch a piece of the apron, which actually assisted in Charlie's brilliant escape. Barber Ken was now holding clippers in one hand and an apron in the other, completely disabling him from further attack.

As Charlie slid down the chair, he landed on the foot pedestal, which acted as a springboard, propelling Charlie instantly through the air and landing him across the laps of the three men sitting next to Charlie's father, one who was holding a nice, hot cup of coffee. As the hot cup of java dumped on the men, they immediately let out a choir of yelps and curse words. Within seconds, the barber shop resembled that of a home that had been ransacked. Magazines, torn aprons, knocked-over chairs, coffee-stained men, and one red-faced father were all heaped together as Charlie was successful in his escape, although not well liked at this particular point in time.

Charlie had always been a good boy. Rarely had Charlie used profanity. As his father would say to others, "We never use profanity around Charlie." Charlie always thought this was not completely true, as his father often came up with words new to Charlie that he was not allowed to repeat. However, this time he knew he had heard profanity—and a lot of it all at once. Charlie quickly realized why men preferred barber Ken's place, as no mothers were ever there to tell the men how to behave. Charlie also knew the situation had now transitioned to a matter of life and death, and his every move had to be quick and deliberate. His results also had to leave permanent pain on his attackers, or this event may be attempted again. As the men all tried to capture the crazed child, they flailed their arms in haste. Within mere seconds, the normal elements that make up a simple barbershop had been destroyed, and the perpetrator had flashed through the door only to stop long enough to wave ado and was nowhere to be seen. He had completed his escape.

Charlie never truly understood what consequences his actions could have until the news of the barber shop leaked out. A few weeks after the story of the barbershop had quieted to a tolerable level and Charlie and his father could once again show their faces in town, Charlie's father told the boy he would be well served by joining a team sport. "I think we should sign you up for the swim team," he said.

"I'd like that," Charlie said. Charlie seemed to enjoy swimming and even appeared to be an exceptionally fast swimmer. Bud signed Charlie up for the town's community swim team and took him to his first swim meet.

Charlie, still with his uncut and now long hair, also seemed to enjoy the idea and was readily excited to go along with things. When they arrived at the pool, Charlie immediately ran into barber Ken's son, Clinton. Clinton was a few years older than Charlie and quite a bit taller.

Upon seeing Charlie and after hearing about the terrible mess Charlie caused at his father's barbershop, Clinton decided he would somehow get even.

Another difference Charlie had from others was his webbed toes. An adult may notice and not think his webbed toes were a big deal, but to an adolescent, they could mean disaster if children were around who were intent on seeking out those with oddities to be exploited or exposed in a way as to destroy the victim. Most of Charlie's oddities were generally able to merge quietly in the world around him, but webbed toes … This was an invitation for some of the best teasing known at the time by the other kids, and the opportunity could not be wasted.

Charlie had seen other kids' feet and knew webbed toes were different. Like other kids, he never wanted to be teased, so he never spoke of his oddity. Plus, he figured he could fix the issue by simply separating his toes by cutting the webbing skin. In fact, one evening before bedtime when he was younger, he attempted to use a kitchen knife in the bathtub and gritted his teeth in pain as he cut the webbing. As he did this, the tub filled up with so much blood that it looked like a crime scene. It burned like hell, but Charlie persisted in his task, wrapped his feet in gauze, and limped off to bed. He just assumed it would feel better in the morning.

To Charlie's delight, his feet did feel better in the morning. In fact, he felt no pain at all. But Charlie's delight was quickly dissolved as he unwrapped the bandages only to find his toes had completely healed themselves, and all of the webbing was reattached as though nothing had ever happened. *Damnit*, thought Charlie. *I'll just have to do it again.* Thankfully, he never attempted this mutilation again.

While under secret observation, Clinton watched Charlie closely. As Charlie prepared for the pool, he took off his swimmer's robe, shoes, and socks, and that is when Clinton saw Charlie's webbed toes. Clinton was amazed and immediately seized on the opportunity to destroy Charlie forever by teasing and embarrassing him. Charlie cringed when he heard Clinton yell, "Hey, look, everybody. Charlie has duck feet! His toes are webbed!"

Within moments, the entire pool seemed to be staring and laughing at poor Charlie's bare feet. People were whispering and talking aloud and direct at the same time. The scene was utter chaos, and Charlie tried to flee the scene. Clinton grabbed Charlie, and he, along with several other children, threw Charlie into the pool and began repeatedly dunking him. Each dunk lasting a little longer than the previous, giving him little time to take breaths between. Bud rushed to Charlie's aid, but the crowd was too large to get through, and they actually seemed to be enjoying the other children's hostilities toward the odd child.

Charlie was under attack, on his own, and in real fear for his life for the first time in his young life. All of a sudden, he felt something inside him shift as power came upon him, and then the half dozen kids who had been dunking him were thrown off him and from the pool. Two of the children flew about ten feet toward the edge of the pool and were knocked unconscious as they hit their heads on the concrete deck. One of the boys lay motionless on the pool deck, while the other boy was also out cold but had bounced back into the pool facedown and would soon drown if he were not tended to. A third boy flew in the other direction but simply landed in the water fifteen feet away. Charlie realized he had done this somehow without even thinking.

The crowd went momentarily silent, and then mayhem broke out as they watched Charlie's unhuman strength take shape. Mothers screamed for help for their children, and three of the remaining boys swam to once again grab Charlie. Once out of the restraints of the original group, Charlie could not be caught again. No matter how the boys tried to corner Charlie in the pool, he simply swam around them. Several times Charlie actually swam through their paths, knocking them violently out of the way due to his speed. The truly odd thing was Charlie never tried to get out of the pool like most children would have; instead, he used the pool's water to his advantage. Even after several of the injured boys' parents had hopped into the pool with real anger and revenge in their eyes, Charlie simply used the pool's water and his swimming as his defense.

Everyone watched with their jaws open as Charlie maneuvered through the pool. Not only could no one catch Charlie, but he would swim directly up to them, under them, between their legs, and even dive over them, actually teasing them to try and catch him. If they were lucky enough to get a hand on him, he would simply slip away. It was like watching someone trying to catch a fish with his bare hands. The events of this day would make much more sense to Charlie upon his learning more about his ancestry.

Finally, Bud held out the boy's towel. When Charlie reached the towel, his dad made an extra mental note about Charlie not being out of breath. In fact, Charlie wasn't even breathing hard.

During the ride home, no one spoke of the day's events. Bud appeared to be in shock, which was still somewhat the case a week later. Charlie, on the other hand, acted as though the events of the day were simply another form of tag. Other than that, the day was no different than any other day for Charlie, and he'd had fun.

In the delicate world of kid kingdoms, things aren't always simple. In Charlie's case, he had embarrassed Clinton and his friends, and revenge was necessary. During the next school day, these boys sought out Charlie with the intent to harm or humiliate him in some way. Clinton and a group of four boys cornered Charlie in school.

"It's time to pay for what you did yesterday," Clinton, the biggest of the boys, said.

Clinton then shoved Charlie up against a wall, hurting his shoulder. Charlie resisted the urge to rub his shoulder, which would surely bruise, as he looked at them.

"Hold him," Clinton said, and the others grabbed him as Clinton threw a punch at Charlie's jaw.

Everything seemed to move in slow motion for Charlie, so he simply moved his head out of the way of the punch, which Clinton drove solidly into the wall behind Charlie's head. Clinton's hand was broken in the process. As Clinton dropped to his knees in tears, another one of the boys tried to kick Charlie between the legs only to have Charlie once again see the move coming in slow motion. Charlie was able to kick the boy in the crotch first, causing him to double over as he writhed in pain. With that, the other boys released Charlie and ran off.

Aside from the recent problems with Clinton and his friends, life was generally quiet in Charlie's world—odd, but quiet. Events such as the run-in with Clinton and his father were uncommon, and due to the cloud of mystery that surrounded Charlie from people gossiping about recent events, most people tended to keep a safe distance or just become Charlie's friends.

Charlie rarely challenged the world and rarely fought against the natural flow of things. He seemed to intuitively know that going against the grain was futile and simply took too much time and energy. He simply enjoyed coexisting with everything and everyone around him. His family was completely opposite, as they seemed to enjoy arguing excessively. When this happened, which was seemingly every day, Charlie learned to sort of disappear. After things quieted down, the family would go looking for the boy. Unless they stood quietly and just listened, they would rarely find him, as he had an uncanny ability and kind of a knack of disappearing right in front of them. It was almost as though he had become invisible. Charlie would hide on top of shelves, under the back of a couch, in a room's crawlspace, or even sometimes inside the fireplace. The fireplace was actually his least favorite hiding place because of all of the ash dust and how grimy he would get, but in many ways, it was his favorite hiding place, as no one usually looked for him there. Whatever hiding place

Charlie fancied in a moment's need, one thing would always be the same: Charlie would hide with a book to read.

By the time Charlie had reached age ten, he estimated that he had read hundreds of books. He read everything and had an unending desire to read more and more. Charlie was not picky, as he would read anything; comic books, textbooks, books on math, cooking books, and etiquette books, although he didn't much see the point that Julia Child was making and saw her as too picky. He overheard his dad saying one time that *Playboy* wrote some good stories, so he found one in his dad's dresser and started to read it. This was when Charlie first learned photo books are really interesting too. After his mom caught him reading his dad's *Playboy* magazine, he also learned rolled-up magazines could be painful when used to repeatedly whack you over the head.

Out of all of the books Charlie read, he enjoyed reading adventure books and books on historical leaders the most. These books seemed to call him into them, and he read them with amazing ferocity. He read books on good and bad leaders, such as George Washington, Napoleon, Martin Luther King Jr., Julius Caesar, Adolph Hitler, Alexander the Great, Attila the Hun, and others. He focused on how they moved their people using fear, motivation, manipulation, or some combination of all three. Charlie fantasized that his leadership ways would be the best, and if the world followed his ways, the world would be happy. If Charlie couldn't read his books on a certain day, he would become depressed, despondent, angry, and completely lethargic toward anyone around him. His need to read was his passion. He devoured books the way a hungry man attacks a steak or a drunk drinks his beer. He had to read, or he would die.

Many things that he had experienced in life were intuitively different than what was being taught to him. Stories about ancestors made little or no sense to Charlie, but when challenged or questioned by Charlie, the person delivering the information would always quickly and sometimes roughly refute Charlie's opposition. So, after a while, he simply stopped asking. His position usually left him feeling lost and dejected. He would spend hours and hours in his small local library reading about everything and anything.

Charlie especially loved world history. He was fascinated by the vast differences in countries far away, but he really enjoyed learning about historical similarities he had with other people he read about. Going all the way back to teachings from the Bible, Charlie was able to relate very strongly with the ability to heal animals or people he touched by placing his hand on them and feeling their pain or seeing their weakened auras and focusing to reenergize them by focusing away the negative conditions.

These memories polluted his mind this day with the many things he saw that those closest to him never did, including his own family. He had seen people's aura presence and assumed incorrectly and innocently enough that everyone else had as well. His naiveté led to many uncomfortable situations in his life and for his parents even more. Explaining to people why their son would report seeing ill people because of their weak auras simply wasn't the norm unless you were Charlie.

As a child, he would often step away from the family to go and place his hand on a person with a weak aura as a result of age, sickness, or injury. Charlie would report that he was trying to increase the energy flow by placing his hands upon the inflicted individual's area of low energy. As the touched people would give immediate reports of feeling better, Charlie's family still suffered through countless hours of apologies as they were mortally wounded by constantly trying to explain things. The depths of the embarrassing acts by Charlie were endless. The family suffered from deep agony caused by a relentless child's attack against their dignity and understanding of what was happening.

The interesting fact about Charlie's ways was none of the people he touched were ever upset, embarrassed, or even reluctant. In fact, they appeared to enjoy Charlie's ways. Even those who thought Charlie to be odd did not shy away the way Charlie's family did; rather, they invited him to touch them, almost as though they sought Charlie out for his touch and comfort.

Although Charlie's ways caused certain agonies for his family and close family friends, they never scolded the child, as they dearly loved him and believed he would simply grow out of this phase in his life as other children grow out of playing with dolls or imaginary friends. Charlie's friends didn't seem to be bothered by his ways either, as they had grown up with Charlie and had either simply become used to it or numb to noticing it. Either way, Charlie always had plenty of friends who loved and adored him for just being himself.

Charlie's readings taught him that there were both ancient and relatively recent leaders who also possessed these abilities. Finding out that others through history had shared his unusual abilities actually gave Charlie great relief. The teachings from his family and school had never taught him these things, so self-learning from reading everything he could get his hands on at the library was wonderfully helpful for the boy.

Charlie never looked at his oddities as special powers even after learning that many of the world's greatest leaders possessed the same abilities. Instead, Charlie was merely delighted to learn that he could be helpful to others around him.

Charlie remained committed to learning correct historical facts and almost compulsively studied issues until they were resolved. This was years before the internet, which made the entire research process lengthy and somewhat tedious. Later, as computers and the internet evolved, Charlie's research became much easier and the results more explicit, as experts could be called upon and facts easily confirmed or denied. From his research results, Charlie started to realize things were simply not always true about who he really was.

One of the first contradictions Charlie uncovered was the whole story around the Benjamin Tribe in ancient Jerusalem. This really didn't bother Charlie, as this was ancient history that mattered to Jewish people halfway across the world, not to a Christian kid thousands of miles away. Charlie liked to read the Bible, though, and he would come back to the story about the Jewish Benjamin Tribe story often because it simply never had any sound conclusions in his mind.

How could a whole group of people simply vanish? Did someone kidnap or kill them? The Bible, which he referred to from time to time, said that the Benjamins were God's Chosen People. So how could God lose his favorite people? Charlie would think that was like losing a favorite pet. They don't just simply disappear; there had to be an answer. Charlie would eventually come to understand this story and how it intertwined with his family lineage, but right now, his focus went over to a tree full of his favorite fruit: pomegranates.

On this fall day when Charlie was nine years old, he was walking back from his local library in Danville when he became distracted by the full tree of special treats. He had snuck some of the fruit off the tree many times, but this day was different. The walk was always a quiet time for Charlie. The library itself was the last building on the edge of the little frontier town. Upon exiting the building, Charlie's path home always took him along quiet Sycamore Creek where he knew every twist, turn, and waterfall along the way. He knew where to slide down its banks to play with the frogs and tadpoles and where to break off a cattail to shake the plant head into the deep pools to attract goldfish, which were plentiful if you knew where to look.

As Charlie got about halfway home, he would cross the old Freitas Road bridge, hop over the Johnsons' cattle pasture fence, which had been there since the 1800s, grab a pomegranate or apple from one of Mrs. Johnson's bountiful and unbelievably tasty fruit trees, and march through her pastures as a shortcut to get home. Occasionally, a couple of cows would need to be pushed out of the way to clear the path. The cows seemed to like this common occurrence, as it gave them something to do. They were all much taller than the young boy, which they also seemed to enjoy.

Charlie, being a real boy through and through, really enjoyed old Mrs. Johnson's fruit, and she enjoyed watching him climb her trees to get at it. Whenever Charlie saw her, he was very polite; however, he had never asked permission to take the fruit, which was odd. Even more odd was the fact that if any other boys tried to go through her pastures or take her fruit, Mrs. Johnson's hired hands would run them off. She probably would have done it herself, but she was about eighty years old and always dressed in a very fine 1800s Western dress with a fringed white collar and finished off with shiny, black polished lace-up ladies' boots. Charlie would walk through the pasture, hop on the cow patties in the summer, and splash through the mud puddles in the winter. As he climbed out of the pasture over the barbed wire fence, Charlie would always look back toward the old woman's wonderful ranch house and wave to her, and she always stood looking out at the boy through her back window and returned a friendly wave back.

As Charlie walked home, he would smell the outdoor smells of the creek, trees, cows, and fruit and listen to the frogs, grass, birds, and air. As he walked, he would often ponder the questions of the lost tribe. One day while he was walking, the wind started to wisp violently as he was turning to wave to Mrs. Johnson, but the dust that had stirred up from the wind blocked his view, and he could not see her or the ranch house. The next day Charlie saw Mrs. Johnson again in the window, and they waved at each other. That evening, though, Charlie's parents commented on a newspaper story that Mrs. Johnson had passed away the day before.

Knowing he had seen the lady after her death would have freaked out most children, but Charlie never saw things this way. Instead, Charlie was always thankful for having the opportunity to say goodbye to people such as Mrs. Johnson one last time, as he always felt their warmth, kindness, and inner connection. He somehow knew they felt it too even if they never really spoke. For Charlie, Mrs. Johnson's fall passing was perfect timing for her, as coming into fall creates the opportunity for nature to create a new start by closing out the dead in preparation for new beginnings. The wind blew, and the dried leaves wafted downward to earth, dancing their last and finest dance, a sort of minuet, their last encore of a seasonal life cut short due to the arrival of a new season.

For most people, fall was not very eventful, but to Charlie, things were very beautiful. The hot, lazy days of summer were over, meaning the other kids would be ready to play his favorite game, kick the can. He knew he would miss seeing Mrs. Johnson, but a new chapter of his life would be introduced to him as his visions had shown him. He was excited about this as his mind danced though many events with answers yet to be discovered and pieced together.

In the meantime, Charlie would have an opportunity to be just like all the other kids and enjoy a normal game of kick the can ... well, kind of.

Kick the can was very similar to hide-and-seek with only a slight variation. The person who was "it" would stand next to an old can and count to one hundred with his or her eyes closed. While counting, the other children would hide, and then the person who was it had to walk around and call out the children before someone could run in and kick the can, thus clearing the kids who had been found by the kid who was it. This meant the person who was it had to surrender the close proximity of the can in order to hunt down those in hiding.

Because the game was generally played during the evenings, limitations on visibility generally created an obstacle to the person who was looking for the children who had staked out great hiding places. Charlie's abilities to see auras from those in hiding actually gave him a huge advantage, as children's high energy levels actually created such strong auras that they were never really hidden from Charlie. In fact, Charlie never understood why the children thought they were hidden at all. If one of the children was hidden behind a bush or a garbage can, it would appear to Charlie that a floodlight was behind them, casting a huge glow. This obviously gave Charlie an enormous advantage in the game. This, coupled with the fact that Charlie was one of the fastest runners in the group, simply gave Charlie an unmatched advantage that was awe-inspiring to the children playing and others who came to watch the children play.

Children are wise, though, and it didn't take long for the other children to realize that bringing their pets along evened up the playing field. A simple dog introduced at the right time could create havoc for Charlie's abilities, as it introduced new auras from those not in the game. But also, as anyone who has ever owned a dog will quickly point out, dogs are very competitive and love to play games. They just never follow the rules. So as the games would go on over the summer, the other children would bring their dogs. Soon, there were dogs running around aimlessly, throwing auras everywhere. If Charlie saw a kid, it was his job to call that kid's name as he ran to the tap the can and call the other out before anyone else could kick the can to free all of the others still in hiding. When this rush to the can happened, Charlie could be seen running from afar because of his speed, the other child running, and several dogs running and barking, as they all raced from their single magical hiding spots in the universe where they had moments ago lay motionless and silent while waiting to be discovered. They could all be thrust into immortality by the aggressive outside world that kept score of these things if they beat Charlie to the can.

The end result was generally a massive collision of forces as the children and dogs would ascend to the single spot almost instantaneously. Children and dogs would go flying, and shoes, baseball caps, retainers, and other items would be strewn about. The very sight of the point of impact could lead the untrained onlooker to believe they had stepped into the middle of a horrible tragedy where there could be no survivors. The accident scene was abrupt. The loud screams of excitement and the barking of dogs only seconds ago came smashing to an immediate end. Silence replaced the immediate world, as the children and the dogs self-examined themselves to make sure they still had unbroken body parts, feet, hands, tails, etc. Then, almost as magically as the moment started, uncontrolled laughter would erupt from the children—a laughter so pure, so mesmerizing, so simple that God himself must have been playing the game with the children. The same God, the same children, the same dogs who played with Charlie on those long, wonderful summer and fall evenings knew he was different and odd, but they knew they loved him for his differences because he was able to make kick the can amazing.

Charlie was also very competitive and would completely excel in games and sports against the other children even if they were bigger and stronger. He simply had willpower and perseverance to come out on top. It did not matter if his opponents were his friends or his family; he would go at it with full gusto and zest. He cared little or nothing about a prize. It was the simple task of obtaining the victory that mattered to Charlie.

Winning was easy to Charlie and expected every time. During competitions, Charlie didn't just want to win; he wanted his opposition to remember their defeats. He wanted them to cry, bleed, and feel defeat. He hated the other kids during the competitions, and they hated him. As soon as Charlie would step away from the competitions, his whole attitude would change, and he would immediately turn back into a lovable little boy. As Charlie grew older and after he realized he was losing friends and angering family, he realized he must not involve himself for worthless and unnecessary competitions but should instead focus on his friendships and save his competitive behavior for future situations that truly mattered.

Charlie was getting older, and things were changing all around him, making him feel odder by the day. People around him started acting differently. They took interest in the young boy and would on occasion and in an uninvited way, surround him, jabbering away and touching him. It didn't bother or scare him; rather, he felt comfortable, almost inviting to the odd behavior. People close to Charlie noticed it, and it scared them, as they couldn't figure out what could be causing the unwarranted behavior.

Charlie was shopping at the local hardware store one afternoon when others in the store tried to corner Charlie for a moment of his time. A quick glance from Charlie toward those around him would make grown men act like small children, make grown women weep openly, and make other children simply stare at him.

During one of these occasions, Charlie's father rushed to his son's side and garnered a ball cap he had found on one the store shelves on the boy's head in hopes of disguising him from the onlookers. Then his father grabbed his son by the hand and headed out the front door to their truck, unpaid ball cap in tow. People surrounded the truck, making it very difficult for them to drive away. After successfully navigating the raucous crowd, the two headed home. Silence once again filled the truck's cab as it had during the pool incident. The dead air seemed to last for hours, as neither one spoke about the incident.

As they drove home, Charlie began to feel a new energy that he'd never felt before. It was as if he were on fire. He started to perspire, and his hands tingled painfully. His mind raced through what he could only think was a dream. His stomach turned, and he thought he was going to throw up. Still, he did not talk. Lights flashed in his mind. As he looked out the truck's windows, he saw colors so vivid that he knew he must be dreaming. Images of people and animals young and old, big and small moved before his eyes. He blinked several times and then squinted very hard several more times, trying to wash away the sights. He reached for the glovebox in front of him to get a couple of tissues to wipe away the sweat. As he reached for the glovebox handle, the door opened without his touching it, an event not missed by Bud as he drove the truck.

Charlie used the tissues to wipe his brow. As he did, he looked at the side window and thought it would feel nice to get some fresh air. Suddenly, the window started to roll down as if by magic. This was too much to ignore, and Charlie's father, completely entranced by what was happening, accidentally forgot he was driving. Suddenly ... *bam*. His father had driven up on the sidewalk right in the middle of town, completely wiping out anything that stood in their path. Parking meters went flying, a wooden bench broke apart into a million little splinters, the newspaper rack in front of Valley Medlyn's Cafe was no longer recognizable, and an old man using a walker learned to run again, as he had to quickly dive out of the way.

Charlie's father would never discuss the events that led to the sidewalk disaster, but word still managed to get around.

Another skill Charlie seemed to possess was he could make many friends, and some would become best friends forever. Charlie had two of the best friends anyone could ask for. In fact, these friends were closer to him than his own family.

Stew was the funny but weird friend. He had a mixed-up family tree that resulted in his having some odd looks. The best way to describe Stew was through his rather odd appearance. He had heavy, thick black locks that folded to the right side of his head, giving him the appearance of being off-balance. Stew also had extra-large pupils, which made his eyes look tiny. These features on his bright-red face gave the appearance of a kind of wind-burned raccoon. These features, added to the fact that Stew hadn't worn pants long enough to cover his ankles since birth and wore white socks with black dress shoes, gave him quite an aloof appearance. Charlie knew the other kids thought Stew was a complete goof. He was short, about four five if he stood on his toes and had thick socks on. Stew was also about as wide as he was tall, but he was not fat, just big boned. He was born with a slightly shorter left leg, which created a permanent swagger as he walked.

Steve was the good-looking kid in the group. He had normal, light brown hair, which was barber-trimmed weekly. (Barber Ken liked this kid.) He had brown eyes, bronze skin, and a normal build. His clothes fit, and they were even always clean, somewhat abnormal for a boy hitting his teenage years. Stew and Charlie used to joke about Steve's appearance, as he was never muffed up. He was the only kid they knew who could get into a tussle at school, play in the creek when walking home, catch a game of tackle football with his friends after school, and come out perfectly clean and unruffled. His personality was always calm, not necessarily quiet, but calm.

Stew and Charlie knew Steve would grow up and get all of the girls because the girls were already crazy around him and followed him everywhere like lemmings following their leaders over the cliffs into the Artic. Steve was the normal height for a ten-year-old boy. So, from the outside, he was the real deal as far as the other kids thought. Steve and Charlie knew better, though, as they had witnessed Steve's real personality. Steve flat-out enjoyed chaos. If chaos didn't present itself on any given day, Steve would create it. Steve liked to start rumors or play harmless pranks just to ignite and meet his daily chaos quotas.

Charlie knew that he was the one with a truly unique look. His eyes were a very unusual light brown, and when the light hit him directly in the face, it gave the appearance of having no color at all. He also had a longer than normal face, small ears, sturdy chin, and, of course, the long hair. Charlie was average height for his age, but he always appeared to have a wiry frame. He dressed normal, wore matching clothes, smelled clean, had confidence, was extremely coordinated and smart, and spoke gently. People told him that young teen girls would love him. To be fair, people were always very interested in and almost magically attached to Charlie, and most followed him around. However, people seemed hesitant to get close to him. He never understood why exactly, and he really didn't care that much if they stayed away, especially the girls, as at that age he thought they were rather odd anyway.

A couple of years later Charlie and his two buddies would go on their first real international trip. The boys were fifteen, and their high school was sponsoring a trip to London and several French cities in Normandy. The trip would give Charlie and his buddies some desperately needed English class credits, so they decided to ask their parents if they could go. For some reason, they were all fine with sending them on the trip.

The boys seemed lost about the trip and somewhat clueless as to how far a distance they would travel. The group would fly from California where they lived across the globe, first stopping in England and then later skipping across the English Channel to France. The other kids on the trip displayed excitement and wonder; for many, this would be their first trip out of the country. For some, this would be their first time in an airplane. Because Charlie had traveled with his parents, he had flown in planes many times and had even been to Mexico and Canada, so the lack of thought about the trip was probably the correct setting for Charlie.

Things got interesting, however, when Charlie first realized he hadn't even thought to properly pack warm clothes for the trip. In fact, he packed very little for the trip in general. He didn't even look on a map or read up on the trip to prepare properly. This lack of readiness did not slow him down, as he clearly was not the type of person to ever find himself in need. People in many places seemed to always be drawn to taking care of the boy regardless of the conditions in which he found himself or the place where he had traveled.

When the day of the trip arrived, electricity was in the air for everyone—that is, everyone but Charlie. He wasn't upset about going or excited about the adventure. He was just going, and nothing was new.

The group flew through the afternoon and that night, finally landing at Heathrow Airport in London the next morning. The airport was completely mobbed with every kind of person one could imagine. There were people in suits, men from the Middle East wearing white dresses, and women with dark skin who had covered most of their faces with what looked to be beautiful fabric. Police walked with dogs and guns. It was a surreal experience for Charlie, but nothing could have prepared him for what was about to happen.

As Charlie walked through the airport joking around with Stew and Steve, onlookers began to stare and talk among themselves. The whispers quickly increased to rumblings and eventually became frantic. Unaware of what was being said, Charlie became quite concerned as he thought he must have spilled food on himself or his zipper was down on his trousers. None of this made sense. The group tried their best to form a circle around him to block Charlie from the onlookers, who had now started to move in closer and were trying to touch him. The crowd was too large and was becoming too aggressive for his friends and the school group to fully protect him from the touches and grabs of the crowd.

Suddenly, the crowd was pushed back, and a team of police stepped in to examine the situation, provide order, and protect the group and Charlie from whatever was taking place. The odd thing was that the police officers also seemed fixated on Charlie, yet they kept their composure and provided the necessary cover until they finally successfully escorted the group to a room away from the crowd.

Charlie was never scared during the excitement. Stew and Steve said they weren't scared either, but their constant excited babble told a different story. Charlie was a little bit interested in the crowd's reaction to seeing him, as events similar to this had taken place a couple of times recently back in the States. Charlie almost seemed to be learning now from these types of events. He didn't fully understand what was happening yet, and because the other incidents had always happened in his father's company and were never spoken of again, he just filed it as kind of a normal thing some people go through.

This time was different, though, and Charlie felt very odd. He felt very powerful, as though he were back home, and energy was filling every spare crevasse of his body. The feeling was overwhelming, and while still with the police in their room, he suddenly became nauseated.

"Charlie are you—"

Before the chaperone could finish the sentence, Charlie was throwing up. He then began to sweat profusely, became very dizzy, and started to stagger. One of the policemen tried to grab him but immediately drew back, terrified by the touch of the boy, as it felt like he had been shocked. The officer looked as though he had just seen a ghost or grabbed a snake. The policeman could be heard telling the other officers the boy felt slimy and scaly, but the main reason he jumped back was because the energy he felt was overpowering his body, and he felt like he had grabbed a thousand-volt wire. Everyone looked on as Charlie tried and finally found his composure. His friends noticed Charlie's eyes had become very pale momentarily, but slowly, their normal color returned. In fact, where the color usually was, his eyes turned almost pure white and resembled an owl's eyes or cat's eyes as the color returned.

Upon viewing, Charlie thought others would become frightened of him after witnessing this, but the opposite effect took place. The people surrounding him seemed more at ease. Some of the other children sat down in the very places they were standing and appeared to be meditating or falling asleep.

What is happening? Charlie wondered quietly.

No one spoke any further. Charlie walked toward a back window and looked outside. "What is this feeling, this place?" he whispered to himself. "Why is this happening, and why are events like this happening more frequently?" His thoughts went further, as he wondered how or what he could do to make these events stop. He figured these events were somehow caused by something he was doing. However, the next few days would quickly prove to Charlie that his actions and behavior had nothing to do with any of the events that would surround his life forever.

The next day was Saturday, so the group started on their tour early before the usual crowds would show up as they walked through the streets of London. It was a beautiful morning with a crisp blue sky and glowing sun, but a cold wind whipped through the streets. Charlie was cold but didn't say anything, as he felt stupid for not packing enough warm clothes.

The group made their way through the many shops of London and some of the many historical buildings and sights that their teachers had taught them about in preparation of their visit. They finally arrived at the day's main attraction: the Tower of London. The castle was a magnificent building situated along the Thames River with the London Bridge connecting the medieval castle with the new world of London's high-rises. When viewing the castle and the surroundings for the first time, most people responded in awe. Charlie, upon seeing the castle, immediately once again felt nauseated but managed to keep from getting sick.

The crowd once again noticed Charlie as well, but this time they refrained themselves from moving toward him, almost afraid to move in on the young boy. This was the first time he realized his anxiety was what controlled the crowd's energy and excitement. If he became nervous, the crowd would also become anxious and moved to help him sort of calm down. If he stayed calm, the onlookers would watch his every move and only react if they felt Charlie worried. Because this day was cold, Charlie was also cold and was wishing once again that he had prepared properly for this trip.

As he was thinking about a warm coat, a lady asked Charlie in her sweet English voice, "Please take this extra coat I'm carrying. It will warm ye bones."

Suddenly, several people quietly handed Charlie their coats, hats, gloves, scarves, or anything else they may have had that would help him warm up. The crowd had somehow felt what Charlie was feeling and responded. What was really interesting to see was as soon as Charlie warmed up, so did everyone around him. Once Charlie's condition was fixed, Charlie turned toward the castle's entrance. He took his turn in the long line and wished he could just walk in unnoticed. As if told to do so, the line of people waiting to get in the castle stepped to the side and ushered Charlie in without waiting.

"Thank you, thank you, thank you," was repeated continuously by Charlie as he walked past the silent crowd who watched him enter.

This was all very odd to Charlie and his group, but once inside the castle, things became even odder. The volunteers who were in charge of the castle's inner workings and upkeep stepped back and lowered their heads to the floor, never making direct eye contact with Charlie. They spoke not a word but directed Charlie and his group into the inner rooms where only the royal family would usually be permitted. Charlie felt at home. He felt like he would soon see his family walking and playing in the halls.

He thought this to be all very odd until one of the current royal family servants arrived to witness the boy firsthand. The servant immediately stepped back and knelt before the boy. Neither Charlie nor his friends knew what was happening or how to respond. As the group traveled throughout England and even in Normandy, these oddities continued. Charlie understood that some of his friends were bewildered, some were jealous, but everyone was amazed. This continued throughout the trip, and Charlie was never so happy to leave and return home once the trip was over.

The Merovingian Mistress Takes a Swim

One of the stories Charlie stumbled onto was that of Chlodio, Argotta, and Poseidon. Charlie would learn later how his unusual oddities and uniqueness were related directly to events uncovered in these historical events. However, upon reading the story, he immediately knew there was some kind of interconnection. The following presents the historical events.

Turmoil was in the air, as it seemed the gods in heaven were fighting for dominance over the world's inhabitants. For thousands of years, a majority of the world's population prayed to multiple gods and created many objects that the people would focus on while praying. The Greeks prayed to the mightiest god, Zeus, who ruled all of the lessor gods. The Romans followed suit but referred to him as Jupiter.

In addition to Zeus, the people prayed to the lessor gods for specific needs. The people prayed to Victoria before battle and to Somnus for sleep protection. Cupid was the god of love. Athena was the goddess of wisdom. Ceres was the goddess of harvest, and Juno was the goddess of marriage. These gods and goddesses, along with many others, ruled the earth from the heavens for most of world until the Jewish monotheistic movements changed man's relationship with the heavens.

This new belief in one God was no small event, and in fact, some of the most chaotic and upended historical wars took place as a direct result of this new belief.

Both beliefs, many gods and one God, can be traced back to roughly 3300 BC during the Bronze Age. The two religions clashed significantly over the years and resulted in many genocidal wars, but never had the two beliefs collided the way they would one evening in AD 414.

This evening would not end in a battle but rather a trespass. The god Poseidon, also known as Neptune by the Romans, would try to end the spread of monotheism by inseminating the rightful heir to the Jewish people by blending his seed with the Benjamin seed, forever sealing the fate of having multiple gods.

Theodemer was a Frankish king and the son of a Roman commander. As often happened in history, the assumption was that bringing together two family lines into one child or heir would unite Rome with its northern Frankish barbarian neighbors. It is also important to understand that Theodemer was looked at as a spoiled, wimpy rich kid. He led only by the pure definition that there were troops who had to follow him under threat of death for disobeying orders. The truth of the matter was his troops really didn't care for the man, and if he disappeared, no one would care. This, of course, wasn't a new occurrence when wealthy, high-ranking leaders posted their sons to take on leadership roles. Most continued to act spoiled and cowardly in the field, just as they were babied growing up. While Theodemer's father had hoped his son would show military success, the boy actually became the very split whose descendants would lead Rome to its demise.

In the early third century, war broke out, and Roman rule was being challenged by the usurper Emperor Jovinus who had been supported by the Franks until Emperor Honorius replaced him. The emperor followed Constantine's rule of running the Roman Empire from Rome and ruled with military first but without compassion, which ended any risk of true leadership and also ended the emperor's following.

While all of this was going on, Chief Chlodio, king of the Franks, was excited, as he had just been informed by his wife, Argotta, that she was with child and he would soon be a father. That evening, Argotta had little sleep, as every time she dozed off, vivid thoughts of her being attacked raced through her mind. Because she had always lived such a protected life separated under constant guard from threats, Argotta simply put the nightmares off as a result of something she must have eaten or maybe the excitement of the news of her pregnancy.

The air was warm the following morning, and because Argotta was still tired from the sleepless night, she decided to go for a swim. During breakfast, Argotta and Chlodio were surprised to learn they had both shared the unusual dreams during the night. Feeling somewhat concerned, but also feeling there was no real risk because she was always escorted with a protective onlooker, they both agreed that a swim would be fine and would actually do her good.

Argotta had unusual beauty; her skin was a deep bronze, her eyes were a mix of blue-green and deep aqua, and her hair had a natural flow of blonde and light brown. Her visible beauty stunned onlookers, and men would instantly fall in love with the goddess.

Argotta's outside beauty could only be matched by who she was inside. She was full of love. So much love, in fact, that there was no choice other than to share the excess love that poured out of her soul like water flows out of a natural spring. Her touches would magically heal the sick. Her look would transform angry people to happy people, and her smile would brighten children's faces. If you were lucky enough to hear her giggle, you would feel her angelic presence throughout your core. She was clearly sent from the heavens above. Now with a child in her womb, she would soon share her love as never before, and the world would have more love to shed light and melt earth's shadows and darkness.

Being the chieftain's queen gave Argotta certain protection from the public's wandering eyes during periods such as bathing. Argotta could have sold views of her beauty, but she was private, and as queen, her privacy was further protected. Only those closest to her would ever see her naked beauty or touch her voluptuous body with its perfect contours and seemingly sculptured lines. Her breasts were firm and perky. Her buttocks molded her long legs perfectly with her back. Her skin was soft yet firm, and the features of her face were soft but sharp, which give her a look of care and control.

Argotta was always fond of the ocean, as her family memories always took her back to playing at the water's edge with her father and mother as a child. Even when obligations kept her away from the water, she would often let her mind drift to the thoughts, smells, and sounds that her mind's eye would watch.

Argotta, along with her escorts, made their way to her private beach. Without hesitation, the queen disrobed and waded off into the calm sea for a blissful swim. She floated on her back, pointing her closed eyes toward the warm sun. She was calm, and everything around her was so peaceful that she actually started to doze off while she swam quietly. Argotta's peaceful meditations were broken as she heard her name being called by her husband to come ashore and join him for lunch. She happily accepted.

The meal was quiet as the two spoke little, both still occupied by the visions of the dreams from the night before. Following lunch, the two drifted off into a much-needed slumber. Argotta woke as she heard her husband stirring about. She was surprised how late in the day the two had slept, evident by the position of the sun that now lay barely off the horizon. Chlodio had business to attend to, so he bid his wife farewell and promised he would return shortly following his commitments.

Feeling better now than she had earlier in the morning, Argotta would use the evening as the sun sat to take a relaxing swim along the mouth of the Merwede River where the river flowed out to the sea. Argotta was still being accompanied by her maidservants to ensure her privacy and safety. Argotta would relax during this evening's swim and enjoy her privacy as she was still feeling tired from the night before and from all of the congratulatory compliments she received after announcing the news of her conception.

As Argotta started to disrobe in preparation for her swim, something caught her eye just off shore. When she glanced up to see what she thought was a rock poking out of the water, it was gone. Argotta thought her eyes were simply playing tricks on her. She finished undressing and slowly walked into the gentle tides until the only remaining view of the fair beauty was her head as the ocean's body engulfed her. Almost as soon as she was out of helpful reach, the queen felt an uneasiness as the calm waters surrounding her started to feel turbulent and very cold. As she continued wading in the water, something scuffed the backs of her legs. A few feet away from her she saw the outline of what looked like a creature's scaly back gliding just under the surface. A couple of seconds later she thought she felt the skin of a serpent glide along her outline and touch her body. Concern turned to fright as she felt the definite feelings of a serpent glide between her legs, winding around her private regions and actually lightly penetrating her softly as it seemed to inspect her. Shockingly, her fears left her, and she began to become aroused.

As the serpent figure continued to circle her, she felt the skin and great muscles of what she thought was also of a man. The serpent was a Quinotaur, half man and half sea creature. She had heard of this serpent but thought of it as only being mystical because neither she nor anyone else she knew had ever seen one. The serpent-man's strong arms slowly had control of the maiden as he rose from the water's depths and firmly held the princess from behind. The serpent's strong hands caressed her warm body, her supple breasts, her soft skin, and her smooth hair. As he held her in his grasp, his serpentine body seemed to still be circling in the waters below. He did not speak, as there was no need. The maiden was transposed and fixated on his touch. There was no fear, only excitement and anticipation of what was about to happen to her—what she wanted to happen to her.

Suddenly, almost violently, the serpent's underwater body thrust its full man body into the maiden in rapid and long succession. The serpent seemed to know how to fill the maiden's sexual needs to the exact point where his penetration met her point of climax and where pleasure met pain. She screamed in pain and ecstasy over and over. The maidservants watched helplessly from the shore as the maiden continued to cry out in breathless succession.

The servants could clearly see what was happening, but their minds could not believe it. Too far away to help, they could only watch helplessly. As suddenly as the event had started, it was over. The serpent had uncoiled himself and his manhood out of the queen's womb. His task had been accomplished, as his seed had now supplanted itself in the baby alongside of the father's seed.

The queen and her maidservants presented this story to Chlodio, as they were sworn to honesty. They feared they would all be killed for spreading untruths about the queen, but the king had had the same visions the night before so he held back any retaliation until the child could be born and inspected for serpent-like characters.

The year was 415, and Merovech, the son of Chlodio and Argotta, was born in Tournai (present-day Belgium) of both human and serpent character (Neptune demigod beast). The child possessed unusual characteristics, which were both visual and unknown at birth. His visual characteristics included webbed feet and very unusual elastic skin that felt cool to the touch and would stretch under his arms, thighs, and neck, giving him the ability to elongate his body to supernatural proportions.

Chlodio and Argotta accepted the child with the natural warmth and love of a father and mother, yet they knew this child possessed gifts from the serpent god. As Merovech grew, it would become obvious to others that he had magical powers of sight and charisma, which would later enable him to unite the Salian tribes into one Frankish Empire. His name came from the Dutch River Merwede, present-day part of the Rhine-Meuse-Scheldt delta, a main subsidiary of the Rhine, and he would become known as the founder of the Merovingian Dynasty. His descendants would eventually become the Frankish rulers who migrated through Germany, France, and Belgium.

As a result of Merovech's oddities and their usefulness as a leader of his people and a leader in battle, he would be elevated to hero status and was adopted by his followers as their king.

Was Merovech a sacred king with God-given powers from the serpent Poseidon combined with the Benjamin lineage of Jesus, David, Jacob, Isaac, and Abraham and backed by God's covenant? Would a common man have been able to rule these tribes and unite them together in order to beat the greatest military the world had ever seen using divine powers from God's hand of involvement? Were Merovech's powers similar to Jesus's when Jesus, the son of God used his father's divine intervention to change the world a few centuries before?

Merovech represented power as his inner soul fought the internal battle of monotheism verses polytheism. In the end, he would learn to focus all of his energy toward the monotheistic God who, in-turn, rewarded Merovech with unencumbered strength, intelligence, and charisma.

If Merovech had been merely mortal, would he have been able to face battles with the added conviction and confidence necessary to lead common peasants to victories beyond comprehension? Imagine this question in today's world, and compare it with a third-world army attacking one of the superpowers with smaller unskilled warriors, subpar weapons, and no established formal plan of attack and coming out victorious. This takes on a vision resembling the fight David had against Goliath or Jesus verses the religious power houses of his time.

Following Merovech's death, the Merovingian Dynasty, anointed by God's hand and led by Merovech's son Childeric I, would continue to see great victories over the Saxon, Visigoth, and the Alemanni armies, who were extremely skilled and formally led. This established the Merovingian kingdom's territories. As impressive as Childeric's battle victories were, his son Clovis I would be recognized as the greatest ever of the Merovingian kings. Under his rein, Clovis I would go on to lead his barbarian armies to dominate all battles, uniting the majority of tribes throughout Gaul and destroying the Alemanni and the Visigoth kingdom of Toulouse. Clovis I's greatest victory came in 486 when he defeated the Roman Army led by Syagrius, the Roman ruler of modern-day France. This battle forever ended Roman rule over Europe and ended the world superpower of its day. Several years later and following this victory, Clovis I also took on his Christian wife, Clotilda, and adopted her Christian religious ways after defeating the Alemanni in 496 at the close of the Battle of Tolbiac.

After Clovis I died, the Merovingian Dynasty was split and managed simultaneously by his four sons, each ruling their own partitioned states individually but ruling the kingdom as one total power.

Unfortunately for Poseidon, his plan was unsuccessful, as the monotheistic God won out due to the coveted relationship with the Benjamin blood that ran through Merovich's body. The one true God was pleased, giving Merovich both the lineage of the one God and all of Poseidon's unusual traits, which would continue throughout the Benjamins' future lineage, giving true dominance throughout the history of the world. Traces of Poseidon can be found in certain members of the Benjamin line even today, as their inheritance leaves some with webbed toes, elastic skin, the ability to see auras, and the ability to understand other people's deep thoughts simply by a glance.

4

An Evening He Would Never Forget

There was rarely a dull moment in Charlie's life, as he always had a friend or more with him. It was odd that Charlie's friends were often animals; however, this wasn't the oddest thing about his friends. That award went to the fact that all animals, especially animals that lived around water, would always find and play—truly *play*—with Charlie.

This kid simply loved playing in the water, in the mud, and with everything around water. Unlike most people, he wasn't afraid of spiders or snakes or anything.

Charlie constantly heard his mom and dad yelling, "Get those dirty clothes off and get yourself cleaned up," or, "Get out of here with all of that stinky mud."

When Charlie was a young boy, he would come home for dinner after playing in the local creek talking about the events with his family. He would say things like, "I played with a bobcat today with a stick." His family would look at him as though bugs were climbing out of his nose. The events Charlie discussed were so unusual that his parents simply ignored them, as they felt the stories were simply those of a child's active imagination and again hoped it was a phase Charlie would grow out of, which, again, he never did.

Many times when Charlie would return home a muddy mess after playing in the creek, his mother would make him stand out back in the yard while she hosed him down before letting him in the house. She was often irritated and embarrassed by the boy's disregard for cleanliness, but she envied his ability to ignore other people and simply enjoy life for all its worth. He was a good-natured boy and would giggle as his mom hosed him down, which, in turn, would make her laugh along with him.

As the boy grew older, an occasional story would surface from Charlie's parents' friends talking about seeing the boy playing in the water with wild animals. One such story arose with Charlie racing a river otter and a beaver upstream in the murky creek with a marmot and raccoon running along the stream's edges trying to outrace the child.

At one such event, Charlie's friend Steve yelled out, "Go!" And the two would come plowing toward him. Water and mud were flying everywhere until they reached the finish line where Steve stood to determine the winner. On another occasion, Charlie was spied by locals as he was playing tag along one of the deep pools in the creek with a red fox and what looked to be a muskrat. No one could figure out why these animals acted as pets around Charlie. If they occasionally called out to Charlie, he would happily wave back as if he simply didn't know better. If asked about the topic, he would have responded from the innocent assumption that everyone played with wild animals.

Like many young boys, Charlie would join the scouting ranks of the Indian Guides, Cub Scout, and Webelos. During campouts, Charlie seemed to attract all kinds of wilderness critters. The other kids loved seeing and playing with the animals, but their parents … not so much.

Unfortunately for Charlie, he was barred from joining Boy Scouts. Not due to any misbehavior but rather because the other boys' parents were scared to death of the animals that would seek out the boy anytime he went camping. When they had an opportunity to be around Charlie without their parents' knowledge, the other boys found these animals to be both highly interesting and highly entertaining and learned to enjoy the events, giving Charlie his own scouting experiences.

There were even stories of cougars, bears, and badgers entering the camps and playing with the children, especially Charlie. On one such camping trip to Colorado, a small herd of bighorn sheep entered the camp and allowed the young boys to ride them along some very steep canyon passes, almost killing the scout masters from heart attacks as they saw the events unfold upon returning with firewood. The boys could be herd hooting and hollering like cowboys. "Yip, yahoo, hooray!"

The adults were yelling out to the boys: "Get away." "You'll be killed." "Watch out." "Run."

The excitement was both nerve-racking and exhilarating. No one had ever seen anything like this before or since.

Charlie also seemed to have nature track him down in the ocean, like the time Charlie's parents took him and a couple of the neighborhood kids to play on the beach in Santa Cruz. Most animals enjoyed Charlie's company, but not all of them. The day started off seemingly normal with the kids playing on a couple of the boardwalk rides and overeating their limits of cotton candy and other assorted wonderful-tasting junk food. The boys decided to start splashing along the waves on the ocean's edge on the beach and eventually made their way out to play in the deeper surf.

As Charlie played in the water with his friends, several seals started popping their heads up out of the water around the boys. The odd event attracted onlookers from the pier above the boys as well as people on the beach.

"Look, those seals are playing with those kids," shouted one onlooker.

Charlie's two buddies became uncomfortable with the seals and made their way back to the beach to the safety of their beach towels. By the time Charlie's parents realized the spectacle was actually their son, a large crowd had already gathered. People were laughing and cheering Charlie and the seals on as they were obviously once again playing Charlie's favorite game of water tag.

Charlie's father yelled out to the boy, "Charlie, come out of the water."

Charlie was having too much fun, though, and never heard Bud's call. Over the years, Charlie's parents had heard about such escapades involving Charlie playing with wild animals but had never seen one of these escapades themselves. Sure enough, there was Charlie diving down, flipping back up through the water's edge, and tapping on the seals as he came flipping out of the water. The seals were having a blast as well, as they swam briskly chasing the boy. Charlie's parents were stunned and speechless as they watched the events from the water's edge.

Suddenly, as fast as the events unfolded, everything suddenly changed as the crowd watching from the pier above started yelling out, "Shark! Kid, get out of the water. There's a shark. Get out!"

Women were covering their children's eyes or their own if they were by themselves. Men were trying to wave the boy back to the beach but to no avail. Everyone was panicking except for Charlie, who was now too far away from shore for anyone's protection and would obviously soon meet his final fate as the shark drew within striking range. Charlie was surely done for, and neither the crowd nor his parents could help.

As the shark zeroed in, the seals quickly recognized the danger and scattered in many directions, leaving Charlie to face off with one of the largest great white sharks ever seen in the area. Upon finally seeing the danger that approached the boy, something unbelievable happened. The boy swam directly at the shark's opening jaw only to slap the shark's nose as he abruptly swam past him. The shark lunged at the boy as he passed by, missing him completely. The shark quickly turned to give chase, but every time the shark appeared to close in and take a bite, the boy quickly turned to safety. The boy was swimming back and forth under the pier's pylons, and the crowd was running back and forth above, trying to see if he made it out okay. Each time he reappeared, everyone cheered with excitement.

As excited as the crowd was, they still felt he had no chance for survival, as he was swimming the wrong way and was heading farther out to sea and farther away from safety. He was swimming so well that the shark finally gave up and zeroed in on one of Charlie's playmate seals. Realizing this, Charlie set out to once again distract the shark by swimming up behind it and smacking it playfully on the tail fin. The crowd went silent with the exception of one of the old-timers who stated," What in the hell!?"

Upon being smacked by Charlie, the shark seemed so shocked by the events that it gave up on the seal chase and immediately returned to safer waters in the deep sea.

Once Charlie returned to the beach, he was greeted with a hero's welcome and roaring applause. People, including Bud, stood frozen in their places as Charlie walked toward his dad's awaiting towel. Charlie wrapped himself with the towel to dry off and turned and looked out onto the shoreline. The seals had regathered, and with their heads slightly poking above the waterline, they all looked at Charlie. The boy waved, and the seals submerged and were gone.

Other water events always seemed to present themselves to Charlie. One such event happened when Charlie was in his early twenties during a week when a crazy storm passed through near his home. The front brought more bad weather than had been expected and stayed around longer than was predicted.

The rain had been pounding down for several days, leaving river beds above record crest lines. Most of the roads in the area were literally underwater and not passable by automobiles. Even though drivers were being told to stay at home until safer conditions arrived, many people didn't heed the warnings and ventured outside. Charlie had just turned twenty years old and had to grab a couple of supplies from the local grocery store before a date one evening. His girlfriend of two months had promised him "an evening he wouldn't forget." Man, was this an understatement. He was staying at his parents' house, and they would be out for the evening, leaving him in charge of the house and the dinner he would have to make for his girlfriend.

Charlie's culinary skills included cooking an egg and some toast for breakfast and boiling water for mac and cheese. If he really wanted to impress someone, he may even step out of his shadow and cook a burger. Everything else had to be created by someone, preferably anyone else, or anyone eating may be accidentally poisoned by his results.

Case in point: Charlie's last girlfriend had dumped him after becoming violently sick due to getting ptomaine poisoning caused by eating undercooked chicken Charlie had tried to cook with the hope of creating chicken cordon bleu. Charlie, being of French descent, felt it was in his genes to create such a meal. In his defense, his girlfriend should have known there was risk associated with Charlie's chicken preparation when he asked her how she liked her chicken cooked; rare, medium, or well-done. At any rate, her response had no meaning because however Charlie prepared it was how it was served. After receiving a barely warmed chicken, his girlfriend Tammi ate the meal. Later that evening, Tammi concluded that living her life in a bathroom hunched facedown over the toilet was no longer worth the relationship and abruptly informed Charlie of this conclusion.

So today, being promised "an evening he would not forget" with Tammi, Charlie felt he needed to step up his game … and not serve chicken. Being a crafty young man, Charlie would go to the best deli in town, or at least the closest, and buy a premade meal so that he would simply have to heat it up. At the deli, he found the perfect meal. For an appetizer, he purchased nacho chips, cheese sauce, and hot sauce. He thought about it for a while as he noodled what would taste perfect as the main course and go with the nachos? After considerable thought, he came up with the idea of serving a shrimp and crab salad. After all, seafood goes great with nachos, right? Because he was on a budget, for desert he would purchase a large can of fruit cocktail. He would, of course, pour the fruit into a lovely bowl for proper presentation. To top off dinner, and because Charlie wasn't old enough to purchase liquor, Charlie would serve up a bottle of twenty-five-year-old cabernet sauvignon that he would "borrow" from his dad's collection while Bud and Josephine were away. After all, this would be an evening he would never forget, so everything had to be perfect.

Upon Charlie's return home, he noticed how high the creek had swelled due to the heavy rain behind his house in the thirty minutes he had been at the store. Because he was so focused on preparing the meal, he hadn't noticed the car in the road that had stalled along the creek. Charlie took his groceries inside and started the preparations.

About thirty minutes into the cooking, Tammi arrived expecting the aroma of something other than what really hit her when Charlie opened the door. It was a confusion of burnt cheese sauce mixed with strong fish smells from the shrimp and crab that Charlie had dropped into the deep fryer and the can of fruit frying in a sauce pan. Noticing Tammi's instant concern, Charlie decided opening the wine was his only recourse. As he placed the bottle into the automatic wine corker, he hit the wrong direction. The cork was instantly pressure pushed into the bottle. Upon seeing this, Charlie reacted by trying to remove the bottle at the same time, which immediately broke and shot wine throughout the kitchen and all over Tammi's beautiful white dress.

"Charlie!" Tammi shouted. "Look what you've done to me. My God, how could you be so dumb?"

Tammi stomped off down the hall to the washroom to clean up. At the same time, while Tammi continued screaming at Charlie from the back hall, he started hearing screams coming from the swollen creek.

"Help me please … Please help. Help."

Hearing this, Charlie flew out the back door to investigate, leaving his wine-covered date in the house along with the burning dinner.

Unfortunately, Tammi never heard the screams and was left with the belief that Charlie, under duress from embarrassment, had left so he wouldn't have to deal with her or the mess. Tammi called out to Charlie several times.

"Charlie? … Charlie? … Where the hell did he go?" After waiting for a period of time and believing he wasn't coming home, Tammi, who was completely irritated, wrote a nasty note and left.

Once at the creek, Charlie evaluated the situation. The stalled car along the creek was now almost completely submerged with its occupant struggling to keep her head above the water.

"Hang in there, lady. Help is coming" Charlie exclaimed even though he really didn't have a plan.

People watching the events unfold were unable to provide any help, as the water was too deep and the current was simply too strong. Charlie's heart raced, but he was very comfortable with the water. He actually preferred his ability to swim over walking, so he jumped in the water with little hesitation. Charlie, who was used to seeing underwater, opened his eyes and quickly realized he couldn't see a thing due to all of the mud in the water. He quickly popped his head out above the water so he could see and yelled out, "I'm coming, lady. Hang in there!" He fought the current and actually swam upstream to reach the car's door. Upon reaching the car, he opened the door, freed the young lady driver, and held her with one arm as he once again swam up current to the nearest land protrusion.

"Thank you," the woman said through her coughing. "You saved my life. You were amazing."

Almost immediately upon removing the young lady, the river had capsized the car and took it to its depths, completely removing it from sight.

Charlie had saved her from certain death. The onlookers were stunned and speechless. The young lady, after realizing the amazing events, held Charlie and gave him the softest kiss he had ever experienced.

While Charlie was talking with the girl, the local news showed up and started asking the onlookers a bunch of questions.

"Hello, I'm David Duncan with Channel 2 Eyewitness News. Can anyone tell me what happened here?"

No one was able to talk.

David continued asking more questions. "Are there any people in the car?"

Finally, one of the witnesses answered, "No the man over there saved that woman. Somehow, he swam up the river and pulled her out of the car to safety."

How had Charlie done this? By all accounts from the onlookers, as was reported to the local press, Charlie had possessed superhuman abilities in this rescue.

Another witness said, "He looked like a salmon as he wiggled back and forth and flew out of the water as he went over logs and debris in the river to get to the lady. There's no way to explain what I saw."

Yet another bystander noted, "His feet never kicked, and his hands never paddle as most people would ordinarily. Instead, his arms seemed to work together, as did his legs, in very controlled unison—much like the fins of a whale or a dolphin." The man then sat down in a puddle, kind of mumbling along incoherently, appearing to be in shock.

By the time David and his news team were able to slip away from the crowd to interview Charlie and the girl, they were gone.

The girl Charlie had rescued was shivering, part from fear and part from the cold water, so Charlie took her to his house to help her dry off.

"What's your name?" asked Charlie.

"Kelly. What's yours?" she asked sheepishly.

"I'm Charlie ... Here's a towel. You can dry yourself off. If you want, I can toss your clothes into the washer. Do you want me to call anyone for you?"

"No, I'm fine," responded Kelly as she stepped into the next room to remove her clothes and wrap herself in the dry, warm towel.

There was an instant connection between Charlie and Kelly, and she was in no hurry to leave.

"Do you have company?" Kelly asked, noticing all of the food and the extra place setting.

"Oh," yelped Charlie as he remembered he had left Tammi to go help Kelly. He yelled out Tammi's name several times as he looked for her before seeing the note she had left behind.

Noting that Charlie's calls went unanswered as she stepped back into the room with him, Kelly grabbed Charlie and chanced a long, slow kiss on his lips. As she kissed him, her towel slid off her body, revealing to Charlie the lushest body and tenderest spots he had ever seen.

The house looked like a disaster area. His intended meal was everywhere, and his intended guest was nowhere in sight. Food sat burning on the stove. However, the two noticed none of this as they head off to Charlie's bedroom where they engaged in an immediate and passionate love affair.

When the two came back to their senses, they realized they had to stop the cooking and clean up the kitchen.

After loaning the young lady some of his clothes while he dried hers, Kelly looked around the kitchen and immediately decided Charlie had no idea how to cook. Kelly took this opportunity to fix Charlie a real meal fit for a king; after all, he was her hero. Looking around at the other food that resided in Charlie's cabinets and refrigerator, she summoned up a wonderful meal consisting of smoked salmon and a nice salad.

After eating dinner and enjoying a bottle of wine, Charlie and Kelly found they were natural friends and shared stories and laughs. Charlie, still remembering the kiss and the lovemaking that he received earlier, was hopeful he would receive more. He would not be disappointed, as the wine proved capable of unwinding any inhibitions, and the two were soon once again in the passionate holdings of one another beyond boundaries.

After they had finished their lovemaking, Kelly took a shower. While she showered, Charlie laughed to himself as he remembered Tammi's earlier comment about a night he'd never forget. Tammi had been correct with her statement, but it was Kelly he was now remembering.

Later, Charlie sat in bed and reflected on the afternoon's events quietly in his mind. *What had happened?* He remembered how it felt to swim in the creek. He remembered instinctively dodging trees and debris as he swam. His eyes were open, but the water was so dirty and murky that he couldn't see. Yet, he could feel the presence of the approaching obstacles. The feelings came from every inch of his body, almost as though the very hairs on his body could feel the presence. He also remembered not having to come up for breath, as he seemed able to breathe underwater the same as he did out of the water. He recalled his body gliding through the current in an easy motion, as if all of his muscles worked in unison and had come together as one. The odd thing that he couldn't figure out was how he originally knew Kelly was in trouble. She had been a good distance away—too far away for most people to have heard her. Nonetheless, he was happy he had heard her screams.

Charlie's thoughts came to an abrupt halt as a sudden pounding on the front door jolted the two out of the bed. Charlie threw on his clothes as his young guest retrieved her now-dried clothes from the drier. Upon opening the door, Charlie was met with a slew of reporters with bright lights and cameras being shoved in his face. These people had already interviewed the onlookers and now wanted to hear from the hero and the damsel herself about the events that had unfolded in a shocking display in front of them.

Benjamins Become the Frankish Barbarians

The next day, Charlie was in class. Some of the kids had tried talking to Charlie about the events they had seen on the news, but he brushed off their questions. Because they knew Charlie hated attention such as this, they left him alone.

Thankfully, Charlie's history professor, Mr. Hunter, broke the topic as he asked the class, "What comes to your mind when someone says the word *barbarian*?" Most of the kids envisioned big, tough, archaic sorts of people with hairy bodies who carried spears and were intent on hurting or killing others.

One of the boys named Kyle said, "I'm pretty sure my neighbor Mr. Rich is a barbarian. He's always yelling and chasing the kids in the neighborhood."

Mr. Hunter went on to talk about how people certainly don't ever envision soft, civilized gentlemen when they hear the word. Barbarians were usually thought of those people belonging to an outside tribe of non-Roman, non-Greek, and non-Christian civilizations. These people had no formal civilized cultural upbringing and probably ate their own children to appease their gods. These people were bandits, nomads, and savages. They would kill the men they caught, rape the women, and enslave the children. Fear was instilled in the civilized world of the Romans to never step across the border into the barbaric world of the Franks.

The Romans referred to everyone outside of their jurisdiction as *barbarians* in order to scare and dissuade their soldiers and citizens from drifting outside their borders. As Mr. Hunter continued telling the class about the barbarians, Charlie's mind kept slipping into thoughts of the people of the times, and he couldn't help but intuitively feel as though he were somehow related to these people.

The barbarian title may have been useful for the purpose of instilling fear to maintain order within the cities deep into Roman areas; however, citizens living along the edges shared by the barbarians certainly learned very quickly the title did not exactly have its facts firmly in reality. This has been proven many times through history, as those who were overrun and captured by the Frankish barbarians rarely returned to Roman societal beliefs or customs, while the opposite happened when Frankish villages were over taken by the Romans.

Upon capture, the Franks did not enslave the prisoners. In fact, people caught were generally educated and then made the conscious decisions to stay. Even during times of conflict between the Romans and the Franks, history shows the Romans fought under strict orders, while the Franks fought with passion and belief. The Franks understood why they were fighting and what they were fighting for, so they believed in the cause and the final goal. In the end, this very premise is exactly what would ultimately lead to the demise of the Roman Empire following a war with the Frankish Merovingian-led barbarians.

It was this passion by the Frankish people under the leadership of the barbarian Clovis Merovingian that led to the fall of Rome in AD 486 when the two rivals clashed along the Rhine River Valley in the ancient city of Cologne. This same passion would continue over the centuries and would ultimately lead to the Carolingians becoming the emperors of western Europe during the eighth century through the medieval period and ultimately merging with the Nordish kingdoms.

Stories about the Benjamin Tribe are scattered throughout the Bible in the books of Genesis, Judges, Deuteronomy, 1 Kings, 2 Kings, Psalms, Jeremiah, and Esther and teach readers that people have good and bad in them. These stories are rich in content, thoughtful, and thought-provoking, as they help to civilize mankind. To an untrained person, the Bible's stories about the Benjamins end, and the tribe seems to simply disappear without any evidence of their survival in recorded history. Trained historians, on the other hand, understand that history is not only evidenced by written records, which this period lacked considerably, but also by analyzing changes in culture and habits over time in geographic areas where it is believed certain people migrated. Traditions such as how people dressed or how they focused on their families are documented by how people were buried, how they were dressed, and with whom they were buried. Jewish customs found family members buried together without military garb, while native tribes and Romans did not mirror this culture.

Also, when historians can't find written history, they look for religious indicators. Were multiple prayer artifacts found or only one? As has been noted throughout history, the Frankish and Nordish people started out as people who worshiped multiple gods, sacrificed their own children and animals, and carried with them many pieces of religious trinkets relating to many gods. If this changed over time in specific areas where it was thought the Benjamin Tribe traveled, then proper conclusions would have to follow from the burial artifacts found.

History shows us that as the Benjamin Tribe traveled further and further in time throughout distances far away from their homeland and trouble, they seemed to try to melt into obscurity. They crept deeper into the countryside wherever they ventured. After a couple of centuries of traveling over the many mountain ranges and river valleys, the Benjamins started to thickly inhabit the areas of the Franks and Normans in what is modern-day northwest Germany on down to modern-day Denmark.

The Benjamin Tribe was the antithesis to the core of Roman beliefs, political direction, religion, family beliefs, and general human values. For these reasons, the Romans had to title anyone outside of territories of Roman rule as barbarians. Many historical scholars have documented the obvious changes in northern Gaul, which mirrored Jewish traditions, and have led these historians to believe that most of these barbarians were actually the direct lineage of the Benjamins. This conclusion presents itself in great detail during the time when the Merovingian name ruled the Frankish people.

As the tribe continued their blending into the new areas among the natives, they started leaving their Middle Eastern namesake behind and taking on new names. Their names became the names of the towns where they resided. They were happy with whom they were and needed no namesake to attach themselves to their royal history—a history carved out by their holy father, their one true God.

Some of these new Jewish traditions that were being taught to the Frankish people were extremely different than their past beliefs, such as family values and monotheism. These values are assumed to have been accepted because they offered enormous civility among people who desperately wanted it. The concept of putting family first seemingly changed these villages overnight. It was taught and happily accepted that women were as important as men and children were not to be sacrificed to an angry god, as the real God was a loving God. The Benjamins also taught the natives that believing in many gods was weaker than having one almighty, all-powerful God.

As these native people, whom the Benjamins had met during their travels, learned about the one, almighty Jewish God and recognized the covenant they shared with God, they wanted the same relationship. During this time in history, teachings of Christianity were also making their way into native areas along the borders shared with the Romans. Because these natives were learning that Christ was indeed of the Benjamin lineage, they came to accept Christianity as their way into a relationship with God, which offered them the ability to enjoy the benefits of the covenant the Benjamins had.

The native villagers and the Benjamins melted together, and together, they enacted the Benjamin and Christian ways, which left footprints for historians to trace centuries later. Without the Benjamins' name written in logs detailing their travels, historians were still able to track the exact routes the Benjamins took due to changes and adjustments to the traditional tribal ways of living. Progress was quickly and forever changed by the native tribes, making it easy to trace by historians. Due to the addition of new DNA capabilities, old historical hypotheses become more documented.

One of the greatest successes the Benjamins were able to achieve was to teach the natives to read. By establishing reading and writing skills, the natives could be taught about many things that, in the past, would have been foreign to their abilities to understand. The ability to read and write is paramount when facing an enemy, and communications are expected to be properly carried out without confusion.

As these tribes and the Benjamins continued to grow together, they started to be called Frankish, or the Franks for short. Also, as the centuries distanced the families from their homelands, the tribe started to identify themselves with their new lands. New family names were related to and named after the areas where they traveled.

Over the years, the family name would adopt the namesake of Chief Merovech, from which the Merovingian Dynasty derived its name. Merovech was the leader of the Salian Franks. Although his name was cast onto his people, the tribe's leadership by his son Childeric I, who reigned from 457 to 481, established the landholdings for the Merovingians with battle victories against the Visigoths, Saxons, and Alemannis.

The Benjamins, now under the name of Merovingian, also knew that the faster the native tribes became one group, the better their chances for survival were if other tribes or the Romans attacked.

The Merovingian traditions of full inclusion would show up, as the Merovingian name represented all people of their kingdom. These traditions of openness and inclusion, which were hugging and protecting the barbarians, would quickly go on to rule western Europe after the Merovingian leader Clovis, in the Cathedral of Notre-Dame de Reims, converted his kingdom to Christianity on December 25, 496. The baptism of Clovis was performed by Saint Remigius, which quickly covered all of the barbarian Benjamin lands.

In the year 486, the Roman Empire still ruled southern Europe, but the farther their empire tried to push north, the more battles and territories the Romans would lose to the proud-minded barbarians. Losses were not primarily due to deaths from the battlefields but had more to do with dissentions from the warriors and the families who traveled with their warrior husbands. Accords of Roman soldiers were being introduced to the northern Frankish ways where women and children were treated with respect and kindness. They shared the food, lived together as they traveled, learned to hunt and farm, educated each other, and even prayed together.

These practices were not common among the Roman Army, and in times when money was owed to the soldiers and was not paid or when soldiers were away from their families for extended periods of time, especially during harsh winter months, desertions were common. When rumors of a better life in the opposition's military circulated through the camps, desertion from the Roman Army was frequent. This was also during the period of history when the average person lived to thirty years of age—hardly long enough to waste time living in harsh conditions.

This was the leading foundation of the Dark Ages. Stories of haunted forests, demons, dragons, trolls, and gremlins were concocted to keep the soldiers together and detour them from stepping out to the opposition. This creative fearmongering helped the Romans band their army together in some areas but ultimately failed as more and more deserters found the truth.

As an ancient republic, the Roman Empire never developed a formal state-mandated educational system. So, the farther a family was out on the fringes of the empire, or if a family was poor, it was highly unlikely the children, or parents for that matter, were educated. On the other hand, the Merovingian barbarian people pushed many advances throughout their kingdom. As the centuries progressed, future lineage such as Charlemagne would continue offering reforms, which included mandated education, monetary systems, religious reforms, and many other practices never created before.

When you combine the progressive thinking nature of the barbarian Franks verses the restrictive controlling Romans, it is obvious why one group was having vast successes, while the other was quickly moving into obscurity.

As Mr. Hunter closed off his lecture, Charlie quietly closed his books. He was feeling strange again, as some of the stories Mr. Hunter discussed from their textbook actually matched the visions Charlie had seen many times over the past years. Charlie didn't know his lineage yet, but he was starting to understand there might be some connections because the history he read about agreed with his values. He now started to believe he was being guided by some kind of holy intervention to find information for which he never knew he should be searching.

6

The CIA Takes Notice

"Son of a …" Charlie exclaimed as he shifted quickly in his chair, knocking his food and drink everywhere.

"Charlie!" Charlie's mother interrupted, shouting back. "Don't use that language in our house."

Charlie had been at his parents' house having lunch while watching the national news on television when something shocked him. Charlie didn't respond to his mother at first, as he sat glued to the television, while his drink spilled on his lap. The news was replaying a video of him swimming like a dolphin up wild floodwaters and pulling a girl to safety from her car. This didn't bother him, as he had already seen it many times. What alarmed him was the news story was also showing clips of where Charlie lived, worked, and attended school. In every clip, there was the same man in the background. The man wore black clothing and a hat. He looked like a shadow.

This man was the same man who had confronted Charlie many times over the past few weeks. Every time he came around, it spooked Charlie, as his instincts told him this guy was trouble. The man would act nice and was very polite but almost in a patronizing way. Charlie knew immediately this news clip would cause attention he did not want or need. A minute later, he finally came to his senses after he realized his lap was cold and wet.

Charlie's mother asked for his attention several times. "Charlie, what is it? What was on the TV?"

Charlie still didn't respond, but his mother could tell something had disturbed him considerably. His face had turned to a pale, pasty white, as though all of the blood had left his body.

"I have to go, Ma," was his only response as he stood up from the recliner, wet pants and all, and hurried out the door.

Charlie knew he couldn't discuss what he had seen on the television because he didn't want to upset his family or cause unnecessary worry. What he had seen, though, was so odd, so incredibly disjointed, that he needed to take a few moments to piece everything together. What he witnessed on the television in itself was not bad, but it was seeing the man in the background that disturbed him.

Stepping back in time over the past two months, Charlie began to put things together. After rescuing the girl from the flooded creek had made Charlie sort of a local hero, people wanted photos with him, and some even wanted his autograph. The trashman took his photo, his neighbor got his autograph, and even his friends wanted his picture. They also expected Charlie to start paying for their lunches together. They just assumed heroes were always paid, so he should now have extra money to pay for their meals. They weren't paid, though, so Charlie was just as broke now as he was before.

Anyway, as sometimes happens with newfound fame, some of the wrong types of people started to come around. The first person who tried clawing back into Charlie's life was his girlfriend Tammi—the one he'd left standing in the kitchen as he ran out the back door to help the girl in need. Tammi was surprised when she heard what Charlie had done, and then seeing the beautiful young lady Charlie saved hanging all over him made Tammi completely jealous.

Tammi instantly felt sick about dumping Charlie, as she was missing out the limelight. Now she desperately wanted him back in her life. She had always loved any attention that came her way, and if a camera was involved, she would go a bit nuts. Her narcissistic ways were a big turnoff for Charlie, and he was glad she had left. Charlie really didn't care for the attention—or Tammi, for that matter. So, after a couple of weeks with some rough conversations that led to the usual name-calling from Tammi, objects being thrown at Charlie, and threats of her going to the news with made up stories of abuse, things finally just quieted down and she stopped coming around.

Then the phone calls started. The first few came from a professional recruiting agency inquiring if Charlie had any administrative background and was looking for a new job. Charlie, being young and naive as to what he wanted to do for a career after college, said he wasn't looking for a job but would listen to see what they had to offer. The woman on the phone who called quite a bit always sounded incredibly sexy, and Charlie couldn't help but imagine the voice being attached to an incredibly sultry-looking female of about thirty years of age. He would ask open-ended questions simply to hear her voice ramble. He never really even heard a word she said—only how she said the words.

He thought, *Where is she from? Is she from eastern Europe? Maybe southern France. Maybe even Italy.* He wanted to ask her but thought she'd see through his plot of romancing her and figured it would be wiser to play the interview along rather than being too assertive too early and forever ending his chances of meeting her.

After a lengthy discussion, which felt so incredibly short to Charlie, she told Charlie the position was for an administrative position with the Central Intelligence Agency.

Charlie responded with, "Uh-huh, cool." Then his mind woke back up as he realized what the voice had said. "Wait. I'm not interested in becoming a spy," Charlie said hurriedly.

"You don't have to be, and that is not the job being offered, so don't worry," she told him.

Charlie's intuition led him to believe she was lying and the agency really wanted Charlie as an agent and was very interested in his capabilities. She continued her pursuit of Charlie over the phone.

"At the CIA, we employ thousands of people who have nothing to do with spy operations, but instead manage the day-to-day processes and paperwork. We were referred to you from a past employer of yours and would like to interview you."

He thought this was odd, as he felt that the caller had an awful lot of information on him for this being a first call. However, he also realized he thought he could possibly improve himself by getting a better job than his current job as a part-time grocery store stocker, which didn't pay well. So, what would it hurt to go through an interview?

The caller set up the appointment, gave Charlie the address for the interview, and simply said, "Please don't tell anyone who you are interviewing with, as we never disclose this information." Then she simply hung up the phone.

Three days later, Charlie was alone in a room, sitting at a desk and filling out the longest job questionnaire he had ever seen. Two hours later when Charlie had completed everything, the interviewer came in to discuss the results. Charlie was disappointed the person interviewing him wasn't the mystery lady from the phone. The interviewer was a cold man in his midfifties. He was tall and slender but had deep eye sockets. Charlie could not even see his eyes, as if that even mattered because the man rarely looked him in the eye. As Charlie listened intently to the interviewer's questions, he wondered where some of the questions came from, as a lot of the information the interviewer was using was information that wasn't part of the questionnaire Charlie had completed earlier.

The man spoke quietly but very directly, forcing Charlie to intensely focus. "Charlie," the man asked, "do you ever wonder how the world really works?"

"Not really," Charlie responded while at the same time thinking to himself, *This dude is F-R-E-A-K-Y.*

The man continued. "Charlie, when a person is born with special abilities, those abilities should be used to benefit his country, don't you think?"

Charlie didn't answer, just listened as similar questions continued. It felt to Charlie like the interviewer knew Charlie better than he knew himself. This made Charlie uncomfortable, almost threatened.

That being said, Charlie told the interviewer after the discussion that he was not interested in the job offer but thanked the man for his time and the opportunity.

Over the next several days, Charlie went about his usual life, never discussing the interview with anyone as he was instructed. That's when he started to feel uneasy in his surroundings. When he would come home after work, he felt as though something had changed. He looked around in detail and couldn't find anything out of the ordinary. When he would walk down the street, he felt as though someone was watching him. He started to think he was becoming paranoid.

Finally, these insecure feelings left him until the night he returned home and found the man who had interviewed him sitting inside his apartment on his couch.

"Charlie," the man said, "how are you doing? I'm sorry if I frightened you by being in your home, but the front door was wide open. When I called your name, no one answered, so I figured you must have stepped out with the intention of coming right back. I just decided to wait."

"Hel-hello," responded Charlie in a very nervous voice. "I'm just getting home from work and didn't realize the door was left open." Charlie knew he had locked the door but went along with the conversation and listened to the man.

"You should be more careful, Charlie, as you never know who will come into your home if you leave doors open. You see a lot of nuts on the news every day, and you don't want to run into them when you come home from work.

"Anyway, Charlie, I was on your side of town today on another matter, and the agency asked me to swing by and see if you would reconsider working with us."

Now somewhat fearful of saying no, Charlie felt he better say he was still thinking it over, which was his current answer. He just wanted this man, from whom he felt deep danger, out of his place with as little friction as possible.

Hearing Charlie's answer, the man instantly stood up and became aggressive, presenting himself in a hostile, confrontational manner to Charlie. "You don't have a choice in the matter, Charlie," the man yelled. "We tell you what to do. You don't tell us!"

The man put his hand in his pocket. Charlie feared he was reaching for a gun, which made him react in a way that he never knew possible. Charlie made motions as though he were holding the man, but they were ten feet apart. Charlie's arms reached out to the man and threw him back against the wall next to the front door without ever actually touching him.

Charlie had lifted this man, who he guessed weighed somewhere around 225 pounds, and threw him across the room to the wall nearly twenty feet away. The same muscles that had created the hero when saving the girl were now working in unison to overpower this unwanted intruder.

As soon as the man hit the wall, two other men appeared with weapons drawn and pointing directly at Charlie. They helped the stunned man to his feet and said little to Charlie as they carried their dazed friend outside to a waiting van and sped off into the night.

Charlie had shown these men and himself the real Charlie. Charlie had unleashed his personally unknown strength and raw power, and it scared him. He knew how terrified the men were as well because one of them nervously stuttered, "L-l-look at his eyes. They look like cat eyes."

Several weeks had passed since the incident with the intruders without any further problems, so Charlie thought things were getting back to normal until the late-night calls started. The phone rang at eleven o'clock at night, and the unknown voice on the other end of the line said a man would call Charlie in the morning to set up some tests that would be performed on Charlie at his college. As Charlie tried to object to the tests the voice said sternly, "You will show up for the tests tomorrow. *Understand?!*"

Charlie understood. He knew he was walking into a trap. However, he knew this time no games were to be played, and the directions were to be followed. Charlie asked who the person was who would be calling in the morning but was only told to take the call and not worry about the identity of the caller. Then the phone went dead.

Charlie's night was horrible, as he tossed and turned all night worrying about what the next morning would bring and how his life was spiraling out of control.

Tired and angry, Charlie decided to take a chance so when the phone rang the next morning, he barked out at the unknown caller. "I'm not going to talk with anyone or take any tests until I get some answers. I need to know what these tests are about and who wants to see the results."

Charlie's plan failed miserably. The caller made it completely clear that it would be a grave mistake on Charlie's part if he continued his games. "Charlie?" the voice asked. "Do you love your family? Do you love your country? Go take the tests, Charlie, and everyone will be okay."

Charlie remained silent, unable to conclude whether the caller was asking real questions or making threats. With that, Charlie went to the college for the tests.

When Charlie finally showed up for the tests, he was recited a biography of his life from the time he was a little boy to the current date. The people giving the tests gave a fascinating, detailed description of his life's historical events. Their information was unbelievably accurate. They knew things from years earlier that Charlie had forgotten about. He wondered how they could possibly have this information with that level of detail. The details, many of them very personal, went well beyond random data gathered, and much of it no one knew about—or so Charlie thought.

It was the most amazing experience of his life. He also became very embarrassed, as he knew there was other personal information that was not mentioned but was probably known by these people. Compromised from this knowledge, Charlie realized quickly there was no hiding from this any longer.

Comments during the testing indicated that they knew about Charlie's unique sight, smell, strength, and other abilities long before Charlie's arrival to the college for the testing.

The man in charge of the meeting seemed to be a kind man, truly interested in Charlie's differences from a scientific point of view. Charlie was ushered into the room by the man and led to the biggest, most comfortable leather chair he had ever sat in. The lights were turned down in the room.

"Charlie, I'm going to ask you to watch a few video clips with me, and then I'd like to ask you a couple of questions about what you saw when we are finished watching them."

"Okay," Charlie answered as he sat there somewhat quizzically.

As the movie clips played out, Charlie began to realize he had been tracked and observed by others for years. He was angry but intrigued as he watched the difference between himself and his friends. What he had thought to be just minor differences with others proved to be major differences when shown in direct context. Charlie leaned forward in his chair to better focus.

The man asked, "Any comments you'd like to make, Charlie?"

"No," Charlie responded sheepishly.

"It's really interesting, isn't it," said the man.

The man also provided Charlie with several tests that had been prepared long before Charlie's arrival. They were in neat order just waiting for his eventual arrival to the college where the agency could finally test his unique abilities.

While the tests were being completed, Charlie, for the first time in his life, truly understood just how different from others he was, especially how different his vision was. Growing up with his visual differences gave young Charlie many laughs, as he used his differences to play games and pranks on others. But now the government wanted them to be used only for government purposes.

The people performing the tests asked Charlie to explain some of the observations or pranks he had pulled, especially during his school years. Charlie talked about how his school days were always a recipe for pranks and laughter for the young boy. A simple example would be how schoolchildren were always confused during interactions with the opposite sex. Charlie further described how he recognized their confusion from what their auras were showing him.

It was always really funny when one of the couples was in each other's arms and another person arrived on the scene. The couple would act out all the proper etiquette, but their energy levels would reveal completely different desires, as one of the coupled people's energy would strongly reach out toward the third person who just arrived. After seeing the auras, Charlie often asked his friends why they kept dating each other when they were obviously interested in someone else. They would respond in a bewildered way as to how Charlie could know their inner thoughts, but out of embarrassment, they would completely discount his questions and deny any improper feelings they had outside of the relationship. After many such occurrences, Charlie's closest friends started to become quizzical about his abilities to see their true feelings. Once they understood his assertions were correct, they would confide in him about their true thoughts about their relationships. Charlie's friends kind of classified his interpretations as merely an ability to follow a hunch about people.

The people currently testing Charlie seemed extremely interested in this specific ability, as they asked Charlie several questions.

"Charlie, do you know what I'm thinking?"

"No," Charlie responded.

"Do you know what I'm feeling?"

"Somewhat," Charlie again responded.

"What do you mean?" asked the man with his eyebrows now lifted.

"I know you are really interested in these tests and our conversation because your energy levels expand greatly and are visible in your auras."

"Fascinating. Please tell me more."

"I know you do not like having the man at the door watching us, as your aura drops instantly anytime you glance over there."

"Is there anything else?"

"Well …" Charlie trailed off as though he didn't want to say.

"Go ahead, Charlie. We don't want to keep secrets here."

"Well … You really like your assistant, and she really likes you."

With that, the two blushed and smiled uncontrollably as they walked away in opposite directions.

Charlie continued his discussions about his youth and his observations about his friends and commented about how some of them would go as far as to say that Charlie had a strong ability to understand women. In reality, he was seeing their true thoughts because of what their aura energy levels were telling him. It was also doubtful, even with his ability to see auras, that Charlie was any better equipped to use this extrasensory gift to understand girls any better than anyone else.

He would say to himself, "Me, understand women?!" Wow, were his friends clueless. At that age, he didn't know how to operate most kitchen or restroom appliances let alone understand women. In fact, twenty years later, he still wouldn't understand women. He laughed to himself as he thought about how life hadn't been a complete waste for him because he had learned how to operate a toaster without supervision.

Charlie was surprised to learn how important these observations were to the people testing him. They asked Charlie to get back to the stories of Charlie's friends' dating rituals.

Charlie discussed how his buddies started to realize that his gift of vision was much more than an ability to understand women. It was also an ability to see when the girls had a real interest in someone. Charlie's friends started to rely on his vision more and more as they realized he could tell when a girl was angry, uninterested, or scared. Low energy levels reflect someone being tense. High energy levels indicate comfort.

When his buddies were interested in someone, they could find out by asking Charlie if the feelings were mutual or if they were wasting their time. At first, Charlie had fun sharing what was happening, but then he had started to recognize things going on around him that made him extremely uncomfortable. There were times when some of his friends' girlfriends would have very strong energy levels around guys other than their boyfriends. For obvious reasons, he would not want to report what he was seeing. The problem quickly revealed itself as a no-win situation for Charlie. His friends now knew Charlie had this ability, and when Charlie would say he couldn't see a girl's aura, his friends knew he was lying. If he said nothing, his friends would become angry for not warning them that their girlfriends were becoming interested in others.

Other oddities introduced Charlie to some new challenges during his high school years. He noticed that the guys' and girls' auras changed quite quickly, indicating that their attention was shifting between other people very often. It would even shift back to someone the person had been interested in previously. It was very interesting to him because happiness followed the auras. If two people shared the same aura intensity when they were around each other, they were as happy as could be. Once one of their auras shifted to someone else, the intensity changed, and they would stop getting along as well. Once their auras were showing moderate attraction to each other, they would get along better than when one of their auras was fading, but the relationship was only as friends. They couldn't hide their feelings from what they were saying with their auras, and Charlie knew when to hang out with them and when to stay away.

An unexpected problem surfaced when Charlie was a senior in high school. One of his closest buddies started hanging out with a new friend. Energy levels had never presented themselves to Charlie incorrectly, and what he was seeing caused him great confusion and concern. All of Charlie's life energy levels revealed who liked whom and who was comfortable with whom. Girls tended to let down their guard more than boys and were genuinely more affectionate than boys and, in general, posed much stronger energy levels. Often, girls were harder to read because it was difficult to understand where their comfort levels stopped and their compassion levels began. This also made it more difficult to tell if a girl was physically interested in another girl or just wanted to be buddies. Boys, on the other hand, never became fully comfortable around other boys unless they were being submissive.

Although Charlie's ability usually helped his dating life throughout the years, it also caused him great angst. When he wanted a relationship to work, he could see right away when it wouldn't. The major lessons that he learned from his abilities took place the year earlier when he first started attending college. Charlie would experiment by pushing the limits on what he was seeing from the energy levels and ask girls and their friends many questions. He quickly learned that most people are afraid of what they know to be true, and they usually do not want others to know their true feelings. Charlie's experiences and directness also cost him many slapped cheeks while he learned how to deal with his visual gift as it related to dating.

Charlie's gift wasn't used solely for dating purposes, as it presented many unusual situations for his family and others close to him as well. Charlie's family saw firsthand events unfold many times over his adolescent period. Things such as Charlie finding lost children in national parks, finding lost animals in the neighborhood, seeing deer at night on the sides of roads, and warning his parents of any upcoming dangers in the road so they could slow down while driving. He once saw a bear on a school trip night hike when others in his group could not and was able to warn his classmates and teachers.

When he was four years old, he alerted his mother that he saw the aura of a man on a park bench off in the distance in a park. His mother initially didn't believe him. It was a very cold winter day, and she couldn't see anyone. Upon further inspection, she found the man and alerted authorities. Unfortunately for the man, he had passed away earlier that day before help could be reached. Unfortunately for Charlie, this event became publicized in the local news, which also led to one of the first confirmations that Charlie may be the gifted Benjamin the CIA was looking for. Their research had estimated this individual may be alive today.

Probably the oddest event that was witnessed by Charlie's family happened to his father while he and Charlie were on an archery hunting trip in the Olympia National Rain Forest in Washington State years earlier. Anyone who has ever hunted using archery knows the drill. You put on as much camouflage clothing as possible to stay warm because you'll be sitting in a tree stand all day. No matter how much clothing you have, it's never enough, and you'll freeze all day. You won't freeze to death, though; that would be too easy. You'll only freeze just up to the point of death, but you'll survive just long enough to catch pneumonia. The reason you'll be so cold is because it's a known fact that there has never been a hunting trip when it hasn't rained or snowed the entire trip.

The hunting rule book says it must rain hard enough for the water to soak you through all layers of your protective clothing and reach your skin. Then, and only once you are soaked thoroughly, the snow is allowed to start. Snow on a hunting trip serves only two purposes. First, it is designed to freeze your already-soaked clothing. Second, it is designed to change what everything looked like when you entered the forest, as it is magnificent at covering the trail markers you set coming into the forest. Once the trail markings are covered, you will be thoroughly lost for several more hours to ensure you become sick enough to actually say you were on a hunting trip.

Hunting boots must also be worn to ensure they fill up with enough water to freeze your toes off. It's common knowledge that when a forest ranger happens upon people in the forest who claim to be hunting, the ranger will ask these people to remove their boots and show proof of their toeless, numb foot stumps. If they take off their boots and they have all of their toes, it proves they are not hunters at all and are immediately arrested.

The final thing that was always done right before an archery hunt was to apply a heaping amount of skunk oil to themselves. Yes, skunk oil. Apparently, humans smell worse than skunks in the forest, so adding a little skunk perfume was what would bring the animals closer to Charlie and his father. With guidance like this designed to help Charlie understand animals, is it any wonder Charlie didn't truly understand women either? A side note worth mentioning here is skunk oil can be purchased at any outdoors store and is a must have when you feel like playing a prank on any of your friends. It's also helpful to know that when body temperatures rise, so does the level of the skunk oil aroma. So, if you opened your friend's locker and dripped a drop or two into their shorts, they would become somewhat embarrassed after they started sweating while exercising in their gym clothes.

Anyway, Charlie and Bud had set up their tree stand and were ready to wait out their prey. It was always boring as hell. The first time Charlie had ever been in a tree stand, he was afraid he would fall asleep and roll off and die. After several of these cold, damp hunting trips, his fears changed from falling out of the tree to having a fear that he would *not* fall out and die. In fact, Bud could never figure out why Charlie would always place sharp objects under the tree stand, but he was just ensuring that if he fell out of the stand, he would land on the sharp objects below and have a swift death. He didn't want a slow death; just a quick one would do.

Now let's get back to the story of the Olympia National Park trip and what this had to do with Charlie's visual abilities. Bud and Charlie had been out all day in a typical rainy, snowy day when Charlie saw something in the distance. He whispered to Bud, "Dad, look over there. I think a bear is coming toward us."

Bud couldn't see anything yet, as it was too far off in the distance. His response to Charlie when the boy saw something that he didn't was always one of mentorship and guidance from a father to a son. "Shut up, dumbass. There's nothing out there."

Because Charlie was only seeing the energy levels the animal was emitting, he couldn't tell exactly what it was, but it sure looked big. Here's another side note to help you understand how Charlie saw things: Imagine driving down a long highway during a hot afternoon and seeing heat auras rising off the hot road in the distance that give a foggy or blurred type of appearance. Charlie simply saw these types of auras on everything. The stronger the energy, the stronger the auras. That same wavy fog appearance was how Charlie would see energy levels on people, animals, and all other life forms. Because of this ability, he often saw the energy far earlier but could not tell what the object actually was.

This was the case with what Charlie was seeing now. It was starting to become dark, which helped his vision but hurt his father's. The two stayed as quiet as possible so the stinky skunk perfume covering their frozen bodies could do its magic.

As the object came closer, Bud whispered, "It's another hunter."

Charlie whispered back to Bud in his typical smart-ass way, "If it's another hunter, we should probably put a couple of arrows in him to put him out of his misery."

Charlie's father never appreciated the boy's subtleties or sense of humor, but Charlie always thought he was funnier than hell. The object came closer yet. Both Charlie and Bud were seeing it clearly now, but neither could figure out what they were really seeing. Was it a bear or a man? It was now within thirty feet of them, and they still couldn't tell. It walked upright like a man and had a huge upper body, but it also had long hair like a bear.

Charlie thought it was just another one of those damn hippies, so he told his father, "I'm going to shoot him." Charlie never understood hippies.

His father, also not a hippie fan, informed Charlie again, by saying, "It's against the law to shoot hippies out of season."

Charlie thought, *Damn rules and damn hippies!*

Whatever this thing was, it also had the most noxious smell that the two had ever been around, including Charlie's feet. This was the first time Charlie understood why putting skunk oil on was helpful for hunting. If the animals smelled the two of them with their skunk oil on and then smelled this thing, then they would win a pretty smell contest.

The man or animal finally stood directly below the two hunters perched in their tree stand. Charlie's father and Charlie were completely dumbfounded as to what they were seeing. They both knew they would be stuck in that damn tree if it didn't leave soon, though. All Charlie wanted to do at that moment in time was to get back to the dry car and turn on the heater. So, hoping to piss it off and get it to leave, he did what any fifteen-year-old would do. He poured his soda on its head.

Later that evening, after watching an angry predator trying to shake the two from the tree, Bud informed the boy that his mother surely must have had an affair early on during their marriage, as Charlie couldn't really be related to him. Bud said, "I can't prove it, but there is no way someone like you could have ascended from my family's loins." Several years later DNA testing was made available to the general public, and Bud would learn just how much Charlie represented Bud's family lines.

In the meantime, this thing grabbed hold of the tree and started to rock it back and forth, snarling the whole time. Now, ordinarily, Charlie wouldn't have minded the rocking of the tree. He had always tossed things out of the tree house back home onto his brother's head, and his brother would respond by trying to shake Charlie out of the tree. What concerned Charlie here was that the tree he and Bud were in was a rather large redwood, and this thing was successfully shaking it rather well.

Charlie responded by telling his father, "You should climb down there and discuss the situation at hand with this thing and see if the two of you can come to an agreement."

Again, Charlie's father mentored him following his remarks. "Shut up, sit there, and hang onto the tree."

Even though both had their bow and arrows, they knew not to dare shoot this thing. It was much bigger than any bear they had ever seen, and the only damage they could do was make it angrier. So, they held on and waited for it to leave, which it eventually did. It was good that this thing didn't climb trees, or they would have been stuck.

As the thing walked back into the forest, Charlie's teenage humor trickled through his brain. He asked his father, "Should I put an arrow in its ass?"

Bud's response was a silent stare, but Charlie knew what his father would have said if he had not been shaking too much to speak: "Shut up, dumb ass!"

The two never could figure out what the thing had been exactly. Charlie knew one thing for sure: whatever it was, it was the older brother because the way he shook that tree sure reminded Charlie of his older brother William whenever he got angry with Charlie.

Bud never liked to believe in the young Charlie's visual differences. Whenever Charlie's mother or friends wanted help finding a stray animal in the dark, they would ask for the boy's help. Bud, on the other hand, would try to defer the entire conversation anytime the subject matter came up. Bud would exclaim that Charlie just had very good night vision. Charlie could count on one hand how many times his father ever asked him to use his skills to benefit his own interest, but this was one of those times. Bud would not come down from the tree stand until Charlie was no longer able to see the energy levels from the thing that had paid them the visit.

It was now pitch-black outside, and Charlie's father was dependent on the boy's vision and wanted to know everything he was seeing on the way back to the car. He asked Charlie at least fifty times, "Do you see anything?"

Charlie would say, "No, I don't see anything," becoming angrier and angrier each time Bud asked the question. Finally, after being asked so many times, Charlie realized how numb and sore his feet were. He finally exclaimed, "No, Dad, I don't see anything, and I can't feel my fricken toes anymore either because this stupid trip has caused them to fall off!" But he hadn't said *fricken* and instead he used the real f-bomb. He thought that was allowed among men in the wilderness. Apparently, his father hadn't read that book.

When Charlie swore, his dad yelled at him and asked why he talked like that and who had taught Charlie such foul words. Charlie thought to himself that it was his dad, his brother William, the kids in the neighborhood, and even his preacher once after Charlie had dunked a squirt gun into the holy water bowl at church and started squirting people one hot Sunday. Poor old preacher. Charlie wondered if the preacher was still in therapy of if he ever fully recovered. Charlie thought he shouldn't answer his father's question about the swearing and felt he should just ignore it all and get them back to the car.

The two had their flashlights on so they could navigate the darkness and get back without too much difficulty. It was unusual for Bud to be as alarmed as he was. They had come upon many bears and other aggressive animals during hunts in the past, but this was different. Bud wanted no part of this thing or this trip any longer. The two left the tree stand and most of their supplies back in the tree. The only things they took out were their bows and arrows, the flashlights, and, of course, Charlie made sure to take the remaining skunk oil. On the way back to the car, Charlie only saw a couple of little energy balls, most likely a family of raccoons, and one big energy ball that moved like a deer.

When they made it to the car, Bud got in and drove off faster than Charlie ever saw him move. His father didn't talk much while driving for the first hour or so, and then when he started talking, he couldn't shut up. In the end, he vowed to never discuss what they had seen, and he held true to that vow until his dying day. Right before he passed away, he murmured out to the family all that he had seen and experienced in life. His very last comment was, "Charlie and I saw Bigfoot!"

The people testing Charlie's abilities were actually very nice, and they had a true interest in understanding him and his capabilities. He told them his stories, and they took lots of notes and asked a ton of questions. They made Charlie feel comfortable as he shared other stories with them that he had never shared with anyone else before. He even felt somewhat relieved to be releasing so much of what had been locked inside him his whole life.

Charlie never lost his desire to use his abilities to prank those around him, and he had been very content with his abilities. He also learned how to keep quiet about his abilities, as he did not want people he worked and lived with to feel threatened by his abilities. He also did not want to reveal the advantage within him that divulging things would reduce. Only those individuals who were very, very close to him knew about his abilities. This secret group was interested in Charlie's pranks only to the point of how his abilities could be useful helping the agency.

The CIA approach was very interesting. When individuals were found to possess oddities or unique abilities, they were secretly tracked and observed. The different circumstances around their skills were categorized and basically filed away until a situation arose when they need assistance. This is what happened to Charlie.

It was in the fall of 2001 when the secret calls really started to become pushy. America had recently been attacked in New York City, and for the first time in its history, America was faced with a new type of war called terrorism. The problem was no one knew how to identify terrorists before they did something awful. A terrorist may be a coworker, a neighbor, or even a family member. If someone had the ability to see auras and identify liars or interpret motivations, that person could be a great asset.

The interviewer's intent became clear to Charlie. He was being asked to view interviews with terrorism suspects to identify if they were revealing all they knew, whether they were lying during interrogations, and identify if they had additional information they were withholding. In layman's terms, Charlie would be the human equivalent to the US Customs and Border Protection drug-sniffing canines. These dogs sniff out things and alert people to what is unseen by humans. Charlie would be using his visual abilities to identify what others could not see.

But how would Charlie accomplish this without giving out his identity and damaging his life or his family's safety? Don't misunderstand. Charlie was interested in the welfare and safety of his country, but he had his family to consider, and he didn't want to jeopardize their safety and well-being either. These people would not take no for an answer, and Charlie knew it could threaten his family's safety by members of the agency if he didn't acquiesce to work with them.

Details of how life went on from here cannot be disclosed for many reasons, but it was never boring for Charlie with many captured people who had been accused of terrorism. Some were innocent and simply in the wrong place at the wrong time. Others were guilty, nasty people filled with nothing but true hatred. Some of the interviews took place on US soil, and sometimes he would be offshore in other countries.

More and more, these conversations would take place in public areas, and sometimes they would take place in the confines of heavily guarded prisons. Many times, Charlie would be directly introduced to the people, and other times he would view them from a distance. But the reason for the visual observation interviews was always for the same purpose; to evaluate them from an honesty perspective and determine if there was more they could offer or if there was something they were hiding.

Charlie never predetermined what the results would be from his observations because he never had any complete data on the subjects he was asked to evaluate. He only revealed what he was witnessing. The final evaluations were determined by those who collected all of the data Charlie shared.

During this period, Charlie was also asked to travel extensively. He was not only asked to interview possible terrorists but some corporate executives of multinational firms and even select high-ranking members of the US Congress.

So here he was in late 2001 after planes were allowed to resume flying in the US skies, and Charlie was about to walk on a plane heading to meet with members of Congress to discuss business in Washington, DC. Charlie knew the world was often very different than what was seen though one's rose-colored lenses. These members of Congress had a great responsibility: to protect the country against further attacks and identify these invisible enemies, some of whom lived among the locals. Charlie's government rap sheet conveyed his very private visual differences, and these capabilities popped out to some secret divisions like a firework display full of glitz and excitement. Charlie's world changed overnight.

Charlie had no problem with the government asking for his assistance, especially with respect to what happened to the people in New York City.

Knowing what he knew now, if the government had asked him after telling him honestly what they wanted him to do and why, he would have said yes to help them without hesitation. It's never the intent of someone to not want to help; however, sometimes when a poor methodology is used by the asking party, the person being asked has no way of saying yes. The resulting sequence is like a game of cat and mouse. Combine that with a love of practical jokes and general dislike of people who abuse government power, and your personal information is a way to corner you to work for them. You have the making of a sequel to the movie, *Catch Me If You Can* in 3-D.

In the end, Charlie realized the CIA didn't really have all the details of his full range of powers. They knew this, and it scared them from being too direct. However, he felt that in some ways the agency actually knew much more about him than he knew about himself. He knew they had extra details of his ancestry, which neither Charlie nor his family were ever aware of.

The CIA would continue to sporadically observe Charlie. During their investigations, they found very unusual characteristics that Charlie possessed and were identical to some of his direct ancestors. The CIA knew about Charlie's true family lineage but never revealed it to him, as he had demonstrated no knowledge as to family relations. The CIA felt this knowledge, if leaked, could become a significant risk to Charlie, his family, and America. So, the CIA kept the facts around Charlie's lineage and unusual powers classified.

Although Charlie's family lineage and events had been recorded throughout history and included members of the Benjamin, Merovingian, and Carolingian families, Charlie and his family had no knowledge of this. Some of the direct people included individuals such as Charlemagne, William the Conqueror, and King Stephen. Charlie's lineage directly included emperors, kings, and queens from the Vikings, as well as France, England, Germany, Israel, and Rome. His ancestral records also included direct bloodlines from the Jews, Christians, and Cathars. All fights that involved his ancestral lineage were fought to protect the bloodline dynasty directly or as warriors protecting the kingdoms with whom they sided. All of these facts were known to the agency but not to Charlie. The agency was also hoping to learn if Charlie had other powers. They were very concerned that if Charlie ever ended up in enemy hands, he could become extremely dangerous.

The only thing Charlie knew was that if he was going to ever get control of his life again, he would have to fully cooperate for his and his family's protection. And he did this as faithfully as possible.

Battle of Soissons and the Fall of Rome (AD 486)

A s Charlie continued learning about his personal lineage, his readings would bring him into stories of family members and direct accounts of their actions by firsthand witnesses. Many of these stories amounted to little, but others changed history in a big way.

One such event Charlie learned about was the Battle of Soissons. This battle was headed by Charlie's ancestor Merovingian King Clovis and his army of barbarians against a much more formally trained, funded, and armed Roman military.

Charlie read on as he started to put people from his lineage together with historical events. He was still somewhat confused, as he wasn't sure whether these people who had been directly involved with some of history's greatest events were truly Charlie's relatives. But out of pure curiosity, Charlie continued to read.

A still and heavy air surrounded the morning fog in the small Aisne River valley of Soissons, a region of modern-day Hauts-de-France. After years of constant atrocities by the Romans against the Frankish people, the Frankish people were starting to talk among themselves. A confrontation between the leader of the Franks, Clovis I, and the local leader representative of the most powerful military power the world had ever witnessed, the fearsome Roman Army, led regionally by Syagrius, was building and would soon peak in the quiet river valley.

This day was that day. After years of constant isolated conflicts and Roman assaults, which were mainly selfish acts of bullying against the wives and daughters and never led to punishment of the aggressors unless the aggressors were of Frankish blood, the Franks were stating to commit to fighting.

The final act by the Romans against the Frankish leading up to the final upheaval seems to have been a result of torturous act against a young couple in town. Several Roman soldiers had come upon a young man and his girlfriend, and they took a fancy to her. The young duo tried to avoid the soldiers and go around them, but this would not happen, as the soldiers boxed the girl in, separating her from her boyfriend. They started grabbing at her, fondling her breasts, pulling up her dress, and forcing her to kiss them.

The young man was no match for the soldiers, who now held him and forced him to watch what was about to unfold. Onlookers in the town square were also helpless against the might of the soldiers and could do nothing to help the young couple.

The soldiers persisted in humiliating the young girl by stripping her naked and taking turns on her until all of them had finished in her. She remained naked on the Roman road, bloody from the assault. She would live; her boyfriend would not. The soldiers verbally lambasted him for being too weak to help her and then laughed as they mocked him, saying, "This girl will be better off raising our Roman child instead of your Frankish pig." With that, one the soldiers took out his dagger and carved out the boy's eyes.

The boy began screaming in pain, and it looked as though the soldiers would finally leave. Then suddenly, one of the soldiers turned toward the boy with his sword in his hand, and with one heavy swing, he lopped off his head. The boy's young maiden watched in horror, defenseless as all of this unfolded right in front of her and the other townspeople. The Frankish people sought revenge but knew they were severe underdogs against the great Roman army.

At the time, the Franks were made up of multiple independent tribes who lived along the fertile river valley. These tribes were created from nothing more than a hodgepodge assembly of farmers and lowlanders not known for fighting back and certainly not known for winning fights. They were, in fact, considered an unarmed, uneducated group of barbarians as all Romans described the non-Roman inhabitants of the day.

The enraged, overemotional barbarians were being led by the Merovingian king Clovis I and were considered no match for the powerful Romans. Clovis I could not understand the misjudgment and underestimation by the Romans. Surely they remembered just two decades earlier these same Franks were called upon to fight off the attacks by the Visigoths in Gaul who were decimating the Roman Army. In fact, if the Franks had not stepped in and sided with the Romans to push back the Visigoths, Rome would have fallen decades earlier. The Roman underestimation would give the Franks a significant edge, as the Roman soldiers would not be as well prepared for the battle that would soon ensue.

Clovis I gave the Roman leader in the area, Syagrius, the date, time, and location of the battle. Syagrius and his Roman soldiers did not prepare for battle because they knew that Clovis I was really the underdog, and that gave the Romans what they thought to be an unmatched advantage. With this information, Syagrius's men mocked the Franks even harder and drank heavily the night before the fight, thinking this whole event to be some Frankish fool's play. After all, there was no real Frankish formed army.

Syagrius himself was so amused and bewildered by the challenge from Clovis I that he couldn't hold back his excitement. The odds would be strongly in his favor, and Roman bounties would be huge and result in more control of northern fertile lands and a wide assortment of fertile women. Rome would once again grow its imperial reach, and Syagrius would be a hero, which could possibly escalate him to emperor.

Clovis I had anticipated his opponent's lackadaisical response to his calling out the date, time, and location of the fight and used what little time he had to assemble his army by combining most of the smaller Chararic-led tribes. Clovis I had to work diligently to get the Franks prepared. The hearts and minds of the Franks were much more prepared than the Romans, as their hatred after years of poor treatment by the Romans ran deep. There were simply deep wounds that needed to be repaired, and the

Franks were ready to fight to the death for this righteous cause. The real challenge would not be breaking the hearts and minds of the Romans but obtaining weapons for the Franks to fight a fair battle.

It's important to note that the word *Frank* comes from Rome's description of the javelin that these barbarians used as their weapons, hardly a defense against the Roman Army's arsenal. The Franks had little weaponry other than the javelins, so many of them would simply pack linens and canvas with rocks to create makeshift slings and flails. Pitted against an army fortified with horses, armor, bows and arrows, swords, knives, and shields, the Franks would need a miracle.

The fog lifted along the river on the early summer morning of the battle in 486. The armies met eye to eye for the first time, leading to an undertone of laughter by the Romans upon seeing their tattered foe who had awaited the fight. The Romans thought that after this quick dousing of the Franks and the fight that history would report as nothing more than a brief uprising, Syagrius and his Roman Army would soon be enjoying the victors' bounty. This would be nothing more than practice for his men. He really didn't even understand why Clovis I was so dedicated to the fight when, in fact, the Romans presence in the area was actually light and infrequent. He understood the displeasure Clovis I had for the small group of Roman soldiers who had violated some of the Frankish women, but so what? They were barbarians, pigs, barely definable as human. These pigs should be happy that a Roman soldier was even willing to share a bed with their women.

As Charlie read on, he couldn't avoid feelings of loyalty to Clovis I and the righteous causes he stood for. He also envisioned standing alongside of Clovis's men as they fought against the injustices of Syagrius and his Roman military. Things were different more than 1,500 years later for Charlie's world, but he believed in protecting people from current injustices just like his forefathers had.

Charlie continued reading on about how Syagrius fully expected Clovis's barbarians to flee after seeing the mighty force that stood against his men after Syagrius lined up his army against them. Clovis I and his barbarians proved him wrong and stood strong, and the fight took place, making Charlie extremely proud.

At the time, Syagrius could not have known that this battle would become the precipice for Clovis's beginnings as a dominant leader. The fight would snowball into the domination that would become the Merovingian Dynasty and founding of modern-day France.

The battle ensued, and events unfolded. Arrows from Syagrius's archers started the engagement, followed by an arm-to-arm thrashing by trained soldiers against the smaller group of untrained combatants. Clovis's men fought hard and seemed to have been designated as the winners as soon as the battle began. For some reason, the Roman steel swords had trouble breaking the skin of the barbarians. On the other hand, it seemed that every swipe of the barbarians' dull steel knives and every point of their javelins that met their opponents' vital organs would instantly kill them.

The sounds of fighting were quickly replaced by quieter sounds of moans and deep groans from the dying Roman soldiers. Blood was heavy and splattered under the feet of the barbarians' thick-skinned moccasins. As it was summer, the smell of death grew quickly. Clovis I was looking for Syagrius to complete the conquest. Little did Clovis I know, Syagrius had already retreated his position into the arms of the Visigoths for security only to be turned back over to Clovis I to prevent war between the northern Franks and the southern Visigoths.

Syagrius, along with all Frankish tribal leaders who refused to help in the original battle, would be executed over time, and Clovis I would emerge as the leader of the Franks, giving rise to the Merovingian Dynasty, ending Roman rule, and sparking the events that led to the original creation of France.

Charlie slowly closed the book and gazed quietly out the library window at the giant oak tree and watched as a slight wind gently caused its leaves to wave, his mind quietly meditating on what he just finished reading, and his heart was proud.

8

Tracking Charlie

Charlie's reading topics did not go unnoticed by those who continued to secretly track him. Those who followed Charlie worried that he may be learning more about his true historical identity.

The hotel phone rang several times as Charlie fumbled for his room key. After rushing into the room, he picked up and said, "Hello." There was no immediate answer, but he could hear breathing on the other end. "Hello," he demanded once again.

Finally, a dull, quiet, obviously male voice responded. "Why are you in town, Charlie?"

"Who is this?" asked Charlie in a quizzical voice.

Again, the muffled voice repeated the question. "Why are you in town, Charlie?"

Charlie thought the voice was of someone he knew and he was being pranked, so he started calling out several names of his friends until the voice on the other end hung up, leaving only a dial tone.

Charlie asked himself, "Damnit. How could I have been so stupid?"

He realized the CIA had secret interest in him, but they weren't the only ones interested in him. Now a second organization had started to harass him with the intention of gaining control over him.

In addition to these outsiders who had interest in Charlie, Charlie had his own interests. He had graduated college and started his career like any other normal young person, accepting a job in the financial services industry. Over time, Charlie would travel extensively and ultimately quickly rise to the top of his field. As Charlie's career progressed, he would be asked to speak publicly as a subject matter expert in his field. His public speaking engagements would further lead to his being chosen as a lobbyist. He often spoke privately with members of Congress, dignitaries, and heads of state on business-related matters.

Charlie was extremely successful in these endeavors and realized he could easily lead people to vote positively on matters he discussed. This success did not go unnoticed. Charlie went on to be asked to dine with US presidents, vice presidents, cabinet members, ambassadors, and even international heads of state.

Unfortunately, and unknown to Charlie due to his innocent understanding of power, Charlie was about to be introduced to some individuals' nefarious ways, as they sought for power over him at any cost. As a result of these people's quest for power, Charlie would soon realize that he was being watched and was possibly in danger. These people either wanted Charlie to work for them or needed him terminated.

Challenges arose when multiple teams were tracking the same individual, as they tend to figuratively and literally run into each other. This was the case with Charlie. There were not only local and national teams following him but international teams as well. All of this wasn't missed by Charlie, who finally started to clue in to odd happenings around him, causing him to start paying attention to his own safety.

Charlie had learned and now understood what his real relationship to European history was well before he was ever made aware of why Bud was never taught the truth about his ancestors. As long as Charlie and his relatives didn't know the truth of their ancestral rights, they posed no threats and were simply watched and left alone. Although Charlie was naïve to his ancestry, the nature of his relationships with powerful people were seen as a potential threat to those who knew the truth.

Charlie's travels started leading to odd situations for him and his family, which, over a period of time, started to lead to his questioning some circumstances around these events. For example, anytime Charlie would fly for business, his luggage would show up a day or two later with a note from TSA simply stating they had reviewed his bag's contents. Sometimes they would toy with Charlie by taking out some of his necessities, and sometimes they would add items such as bullets or family photos. When TSA would find the bullets, Charlie had no explanations. TSA made it known this would place him on a travel watch list and then let him go.

He had started thoroughly reviewing his luggage and even taking photos of everything packed in his bags prior to travels. When new things showed up and caused more frequent questioning from TSA, he would show them the photos. Their response was always the same. They would lecture, warn, and release him. He couldn't ever find any explanations for these events, so he would just continue about his ways, but he was becoming more and more concerned. Although Charlie was naturally a carefree individual, he took a healthy account of what was happening. He knew his trackers were serious, but he didn't know yet why they were after him.

To further Charlie's concerns and confusion, some odd business meetings would also take place and leave Charlie genuinely perplexed. These meetings happened before he learned of the connections the Merovingians had with the Benjamin Tribe and before he knew the history of his lineage.

One such meeting would take place in the office of a Jewish financial group in downtown Beverly Hills, California. The meeting was set up under the pretense of a discussion about how Charlie would work with their financial team in order to help both firms grow. The reality was different. When Charlie met with the group, he discovered they only wanted to discuss Charlie flying to Jerusalem as a special guest of the Israeli government to see his homeland and take his proper position among Israel's leaders.

"Take my proper position?" said Charlie. "You've got everything confused. I'm not even Jewish!"

Never growing up Jewish, Charlie frankly thought this group was either misinformed or nuts. Through Charlie's readings, he had come across some lineage and historical findings that were different than what he had grown up believing, but he thought what he had read must be factually incorrect.

The Jewish group was extremely persistent, to say the least. They provided Charlie with details of his ancestral connections and multiple books to read with a plethora of information. Everything contrasted Charlie's original beliefs and understanding of who he was but seemed to match some of the current lineage data he had recently read. Out of fear, Charlie would throw away all of the information they gave him as soon as he left their office.

After this incident, Charlie had other similar situations occur, all claiming conflicts with what Charlie had been taught about his lineage as a child. Because Charlie had only recently started to further investigate his lineage, he was somewhat defenseless on the subject. Growing up, Charlie had only known his parents, grandparents, one of his great-grandmothers, and a couple of cousins, none of whom ever discussed family history.

He was intrigued that the new data that was being introduced to him was all the same, but he thought, *I'm just Charlie, a regular kid*. He guessed there was some mistaken identity issue happening that would eventually sort itself out. He had heard a couple of little stories about some distant relatives but very little outside of that. His family seemed normal as well. Most of the events that surrounded his life seemed fairly normal too. With the exception of some of his personal characteristics, which he had long thought of as simply birth defects, he put everything in the back of his mind.

Charlie's life meandered on just like anyone else's. He would eventually fall in love and get married to a wonderful young lady named Sheila. Charlie felt everything was moving in a very normal direction, but his new wife did not. In fact, almost as soon as the young couple was married, Sheila noticed some oddities and became concerned. She started keeping a diary and had tied together some of Charlie's closely timed unusual travel coincidences.

Sheila was amazed by the many odd events that did not alarm Charlie. She figured he had been surrounded by so many odd things during his life that he was now just oblivious to their existence around him, but she was not. Sheila decided to have their home checked for wiretapping or bugs just to make sure there wasn't something bigger happening. Surprisingly, this turned up thirty-six hidden devices. This now caused Charlie to think back to all of the odd events that had happened over the past several years, causing him to stop believing these events were simply coincidences. He was starting to realize he could no longer ignore what was happening around him. The events that he had hidden in the back of his mind would now become a central focus. Out of sincere concern from Sheila, he would work to try and learn what could possibly be behind all of this interest.

Charlie searched his mind, trying to make sense of things and concluded that all of the events surrounding these things seemed to be directly tied to his ancestral history. So, he started there and diligently researched everything about his family in books and on the internet. He soon found that he was the world's worst genealogist. He found nothing and concluded after months of frustrating dead-end trails that he needed to employ professionals to assist him on his quest. This led to several DNA tests and multiple hirings of international genealogy groups to possibly tie up any loose ends that could possibly lead to answers and help identify any questions.

The term *question* would prove to be an incredible understatement. Charlie's DNA revealed his bloodline started in the Middle East, traveled through parts of the Roman Empire, through eastern Europe, over to northern Europe (today's Germany), down through modern-day France, across the channel to England, and ultimately to America. Charlie laughed to himself. He thought he was simply of German and Czech descent because that's what his parents were. Whatever he was would be figured out, but these first reports still gave him no answers to what was happening in his life at the moment.

As the genealogist reports started to come in, Charlie was again taken aback. The first reports that came in from a firm in Israel showed a long history of lineage going directly back to the Benjamin family all the way to 586 BC.

Charlie's first reaction was, "The lost tribe of Israel! How can that be? I'm not Jewish!"

The reports certainly contradicted this belief, but instead of providing answers, the information only created more questions. As more and more reports poured in from several unrelated genealogy groups, Charlie was amazed at the detailed parallels of data they provided. He could read all of the different independent reports and come to the same conclusions. Why wasn't any of this new information ever presented to him? Was what he was reading true, or was it a compilation of mistakes? Was he really of Jewish blood? Why was he raised as a Christian with this background?

He had admitted to himself that he had always wondered where the name Benjamin on his grandma's side of the family originated. Through the geology research, he learned the first record of the name Benjamin was traced back to his ancestor Roger Benjamin. History listed Roger as the first time the Benjamin surname was recorded in England. Private parish records hinted that the boy was named Roger Benjamin as a way to protect the child from being destroyed during a period of Catholic Crusades under the order of France's King Louis VII. Later, Roger's identity and all related history would try to be destroyed during a period of demarcation under the direct orders of King Henry VIII centuries later.

Upon reading the information, Charlie's hands trembled, his heart raced, his throat clammed up, and his eyes watered as he continued digesting the information before him. He wanted to stop reading. He actually wanted to throw up, but he couldn't put the information down and kept foraging through the materials.

Prior to the period of the Crusades, Constance Capet Countess, the sister of King Louis VII, was placed in an arraigned marriage with Eustace Blois, King Stephen's eldest son. The marriage had been arraigned in hopes of binding together the monarchs of the Normans and Franks, creating one grand empire. Primarily due to a great separation of age, Eustace and Constance Capet never produced any offspring, leaving the grand plan in jeopardy of ever being fulfilled. Prince Eustace also became an unyielding child and created despair for King Stephen as he realized his kingdom would ultimately be lost and all plans of his grand plan would go unfulfilled. The king's fears would be realized a decade later when Eustace was poisoned and die without producing a royal heir.

Years prior to Eustace's death, King Stephen would witness many premonitions detailing his greatest fears about his son. He saw through these visions of his son's travels and the havoc he had caused throughout the English countryside and his ultimate death. As these views sickened the king from what he saw his son doing, he became adrift from his relationship with Eustace, causing further and further divide between the two. Many scholars agree that this distance between the two caused Eustace to act more and more menacing, ultimately leading to his very demise. These moments of insight also revealed an odd solution to the king's quest of creating a supreme empire, but what was revealed was so awful that he kept the illuminations to himself. The longer he hid these messages, which he believed were being sent directly from God, the more intense his visions would become.

Finally, and with great reluctance, he shared the dreams with his own wife, Adela de Normandie, who was also called Matilda. He surely thought he was going insane and reached out to Matilda to help him sort through everything. He had no intentions of following through with what the premonitions were telling him and estimated his wife would surely become hostile with the information he presented but would also help him sort through everything.

The visions pointed to the king fathering a child with his own son's estranged wife, Constance Capet, to ensure a master bloodline. To the surprise of King Stephen, Matilda and, ultimately, Constance Capet agreed to the union. Both women agreed to the union to ensure protection and the greater good for the countries under the order of a royal bloodline lineage that would also prevent a transition to the king's cousin and hated relative Empress Matilda. The union would also see strong resistance from Pope Celestine II, as he did not back King Stephen's claim to the English throne, as well as from Constance Capet's brother, King Louis VII. If successful, this child would have the greatest monarchial bloodlines giving him more control than any one person has ever yielded before or since. The child would be born in secrecy in France in 1143.

Upon receiving the shocking news of the child's birth and understanding that this child would not only become the eventual King of Normandy, thus disabling the King of France from acquiring King Stephen's kingdom, but also potentially taking the kingdom of King Louis VII away in the future, King Louis VII was furious. What resulted was horrible. King Louis VII, in cooperation with Pope Eugene III, created a crusade under the false pretense of religious cleansing while hiding the real goal of seeking out and destroying this child who posed a significant threat against both of their powers.

In fear for the child's safety, the countess would secretly send the child to England to be raised secretly by King Stephen and Matilda through their parish on English soil under the assumed name Roger Benjamin. The child would be raised in obscurity until he became old enough to lead his nation and assume the proper skills from King Stephen. Unfortunately, King Stephen would pass away before seeing this quest fulfilled.

The countess herself, never a lineage threat to either the pope or King Louis VII, was not harmed during the crusade and even remarried after Eustace's death. The countess lived her days out in the Toulouse area of southern France, never divulging one of the world's greatest secrets and taking it to her grave. Unfortunately, the citizens of the Toulouse area where Constance Capet lived would spend years under constant religious and political attacks driven by the Catholic Church under the guise of religious order. The area where Constance Capet lived was populated by a small Catholic Church along with a resistance sector of a highly religious and extremely peaceful group of Cathars. This group shared a deep belief in God, the same God the Catholics and Jews believed in, and who were described as the most spiritual Christians in history.

During a later Crusade, the Cathars, under orders of the church, were forced to denounce their belief in their religion and their God or be burned alive. Knowing the Cathars would never concede to these demands, the Catholics would be able to execute the Cathars. As the troops of Pope Innocent III fulfilled their gruesome orders, some started to question what they were doing and began to back off, asking for clarification. The pope, however, only pushed harder. When the pope was questioned as to how to really determine the Cathars' true religious position, the order was given to "kill the women and children, and let God sort out the innocent."

Later in the fourteenth century as the fact emerged that a royal bloodline may in fact exist on the English shores, King Henry of the Tudors and current royal crown lineage tried to once again to end any potential overthrows of the throne. Instead of killing mass citizens and citing a false blame to an innocent religious group, King Henry would instead issue a proclamation to destroy all parsonages and recorded facts relating any parties other than his own interest to the throne. Just like the attempts of King Louis III to locate and kill the rightful heir to the English and Norman thrones, King Henry's extermination of information also missed its mark.

History leads to many clues of Roger Benjamin's existence and relationship as the secret son of King Stephen. The boy was raised without notice or fanfare and would ultimately be buried without a headstone. His death would have gone completely unnoticed had he not been exhumed centuries later where he lay buried under both the royal shields of the Royal English family and the Blois in a grave next to King Stephen.

Fast-forward several centuries, introduce DNA and modern technology, and secrets of the past offer real threats to today's political and religious leaders. Compound this with recorded historical events of supernatural or magical powers that show up in one of the heirs every fifth or sixth generation, and you quickly come to understand why Charlie and the other descendants were being tracked until someone revealed the unusual talents or powers that Charlie was now demonstrating. Unfortunately for the individuals tasked with tracking these descendants, this job could take decades or centuries without any findings during their lifetimes.

Lucky for Charlie's trackers, he and his generational family were somewhat small and consisted of twelve cousins and three siblings. Some difficulties for Charlie's trackers appeared, as there were long periods of age separations between the current lineage. The oldest cousin and first representative of this generation was born almost twenty years before Charlie. This means Charlie's cousins had to be tracked for all of those years. As almost a mockery from God himself, Charlie was the last-born potential heir of the current generational bloodline.

Because none of the prior relatives had shown any unusual signs of oddities, all of the trackers had to continue their daily grind of following people, bugging rooms, flying incognito when any of the people being surveyed traveled, impersonating nurses when one of them fell sick, taking jobs as teachers as they attended schools, etc. This was a twenty-four-hour shift, seven days a week, 365 days a year, and for some, they had already been tracking them for decades until Charlie showed up, a full thirty years from the time they had started tracking the elder bloodline member of this generation.

Once, about a year prior to Charlie's oddities being reported, the trackers became very excited. It had been reported that one of the members of Charlie's generation had started demonstrating odd, magical powers where he could bend steel with his bare hands and make his hands shoot fire.

"Wow, finally," shouted many of the members of the tracking group over their radio frequencies. They were very excited to finally move on to different jobs. Some had spent their entire careers following these Benjamins and were ready to retire.

All were curious about these powers that were being reported now but didn't know what that really meant. After all, it had been more than 250 years since the last recorded event had demonstrated itself. This also meant there was very little current data to work from in analyzing what these powers would look like. So, yes, they were glad to see what this all meant—finally.

There was one big problem, though. The individual they thought had been demonstrating the inherited powers turned out to be performing simple parlor games and magic tricks. He was very good at the tricks, had been self-taught, and really wowed his friends and family, but they were simply tricks. Nevertheless, he still had to be followed, along with everyone else, until someone demonstrated some real powers.

It was a real letdown for the trackers. Some even quit, thinking the people in charge of the operation must have gotten something wrong, as surely something should have shown itself by now.

During the year following the magic incident, as the observers came to call it, weird things started to reveal themselves from Charlie. They were little things, odd for others, but not odd enough for Charlie or what he viewed as normal.

Because Charlie was a calm personality, very rarely did things in his life concern him. When odd things happened either to him or around him, he generally wouldn't discuss it, so, of course, none of the trackers would hear about it. Even if a tracker was perusing Charlie visually, he would often see things his followers would miss because of his ability to see auras, feel the energy waves of the world, and either go with the energy or against it. Weird, yes. Unusual for Charlie, no. So he never discussed it.

Some things came out when Charlie was younger due to his swimming incidents and saving the young lady. At that point, the surveillance teams knew they had likely finally found the person from the lineage they needed to monitor while protecting him from other governments as well.

Charlie never really saw his oddities from another person's point of view, and he never really discussed them with anyone in real depth of detail until he married Sheila. Although Charlie and Sheila grew up thousands of miles apart and were raised under completely different conditions by families with very different backgrounds, the two were very similar. She had been raised on a farm, while he was raised in a suburb, but the differences seemed to end there.

As different as the two could have been, they actually had many deep similarities. Both grew up going to church and had deep spiritual beliefs. Both were honest, sometimes painfully honest. Both were extremely curious people who spent much of their leisure time reading, seemingly continuously. They loved their families, played together, traveled together, laughed together, and flat-out enjoyed all of life's opportunities together.

Charlie and Sheila celebrated their similarities, but after Sheila moved in with Charlie, she really started to notice some of his oddities as they presented more and more difficult situations that Sheila would have to explain. This made the CIA nervous, as they didn't want Charlie's information leaking out.

So, after following Charlie's relatives around for years and years to identify the unusual, now they had to follow the couple to provide protection for them. When Charlie first learned this, he became amused almost in a getting even fashion. Charlie decided he would just roll along with everything and let everything or his wife sort it all out.

9

Was William the Conqueror a Benjamin?

With Charlie's new marriage and life somewhat chaotic and everyone seeming to understand things about Charlie better than he did himself, Charlie did what most other people would do and immersed himself into other focus points. For Charlie, that, of course, meant he would head to his favorite place for quiet: the library. He would grab a fat book on a topic he had never read about and head to the rear of the library. It was always quiet back there and had a great window where he could occasionally look out and see his favorite giant old oak tree that played host to all kinds of wildlife, such as squirrels, birds, butterflies, and bees.

The book Charlie chose was about William the Conqueror and detailed his life, his beliefs, his family, and how he treated others. Immediately, Charlie learned how this man was easily identified as a conqueror because of the Battle of Hastings. However, this man did not live as a barbaric killer as most people think when they hear the title *conqueror*. Really, King William was a very fair leader who followed the rules of the day and greatly respected families, women, and, most importantly, order. Charlie was immediately intrigued about this legend of history and started to identify with his character in much the same way as he had when he learned about King Clovis. Charlie read on.

William the Conqueror's victory over King Harold during the Battle of Hastings would not only leave England under Norman rule but change the face of Europe for centuries to come. King Harold refused to recognize the pope's authority or bring the church's reforms to the newly conquered English kingdom. As a result, Pope Alexander II backed the Norman duke William by giving him powerful military resources, as well as spiritual backing from the church. Harold also refused to acknowledge that William had legal claim to the English throne through William's bloodlines verses Harold's appointment under monarchic rule.

As a bastard child, William would fight for positioning in the family, as well as in his rightful kingdom. Only after receiving confirmation from the pope that William was the rightful heir to the throne did William forcefully attack and battle for his position. William was furious at Harold and held nothing back during this vengeful crusade. After his victorious battle at Hastings, England, William wasted no time in taking possession of all existing castles and building additional fortifications in strategic locations. William's primary challenge was not his military strategy but rather his language. His native language was French, while the people of his new kingdom spoke English.

Nevertheless, William's confirmation of his leadership as a result of his bloodline would disrupt monarchies for all the future. This would ultimately lead to periods of demarcation by illegitimate monarchs wishing to hide or erase the truth. This would impact young Charlie, as unknown to him at the time, his own lineage suffered attacks against its legitimacy from monarchs installed as kings who used demarcation to hide or erase rightful heirship. However, William and Charlie's bloodline would survive centuries of challenges irrespective of these attempts.

Life is funny sometimes—not as in ha-ha but as in odd. People born into common circumstances can only imagine all the good things that surround those they envy. If they see someone famous or wealthy, they naturally envision all the fun that person must have every day. They may reflect on our own lives and believe they have failed or simply have not driven themselves hard enough or far enough.

The firstborn of a royal family would have been the object of such envy. Those around them would have thought the firstborn to be one of the lucky ones, born into wealth and power that others would have to respect. Others would imagine that anything these lucky ones wished would be produced at the snap of a finger.

The reality was often much different, as was the case with William the Conqueror, or William the Bastard as he was known by the people of his day. In fact, as the eldest son of Robert I Duke of Normandy, or Robert the Magnificent as he was affectionately known by his people, life was complicated. William did not want for material possessions; he wanted for respect, which he thought he was due as the eldest son of the monarch. However, his mother was a classless peasant his father loved and held as his unwed mistress, leaving William the nickname of the bastard.

Many would say this error in his father's judgement would plague William his entire life and would especially cause issues for William after his dad fathered more sons with his wife of royal lineage. Others would say William's challenging start probably made him what he would become. William fought and earned everything he ever received similar to the lineage struggles his ancestors faced from their start. His half siblings, who had two royal parents, never recognized William's place on earth and would challenge it throughout his lifetime.

Charlie was amazed as he continued reading and learning about how he shared similar oddities with William. The boy William who would become king was unusual as a child and shared commonalities with Charlie, such as the power of extraordinary vision and clarity.

He was a friend of the sea and was born of a peasant's blood mix. So how could he have become king? Was this God's calling or simply a great series of coincidences? This king was fair to all his people, men and women alike, when others were not. So where did this fairness come from? Was it a result of years of poor treatment for being born a bastard, which gave him empathy toward commoners whom his siblings could not have understood? William was so fair in his dealings throughout his life that he even reached out to the pope for permission prior to bringing the fight to England for the throne.

William's influence was extraordinary throughout England, as his focus on God was without compare during his time period. During King William's tenure, England saw a record number of abbeys and ancient cathedrals rebuilt. The king also introduced new castles to England as had long existed in France. At the time of his death, more than five hundred castles existed across Great Britain.

In a tribute to his heritage, King William ended the slave trade in England. No longer could people be uprooted from their families, beaten, branded, and traded. King William also respected women during his tenure, which was uncharacteristic of most during his time except in Jewish tradition. Even though his mother was a peasant lady, the king never disrespected her. When others did, he had their hands and feet cut off.

There are man's hopes for proper lineage, and then there is God's true bloodline. Man professes to have lineage that follows hierarchal order, but God's way is through nature. He does not care about titles or material effects of power. God's way is always based on common sense natural order. In the end, out of love and interlock, more love is created, and those with the greatest common sense are born and will harness and control the world with common sense and great talent. This was the case with young William as many people never gave him the respect due a monarch. He had been conceived out of what man's order believed was not valuable, but his birth order from God could not be denied.

The king's powers magnified not only historical events but the effects on those around him. Looking at King William's wife, Matilda of Flanders, shows how her regard for him went from resistance when they first met to unequaled love of the man by her end of days. Why did the House of

Boulogne, a cadet branch of the House of Flanders, create the kingdom of Jerusalem after the first Crusades? What was the power William possessed, and what was the connection to Jerusalem? Did both William and Matilda share a royal bloodline that had separated over the centuries only to be reacquainted with their union? King Williams's wife, Queen Matilda, also had ascended from a long line of Frankish royalty, the same royalty headed by the Merovingians and the members of the lost Tribe of Benjamin who ascended throughout northwest Europe.

Why would a Norman king be less concerned with settling differences with neighboring French enemies and more concerned with non-enemies in lands thousands of miles away? Could this have been a plan from God to reconstitute the Benjamin Tribe with sacred lands? We may never know; however, during this period of time, the lineage of William and Matilda would lay the groundwork for future noble leaders—emperors, kings, queens, dukes, and countesses—who would show the path for changes around the world. There would be many.

Witnesses say that William executed God's plan, which gave him the strength of a thousand warriors and the knowledge and intuition of fabled kings before him. Over time, William would be challenged over his rightful place in the world. Time and time again, man would try to push William down, but he would never stay down. In fact, he would fight back harder and harder each time. Williams's biggest fights were with his family members. As they aged and dwindled in number, fewer and fewer would lay claim to the throne that would become William's. However, though the numbers were reduced, the fights intensified.

William had been promised the throne by the dying childless King Edward the Confessor, but Earl Harold Godwinson, who had previously taken the oath to back William's claim to the throne, had reneged against William and ignored the dying king's promise by taking the throne to himself to be the next king. Although this made sense to many, as Earl Godwinson was of proper noble Anglo-Saxon bloodlines from his father and mother and shared direct lineage through Cnut the Great, it was not the true and proper bloodline order.

Duke William, on the other hand, was a Norman, and England had never had a Norman king. William spoke French, so the English people could not understand him. The English system of rule was much more complex and confusing than Normandy. Finally, the Duke was a bastard, hardly befitting royalty.

So, with all of the headwinds facing Duke William, he sought out God as the decision maker in this argument, and the decision landed in the lap of Pope Alexander II. The circumstances clearly indicated that William was the rightful heir through bloodlines. This decision was the proper one, and the stage was set for war between Duke William and Earl Harold.

At the passing of King Edward, the only way Duke William was going to get Earl Harold removed from the throne would be by great force. As Earl Harold assumed the throne, he immediately amassed a great army around him. Duke William amassed his armies across the English Channel and set fire to all of his fleet behind him, a fleet numbering in the hundreds of ships. William wanted Harold dead, and he would get the kingdom. Burning the ships told William's soldiers, there would be no retreat. William the Conqueror went on to face and kill Harold Godwinson in furious fashion at the Battle of Hastings on October 14, 1066, and would be crowned king on Christmas Day in that same year.

Political ways, religious beliefs, and human decency even through adverse times and challenges empowered the traditions of the Benjamins to survive through King William's period. Finding the path of the Benjamin Tribe is now possible through tracking the shifts in cultural behavior that changed the world as the tribe migrated through specific geographic areas. This enabled historians, archeologists, and sociologists to make proper conclusions as to the paths the Benjamin Tribe traveled. They changed the world centuries before the Merovingians, King William, and others arrived and, of course, well before modern-day Charlie appeared.

This Benjamin lineage created a calmer, more just and orderly world for all history to enjoy. Though many challenges would present themselves in the future, the powers as the Chosen People from God's covenant would continue throughout the Middle Ages until persecution in Europe finally forced a new quest for freedom. The Benjamins' migration across Europe and ultimately across the seas to America forever changed the world into a more compassionate place. This path could only have come from the light of God.

Charlie sat motionless as he started to meld everything together from what he had recently learned about his lineage and the oddities he shared with these historical figures. What did it all mean? Why didn't other relatives, including his brother, sister, mother, or father, share some of these oddities? Why him? It started to make more sense why some people had spent years tracking him. He didn't know who he should talk with or trust with everything, but he knew he had to figure it out.

As he sat there, he felt powerful, proud, and weak at the same time. Tears started welling up in his eyes. Suddenly, he felt a great fear that he would die before getting this information out to the world. He thought history should be corrected and the erasure of the demarcation process reversed, but he knew instantly there would be powerful forces standing in his way, as it could mean an end to the very survival of some of the royals currently in power.

10

Frozen in Time

Charlie knew that some people described him as being smarter than others. They always said he was sharp with his answers and generally correct. When events happened around him, he would be the first to respond properly. His responses and actions gave others the impression that he had been given the answers beforehand. However, Charlie never felt or saw his level of intelligence being as sharp as others had reported. In fact, Charlie felt much less intellectual than others around him. He would listen to the words they used as they spoke, and he would occasionally wonder what the words meant.

Charlie's thoughts of slowness extended beyond simple vocabulary. He saw the world around him in slow motion as well. Charlie's views of the world seemed to capture everything around him in a 360-degree view and in perfect clarity. If something was moving toward Charlie, he would see it before others around him and would react accordingly.

This started showing up when Charlie was a young boy when he was teasing others around him. He would poke others and annoy them, trying to get a reaction. In kid kingdom justice, a normal response to being poked or bothered usually resulted in a quick punch in the mouth. This was the intended consequence to Charlie's bothering his friends, and it would have been perfectly acceptable. However, the intended recipient of the punch would have been Charlie who always rendered the kid throwing the punch more than tired from flailing around hopelessly as he easily avoided these attempted smacking's. These events involving Charlie always ended up with no punches being landed and a happy Charlie laughing at the flying missed attempts by a frustrated kid. Witnesses reported how quickly Charlie avoided the punches and always in the right direction. Between punches, the young, seemingly hyper boy would sneak in a couple more pokes to the angry kid and then perfectly dodge several more punches. The other child would grow tired of throwing pointless haymakers and come to a stop, usually buckled over with their hands on their knees, huffing and puffing and very irritated.

Charlie loved this and thought of it as mere fun. Most kids recognized it as Charlie just being obnoxious, and they would forget the event soon after it took place. However, some of Charlie's victims carried their anger and embarrassment long after the events took place and sought revenge. As their anger built, they would sometimes plan retaliatory attacks on Charlie when he seemingly wasn't prepared to defend himself. Even when they sneaked up on Charlie, he would avoid their attacks and move as though he had filmed these events in advance, predicting everything the would-be assailants had planned and every move they would make.

Some of Charlie's frustrated victims often teamed up and conjured plans to get even with him. There would be two, three, or ever four kids surrounding and attacking Charlie at the same time. Onlookers would watch and say, "Charlie is going to really get a beating today." Many felt sorry for Charlie, as they knew he was greatly outnumbered, and surely, he was going to get badly hurt. Others, usually past victims of Charlie's irritations, would say, "Finally, the jerk is going to get what he deserves." Regardless of whose side the children took, most carried some doubts about whether Charlie would be able to come out on top of the situation unscathed as he always seemed to do.

As the kids surrounded Charlie and called him names, he said nothing and just watched their eyes. One of the kids spit at Charlie in anger.

Charlie shifted to the right, and the spit hit one of the other attackers right in the mouth, causing the kid to gag as he tried to stop from throwing up. Charlie and all of the crowd watching started laughing at the spit mistake. This angered the assailant even more, which immediately prompted the attackers to move in on Charlie all at once.

Fists were flying, feet were kicking, elbows were spinning, but none met their intended target. Charlie moved efficiently and avoided all of the pain, and those around him could hear him giggling as the event progressed. The crowd became completely silent and appeared to become hypnotized by Charlie's abilities. It was simply fascinating to watch. As the attackers grew tired from their continuous missed punches and kicks, Charlie moved in and had some fun. He grabbed one kid by the back of his pants and flipped him into a nearby garbage can headfirst. The boy screamed as he was launched into the smelly den. The boy's feet flailed in the air, giving the appearance as though he was an upside down mushroom with legs.

A second boy was thrown face-first into a fountain next to where the boys fought. The boy, now looking like a wet rat, poked his head out of the water, not even daring to climb back out and resume his efforts.

The final two boys involved in the dustup were somehow slammed face-to-face and then dropped immediately to the ground on top of one another in a heap of defeat. They lay there motionless.

The circle of onlookers opened up a path for Charlie's exit almost like a crowd parts during a royal procession. As Charlie walked away from the melee, everyone just stared at him while taking quick glances back at the fallen warriors. No one immediately moved to the aid of the beaten children. Instead, the crowd looked at them as though they were infected with something contagious. They didn't help them but rather dispersed, quietly mumbling to themselves about what they had just witnessed.

Charlie's abilities to see things quicker than others also gave him the ability to hear things a split second sooner than others as well. Conversations that involved Charlie enabled him to have extra time to come up with an answer, usually the correct answer. It was almost as though a comment or question would be asked, and then everything would become a freeze frame, holding everything motionless until Charlie formed his answer, and then everything would move in normal time again.

Because Charlie didn't have the presence of mind to understand that others did not have this ability, he just felt it was normal. As he grew older, he started to realize a difference but never truly appreciated this gift. He still felt mentally slower than others but thought his ability to freeze frame time made things sort of even.

11

Gods and Mortal Men

M en are created very similarly at birth in the sense that most are born with two arms and legs, a head, common sense, and the intuitive smarts to stay away from wild activities and danger. Not Charlie. He liked grabbing at life and riding it for all it was worth. To Charlie, each day was a new opportunity, and he would always try to grab the golden ring. Even when life came at him hard or presented him with challenges, he would attack it head-on and simply laugh things off and keep smiling, almost as though he enjoyed the chaos or drama that often resulted from these events.

Charlie liked to create the events that surrounded him and control their outcomes. It was as though Charlie could look at a river, feel the energy flowing by, and understand that he could stand in the flow and try to push the water back to an obvious no-win situation, or he could throw a canoe on the river and ride it out while using its energy to his advantage. His understanding of how to harness the world's energy gave him seemingly supernatural abilities.

As a young boy, Charlie learned and enjoyed understanding how real energy worked. When he was a young child, he could often be seen moving pencils or paperclips without touching them. He would focus on the pencils, feel the energy coming off his fingers, and focus on pushing the energy into the pencils. They would then start rolling away from the pressure. For the paperclips, he would hold his hand over them, and they would rise in the air. When his friends would ask him how he was doing it, he would tell them to focus on the magnetic feelings and they could do it too. They tried but weren't successful. Life was just that way with Charlie. People often commented to Charlie that what he did was some sort of magic trick.

As Charlie grew, these tricks intensified. He could make chairs slide out for girls, and they would giggle. He could open doors without touch and could warm cold rooms without a heater. He just seemed to always be fun and helpful that way.

Some say the greatest way to God is through music. Regardless of whether that is true, it was definitely the best way to reach Charlie. One summer night while on a walk home, Charlie was passing by a live musical performance. The music was enchanting, but the event was sold out. Charlie would not be prevented from entering and listening, but the security staff at the front doors felt otherwise. Charlie stared deep into the guard's eyes with a terrifying bullet gaze that petrified them where they stood. Never one to steal, and understanding the guard's natural energy to win in situations such as these, Charlie reached into his pocket, retrieved some paper money, and put it into the guard's shirt pockets. The guards let him in.

Other events similar to these, but much more significant, usually involved Charlie going somewhere that he shouldn't have gone, getting caught, but then almost magically getting away unscathed. Case in point, while visiting eastern Europe one time, he and a couple of friends happened upon a political event taking place involving the presidents of several of the surrounding countries. He told his friends they should all go and listen to the discussion. As one would certainly imagine, security was extremely tight. The country they were visiting was part of the old Communist bloc.

Because the police had been trained under Communist regimes, the police officers certainly knew how to intimidate and repel people not allowed at such events. Charlie's friends stayed back and let him go forward alone as they were fearful of the tough-looking police. As Charlie approached the restricted area, he was immediately surrounded by several large and heavily armed guards who called out to Charlie to stop. The main guard immediately stepped up to Charlie and appeared to be getting ready to fully restrict his access. Then the guard simply stopped, stepped to the side, and allowed Charlie unencumbered access. Charlie's friends stood there with their mouths wide open.

Several of the boys echoed each other, "Are you kidding me? How does he get away with this?"

Moments later, as Charlie's friends were standing around gawking about what they had just witnessed, the guards came over and scurried them away.

Several minutes had passed when Charlie reemerged unscathed. When asked how Charlie had gotten past the guards and allowed access, Charlie said he simply uttered the first words that came to his mind in English. He told his friends he knew it was very likely these people did not understand Charlie's language, or they would maybe understand little bits and pieces of it, so what he said would be too complex or confusing and the words would most likely stop them in their tracks. So, when confronted, the first words he tossed out that came to his mind were not even a sentence but rather a smattering of different words mixed together.

"So, what the hell did you say, Charlie?" asked Steve excitedly.

Charlie ignored Steve's question, as he didn't think this was as big of a deal as his friends were making it out to be. Charlie had simply tapped into nature's energy and changed the conversation and the circumstances altogether. When he did this, the guards immediately backed off and let him in for a brief period until they realized what they had done and then came for him. When his friends asked why they didn't arrest him, Charlie said that once the guards had let him in, it would have been extremely embarrassing for all involved if a big scene erupted. Knowing what he had said to the guards was nonthreatening and completely crazy, the guards assumed he was harmless and simply needed to be redirected out of the area. If asked, they could have responded to their superiors with a story that a crazy guy came in and they took care of everything, and the event would be slipped under the carpet so to speak.

His friends asked Charlie again, "So, what did you say to the guards?"

Charlie said, "I simply said, 'Your chicken tastes like licorice toast,' in English and went on about my business. I knew they would have to look up what I said and then ask each other a thousand times if that was actually what I said because it made no sense. In the end, the guards could only come to one conclusion—that I must be nuts.

Charlie tried teaching his buddies that it was more about attitude and confidence than what a person says. Charlie's friends did not speak the rest of their walk back to their hotel.

Other incidents that presented themselves in Charlie's life also involved money. Charlie knew most people thought he was either broke or looking for extra money. However, Charlie always had money, and the more he spent, the more it seemed to just show up. Some of the money would come in the form of cash gifts from people he never knew or had even heard of for that matter. At first, his parents wondered where the money was coming from and asked family members with no answers. As the money kept coming, he would discuss this with his parents, and they would tell him to just enjoy it. They never found any answers about who was sending it, and the amounts were small at first.

After a while, however, the amounts became significantly larger, so his parents took a more active role trying to find answers. Sometimes the amounts were in the thousands, and oftentimes, the money would simply show up in his little savings account at the bank, always with no tracking as to where the money came from or who had sent it. The oddest events of payments involved trips or events that Charlie was involved with that would end up being paid for by unknown sources. After many similar occasions, Charlie's parents asked the police to get involved to ensure nothing illegal was happening, but the police were never successful at finding any answers or wrongdoings. As time passed, Charlie's parents would follow up more often with the police only to be told everything was legal. They also noted they weren't allowed to discuss anything else regarding the situation and told Charlie's parents to ignore their concerns about tracking who was sending the money.

Although some of the unusual events that Charlie faced were just part of his personality, he figured that was the way things were for him. He never related any of his oddities or the monetary gifts to his lineage because early on he never knew the history of his lineage. He certainly never knew any of this could be related to being a Benjamin descendant or a descendant from some very famous people in history.

12

Pepin's Treason and Charlemagne's Reign

Charlie was just finishing a boring book and was getting ready to call it a night and head home for the evening as he laid his head back against his chair and blinked his eyes hard, trying to get them to focus. He was tired and upset, as he hadn't found anything exciting or new for several weeks while researching his past ancestors. As he started to relax, he happened to glance at several books on the bookshelf and noticed one about Charlemagne's life. Thinking to himself that he hadn't read anything on the subject, he decided to take a quick look at some of the chapter headings. Charlie's quick glance turned into hours of deep excitement, which ended with a tap on his shoulder by Mrs. Goal, the librarian.

"Charlie, we are closing. You'll have to grab your things and go home now." Mrs. Goal always appreciated Charlie's enthusiasm at the library and hated to disrupt his reading, but she also wanted him to get home safely before it got too late.

"All right, Mrs. Goal," responded Charlie as he packed up his things.

He then checked out the Charlemagne book, placed it into his backpack, and headed out.

Once at home, Charlie said good night to his family and marched off to bed where he continued reading the book on Charlemagne late into the next morning. The book gave Charlie his first real training on how people sometimes take advantage of others to get ahead. Charlie was also curious as to how close friends and family sometimes try to take advantage of one another for selfish reasons. The book described in detail how actions by Pepin manipulated members of the Merovingian royal family to help Pepin himself gain power by falsely claiming Charlemagne was his son and then helping him to ascend to power.

The book opened by discussing treason as most commonly completed by those closest to leaders. The story progressed from there and sighted additional facts as the story continued about how Charlemagne's history started with treasonous acts by others.

This was the fact that usurped the direct lineage of the Merovingian family with lies and manipulation and placed Pepin in charge of the throne. Direct rule would ultimately be given to Charlemagne by way of the puppet master, Pepin, under great scrutiny.

After the death of Merovingian King Theuderic IV, the throne lay vacant for seven years until the Merovingian son, Childeric III, was able to take control.

Years earlier, upheaval from the Merovingian family offspring fought internally for control. This constant infighting created weaknesses in the family that was then taken advantage of, none noted greater than the Frankish Statesman and military ruler Pepin of Herstal. Through a process of diminution, Pepin of Herstal murdered Merovingian King Dagobert II and took over his power but was never given the title of king. Due to public unrest and the fact that a rightful Merovingian bloodline was still alive, Pepin of Herstal's grandson, Pepin the Short, instituted a new Merovingian king, Childeric III. Childeric III wanted nothing to do with being king even though it was his bloodline obligation. Instead, he was retired to the monastery.

The desire to rule was not lost on Pepin the Short, Herstal's grandson, as he petitioned Pope Zacharias in order to betray the Merovingian rule just as his grandfather had. Pope Zacharias was heavily influenced by

Pepin and eventually rendered the statement, "Who should be king? The man who actually holds royal power, or he, though called king, who has no power at all?" Realizing the power that could be gained from a pact with Pepin, Zacharias would go on to betray the papal pact with the Merovingian family and rightful heirs by declaring Pepin the Short king.

Some of the interesting facts that have become foggy in history over the years are how and who the royal blood and lineage carried on through and intertwined with through the years. Also, power was portrayed incorrectly in many ways. For example, it was very important for the church and Pope Zacharias to declare anyone other than the Merovingians, who were the direct descendants of the Benjamin Tribe, as king. By doing this, the royal, God-given bloodline would be diminished, thus allowing the church to take over the appearance of power.

To achieve this, Pope Zacharias would conspire with Pepin the Short to incorporate a plan to have the monarch Merovingian Childeric III in place as acting king. Pepin then worked behind the scenes to reform the Frankish Church, taking more and more power away from Childeric. The plan was designed to reduce the Merovingians' interest and slowly wipe away their visibility while, at the same time, manifest the recognition of Pepin's Carolingians in the face of the people. The other Carolingian family members understood what was happening and revolted against Pepin who had them put down until he was in full charge. Ultimately, Pepin's plan and conspiracy with Pope Zacharias was successful and his self-proclamation of king was confirmed once Pope Zachary deposed Childeric in 751.

The new king, along with the current and future popes, worked together to ensure power under the false self-proclaimed monarchy. In these situations, the real challenge became keeping the true bloodlines hidden. Even though Childeric III was removed from the office, he still possessed the true Merovingian bloodline and was the rightful heir to the throne. He would also father a son, Theuderic, whom history seemed to lose.

Charlie was a very honest person, so these stories of deceit often left him confused. He would read and reread parts several times and pull out other books to cross-reference facts. He also pulled out several life drawings of Charlemagne, Pepin, and the Merovingians for comparison purposes, as historical documents generally described Charlemagne as looking more like the Merovingians and less like Pepin. After reading about the many misdated events around Pepin, his wife, and the birthdate of Charlemagne, Charlie, like the many scholars, used historical facts to determine that Charlemagne could not possibly be Pepin's child. The timeline details also proved further that Pepin was deeply involved with the pope for the Roman Catholic Church, which, for political reasons, needed the Merovingian bloodline to end, ensuring the church's power.

So, who was Charlemagne really? One thing that brought Charlie to this question has been asked over the centuries without answer: Was Charlemagne truly Pepin the Short's son? Or was he actually the son of Childeric III and Pepin's consort, Bertrada of Laon? Was Charlemagne actually of royal Merovingian blood, where Pepin was not? Was Charlemagne actually Theuderic, the son of Childeric III, who simply disappeared at the very time of Charlemagne's arrival? No one knows the date or location of Charlemagne's birth, and Pepin and Bertrada were not married at the time of the child's birth. Did the church under Pope Zacharis and the kingdom under Pepin's cooperation hide the facts around the Merovingians' royal bloodline by claiming Pepin to be the father of Charlemagne to ensure they absconded the power successfully?

You cannot find any depictions of Charlemagne similar to Pepin's lineage; however, there is a striking resemblance of Charlemagne and the Merovingians.

During Pepin's power grab, maximum deception was used at all levels, and it has been considered that a false monarch was placed on the throne.

Charlie paused in his reading and considered it for a moment. It seemed to him that people might never know the full truth of the matter; however, Charlemagne's contributions to the world couldn't be overlooked. If he wasn't originally in the royal bloodline anointed by God, he sure acted saintly.

During this prolonged period of deception, Pope Leo III also understood the church had to become the most important benefactor of this change and could cause the Carolingians to simply rule as the Merovingians had. This would be further demonstrated in AD 800 when Charlemagne, the Carolingian ruler, wanted to be crowned emperor and traveled to Rome. During his arrival, Pope Leo III sneaked up behind Charlemagne and crowned him emperor away from an official event. Even though Charlemagne wished to be crowned, he wanted the event to take place as a royal event to avoid the appearance that the church was at a higher standing than the kingdom.

Upon the crowning by Pope Leo III, Charlemagne became the first Holy Roman Emperor ruling over an empire rivalling the eastern Roman or Byzantine Empire. This is considered by historians as one of the most important moments in world history. When you think about it, the move by Pope Leo III to crown the king was one of the greatest deceptions ever, as the process used by the pope gave the appearance that the church was in charge of determining who gets to be in power. Charlemagne would go on to become one of the most powerful emperors history has ever known. He brought together most of western Europe, brought prosperity and economic stability to his area by instituting successful reforms, and, most notably, became famous for building a standardized educational system with schools and curriculum, thus ending the Dark Ages.

During the Charlemagne Renaissance period, cultural enhancement took place and paved the way for Christianity to have unabridged growth, all under the false belief that the church was in charge. Even more disappointing is the fact that Pope Leo's deception most likely contributed to the ire that led to the unnecessary murders and reductions of other powerful religions of the time such as the Cathars, Pagans, and Jews, as well as some lessor groups simply for not sharing the church's exact views. Leo's imagery displayed the church's power over politics by stating viewpoints of the church that matched the church's ambitions. The church bodies were effective because who could blame God for the mission of sorting these issues out at any price?

Charlemagne was the first emperor to reunite most of western Europe since the founding of the Roman Empire. The kingdoms that divided Europe over the centuries were now being reunited by Charlemagne, the sole emperor of the newly founded Carolingian Dynasty.

Charlemagne's success in spreading Christianity across Europe would go unmatched throughout history. He would give time, money, and land to the church and always protected the pope. He added chapels using Byzantine and Christian designs, educated the clergy and monks, added inspirational music, and standardized their practices and skills using Pope Benedict's rules.

One of Charlemagne's major contributions to the world was his focus on education. He educated both his sons and daughters with the highest levels of education available at the time. This was ironic, as he was called "the man who was the sponsor of medieval education," yet he himself was unable to write, even though he continued to try even into his later years. He built schools and expanded his educational system throughout Europe, modernized current learning facilities and systems, and standardized the information being taught. He added students and provided for the textbooks, libraries, and teachers for his new educational system. He even formed libraries and provided the tools and staff to copy classical and religious literature. He standardized language and created a more pronounced form of condensed writing. His contributions around communication and understanding forever brought the people out of the Dark Ages.

Finally, Charlemagne eliminated gold as the monetary standard and replaced it with a much more available and stable system using silver. Charlemagne continued to show his vast intelligence by standardizing his method of maintaining power, wealth, and efficiencies throughout his empire by perfecting the use of an administration system called *missus dominicus*, the palace inspector.

Throughout Charlemagne's lifetime and empire, his standardized thought processes and systems would create unimaginable results never before seen in the world and would leave his lasting fingerprints on society for centuries to come.

After learning about the Merovingians, Poseidon, William the Conqueror, and now Charlemagne and piecing together his own oddities, Charlie started to understand the CIA's and other governments' interest in him. He felt he was still far from the complete truth, but his intuition told him he was onto something and very important. He knew he was getting closer to the answers he looked for and he just needed to keep pushing. He closed the book softly as he listened to the energy that surrounded him and consumed his attention.

13

God Snickers at Charlie's Pranks

Putting everything together while trying to understand why the CIA was so interested in him, Charlie couldn't help but remember some of the fun escapades he was involved in as a kid. Thinking about these events made Charlie laugh to himself.

Teenage years tend to be confusing for normal kids, and when you add an odd kid like Charlie into the mix along with some cleverness, the fun goes off the charts. Teenagers sometimes don't know their limits and can get caught up in the moment no matter how wild those moments become. Junior high and high school kids are also introduced into new elements such as money and all of the toys a young kid could wish for if they had enough of it.

As a solidly religious kid, Charlie knew it was bad to prank people. However, being a logical kid, he negotiated in his mind that it would be okay to mess with people who either acted badly or played with human temptations. Going along with this thought process, Charlie also decided that because God gave him the ability to see others' feelings through their energy levels that he must want the boy to put it to good use. In his mind, Charlie's pranks were really a mission from God.

So, armed with his odd abilities and a uniquely high level of cleverness for such a young boy, he decided to tempt the other kids. In the process, he would teach them a lesson by taking all of their money.

The junior high school he attended was in a somewhat wealthy township, and the schoolkids he was friends with had developed a small gambling problem that the principal had to deal with. As the principal learned of the problem, he announced to the kids they'd be hauled off in shackles to a dark room somewhere under the school where they would be severely beaten if they were caught gambling. The children all knew this threat was probably somewhat of an exaggeration, but just to be sure, they purposely set up a couple of the slower kids to be caught just so they could see what would really happen. As these setup kids were captured, their friends could hear their final shrieks as they were dragged to the secret room to face their punishment. These kids would usually show up again in a week or two, but their personalities would be somewhat subdued as they reentered the general population, no doubt as a direct result of the severe beatings they had taken while in solitary confinement.

Kids can learn a lot from watching what the process is and what the punishment is when others get taken down by the man. The school's process was simple. The teachers would merely wait a few minutes for recess to start and then would just open their classroom doors and grab anyone they saw pitching coins or participating in other forms of gambling outside their doors. It was like catching fish with a net for them.

It's important here to point out how easy it was initially for these teachers to catch kids gambling. At the highpoint of the illicit activities, if you walked through the school during recess, a fire drill break, or lunch, you could easily find behind every wall or in any back hall many of the students pitching coins at the walls to see who could get closest. The coins tossed were not what you won but were merely the tokens used to settle the bets. Most coin-tossing bets were for one or five dollars, but a toss for twenty dollars was not a rare occasion. If you were the fortunate winner, you could make a good childhood income. As the greed factor grew and the gambling bug blossomed with these kids, more and more of them started playing the game, and more and more of them were being hauled off to the secret room to take their punishment.

Knowing how easy it was for the teachers to catch the kids, the children had to come up with a way to detour these teachers from opening their doors. The solution was actually easy, and once operation *keep the door shut* was enacted, the teachers would never again involve themselves in the affairs of these miscreants.

The most effective clandestine counterintelligence operations involve the use of everyday people and common objects. To prove this point, Charlie had all of the kids show up a little early one day with bags of dog droppings if they had dogs. They were then instructed to empty the joyful bags of stink into the trash cans that were conveniently placed outside every classroom door. The kids were then told to partially fill these cans with water. At the first recess, the kids went into the halls as they always did, but once the last kids exited each room, they closed the doors, and everyone rushed to lean the trash cans loaded with water and doggy delights against the doors. A few minutes later, as the teachers opened their doors at roughly the same time thinking they would be plucking young gamblers from the halls, the kids instead heard terror-filled, hysterical screams from the teachers. The kids could tell exactly which teachers had opened their doors by the locations of the screaming. It was like an orchestra from hell as the initial screaming was replaced with a plethora of cursing as the teachers were now basking in their new delightful perfume. Instead of the teachers reaching out and grabbing their handfuls of daily gamblers, they received a wet, smelly lesson that introduced for the first time in history the idea that maybe kids aren't as dumb as many teachers believe them to be.

Charlie's strategy instantly ended the teachers' goals of catching the young gamblers, as they saw no need to ever deal with such a mess again. Charlie became a hero at his school for crafting the idea. The kids all got a couple of days off because the school had to be closed in order for them to clean the awful smell out the classes. All of the dog owners were also happy because for the first time all of their kids had picked up as many doggy droppings in the neighborhood as they could find in preparation for operation keep the door shut, leaving parents' lawns spotless. Somewhere in the ethers of parenthood, you can be sure the parents found out later why all of the kids had worked so hard.

From that time on, and because teachers were no longer regulating these activities due to more fear of reprisal from the inmates, it became tough to walk through the halls and the back alleys of the school without seeing some of the kids freely and without concern tossing their coins in hopes of cleaning the other kids out. Charlie, never one to ignore competition, also took to perfecting his skills of pitching coins like a preacher takes to the Bible or a drunk takes to booze.

As with all things where over stimulus exists, people eventually became bored and looked for other excitement. After a while, there were only a couple of kids who were constantly winning the tosses, so the winning amounts were dwindling as the other kids became bored. The coin-tossing games simply died a natural death. To once again increase cash flow, Charlie introduced and established new gambling games for his eager audience, once again cleaning out all of his school chums' dough.

One of these other forms of gambling that replaced the pitching game was a game called odd man out. This game consisted of three players who would each shake a single coin in his hand, and all three would show their coins simultaneously. If one kid had a head showing and the others both showed tails, then the one showing the head was the odd man out, and the other two would give him whatever the amount of money the bet was for. Similarly, if he showed a tail and the other two each showed a head, then he was the odd man out and would be paid. As a result of his understanding of math, Charlie quickly learned that if he teamed up with one of the other two children prior to the gamming events and they always ended up with the opposite side of the coin, then they would win every bet and split the day's take, guaranteed.

This is somewhat like playing the lotto in America today. Because if the odds of winning the lotto are three million to one and the winning pot is $10 million, then a wealthy person could buy $3 million worth of number variations, guaranteeing they would net out a cool $7 million of net winnings, guaranteed.

Day after day, Charlie and his friends were cleaning up on the playground winnings. Kids would bring in all of their allowances each week to try and win. Of course, parents were not thrilled with their little Tommy or Suzy coming home broke each week. As complaints started pouring in, a school investigation took place, and the school perpetrators were named over and over but never caught in the act. Before the school could wipe out the small-time crime wave Charlie had been instrumental in starting, they had to catch them first.

Threats of suspension and expulsion were thrown out daily but did little to dissuade the criminals. After initial threats of punishment passed ineffectively, the school administrators started to get crafty. The school hired undercover law enforcement added by some of the schoolchildren who had changed teams against the students to entrap the primary gambling ring. These children who teamed up with the police were primarily made up of students who had lost large sums of money in previous weeks and wanted justice served.

You would have thought that Charlie had been peddling booze or women during the prohibition period by the sheer number of undercover police and turncoat students who plagued the sacred school grounds. For a couple of weeks, it was difficult to find a place to play the gambling games. Kids with gambling weaknesses could be seen throughout the grounds flopping around and talking to themselves while they went through their withdrawals. Kids who had lost their bikes, toys, family televisions, coats, backpacks, wads of money, and other small appliances were now being escorted to and from class. The lawless society Charlie had a hand in initially creating now had a new look and feel, and the lawlessness was now definitely over—at least for the time being. Charlie felt like Doc Holiday with the principal being Wyatt Earp looking now to shoot Charlie down and make a name for himself.

It wasn't all bad, though. Many kids who kept losing their lunch money couldn't afford their normal daily rations and began to lose a lot of weight. During the gambling heyday, Charlie's school won awards for having the fittest student population in the country. The gym teacher received undue praise, and a huge banner was hung in front of the school.

Even though the school faculty was basking in their new awards because of all the skinny kids, they knew they still had to deal with the dark evil that lurked under its surface due to the real cause: gambling. The school continued to pay youthful-looking adults to melt into the school's population with hopes of catching the perpetrators. Schools always overreact, and kids never understand their actions fully.

Charlie thought the school should have added bright neon lights like they have in Vegas to increase tourism and gambling on campus. Charlie told his friends, "We could add more and more games to increase the house earnings. It would be great, and our school would have more money than all other schools. That can't be bad, can it?"

School officials had different thoughts, though, and all of their newfound law introduced itself and started sending some of the children home. With the fear of capture eminently possible, Charlie knew he would be all right. He knew who to avoid because he could see who had tight energy levels, which was directly related to people being deceptive. So, Charlie kept on gambling and winning without getting caught.

The principal and vice principal, knowing that Charlie was the kingpin, were so upset with the fact that he couldn't seem to be caught that they took a different and more direct approach. First, they called Charlie into the office and told him that they knew of his involvement levels and that all of the other children that were now working for them and the police and had ratted him out. They told Charlie he would be immediately expelled when finally caught and that capture was imminent. Only a matter of time stood between now and his getting caught. Charlie asked what would happen beyond expulsion and was told all of his money would be confiscated and used to buy trees and benches for the school. Charlie's parents were also immediately contacted and informed of the severity and the dire situation at school. His parents, also wishing to get into the punishment mode, threatened Charlie with public floggings and permanent home arrest. His parents weren't as concerned with the events at school near as much as they were with the possibility of Charlie being home more and their having to watch him more due to the possible school expulsion, which, in their minds, was most likely just around the corner.

Charlie's brother was cool with everything and started selling tickets around town for people to take tours of the home that housed the next Al Capone. William always enjoyed the position in which his brother Charlie's chaotic life left him. William was that guy who did nothing wrong in life but was famous for having a little brother who always managed to find himself at ground zero of anything that was crazy or wild.

Charlie, on the other hand, laughed to himself. He took the seriousness of these threats as a challenge. He knew if captured he would be making big rocks into little ones, but he loved the adrenalin rush of always being close to the third rail, so to speak. Charlie also knew, though, how much he preferred home-cooked meals verses the thought of possibly having to use a prison shank to get what he wanted from other inmates. So, he thought about his options very carefully but always decided to go ahead with his gaming operations or other wild shenanigans anyway. He would proceed just a little more cautiously. Charlie also decided going forward he would reduce his risk of capture by only gambling with the children who had not been completely corrupted by the adults. Charlie didn't care if he was told on because he knew he would have to be caught in the act in order for the punishment to stick.

What the school officials, police, and other students didn't know was how easily Charlie could identify who was being honest with him and who was not because of his ability to see their aura energy levels. When playing the children for money, Charlie could instantly tell when one of the rogue spy children were setting kids up for capture because of their very thin levels of energy. The more nervous someone would get, the thinner their energy levels became. The more comfortable a person is, the thicker his energy waves became. When he saw these thin levels, he wouldn't get involved in the gaming, and sure enough, after a few short minutes, in came the police to haul kids away—every time.

After a couple of weeks of picking what events he would participate in, he found the school administration to become more and more irritated with him and his ability to elude capture even though he was always right in under their noses. The school was also growing very tired of sending home so many other children each week without Charlie being in the mix. Charlie was again brought directly before the principal and vice principal and was again threatened with public decapitation and ultimately having his remains fed to goats. He asked them if he could donate to the school fund and buy trees, benches, and a bronze water sculpture in the likeness of both men for the school. Charlie's parents raised him as properly as possible, so he felt compelled to share 5 to 10 percent of his winnings with the organization that helped create his current occupation. The principal and vice principal seemed to think about Charlie's idea for a split second but soon dismissed it as probably being a bad idea. During this discussion, the nurse even visited and checked the back of the boy's neck and his head for the numbers 666.

During the next two weeks, the same results were again followed by a trip to the principal's office on Friday afternoon. This soon became the norm. This time the principal informed Charlie that because he had done such a good job eluding everyone they we going to reward him by dropping all accusations against him. Starting Monday morning, Charlie would have a clean slate to work from, and bygones would be bygones.

BS, thought Charlie. *Something's up.*

The problem was that while talking to him, both the principal and vice principal had produced the low aura energy levels consistent with those Charlie would see when someone was lying or dying. Because he knew both men to be very healthy and guessing he couldn't be as lucky as to have them both die over the weekend, he decided their story of letting bygones be bygones to be a well-thought-out story. They obviously had something serious in mind for Charlie Monday morning and thought they would finally capture this smart-alecky kid. When he finally left their office, he felt like a baby seal jumping into a tank with killer whales. What Charlie knew for sure was he would not be coming to school on Monday. He went directly to his locker and took home everything with the exception of three textbooks and headed home.

Monday morning rolled around, and Charlie reported to his mother that he had caught a terrible cold over the weekend. He laid in bed acting deathly ill, telling his mother that the end was soon. (He could really turn on the sympathy switch when necessary). His mother came into his room around noon to inform him that most of his closest friends had been carted off to juvenile hall or sent home due to being caught up in a surprise gambling sting operation that had taken place at school that morning. His mother also informed Charlie that the school had called her to check his flu symptoms very carefully to ensure validity. The principal was very direct with his mother and said her son was the number one reason for the police ambush. They couldn't for the life of them understand how circumstances led to Charlie being out of school that day.

After that, Charlie figured he had caused enough chaos for the school, the administration, local law enforcement, and his fellow students and decided to hang up his illicit middle school activities for good, which he did.

To celebrate his retirement, he decided one last prank was in order to seal the day. Knowing that the principal always used the restroom each morning, he decided to place a couple of ketchup packs that he had brought to school the following morning under the toilet seat. As the principal sat down on the seat during his daily visit, the packs, pressed by his weight under the seat, popped and shot ketchup all over his suit. Upon hearing the news, Charlie laughed very hard to himself as the principal walked past him with his backside covered in red.

Charlie would soon finish junior high school and move on to high school, and no one clapped harder that day as Charlie received his diploma than the principal. In fact, all of the teachers and staff were especially excited by Charlie's final departure. Charlie would miss his days there, but he knew from direct remarks made to him and to his parents by the faculty that they were not going to miss him at all.

Upon graduating from junior high school and preparing for his move up to high school, Charlie's transition was the same as every other child's: getting a summer job to earn some money, going on dates with the local girls, playing baseball, and picking a fight with one hundred-plus members from the local motorcycle gang. Okay, that was a lie. Charlie didn't really have many dates at that age, but he did start a fight with the motorcycle gang.

During his first year in high school, his parents felt sports would not be enough to keep his schedule busy and instead opted to keep him occupied with chores around the family ranch. Charlie really couldn't blame them for wanting to keep him busy at the ranch because there were more than enough animals to keep him occupied. For his parents, it was their hope that these activities would also keep Charlie from having enough time to devise his next crime wave at his new high school, but they were incorrect.

While working at the ranch, he dreamed of playing professional baseball. When his chores were complete, he could be found setting up a target to mirror a baseball catcher's mitt position at home plate. He would walk off the necessary 60.6 feet between the pitching mound rubber to the batter's box and throw rocks for hours until nightfall. Over his time of practicing his targeting and delivery, he became very good at throwing. He became so skilled that he could hit most moving or stationary targets. He even developed the talent for knocking squirrels off phone lines, birds off branches, and biker gang members out of lounge chairs while seated in their club yard chairs.

Yes, you read the last sentence correctly. The local biker clubhouse was located near the family ranch and was an oddity to say the least. The house they hung out in was built in the 1930s and had become completely run-down over the years. A quarter of all of the windows were broken, the roof had holes in it, and a painter would have trouble painting it because most of the wood was rotten beyond repair, yet it seemed to always attract a couple of hundred people to it every Saturday evening for their wild parties.

The point of interest to Charlie and his friends was the fact that multimillion-dollar ranches that were built many years later now surrounded the biker hangout. All of the families feared the inhabitants of the biker hangout, but no one ever dared say anything to them for fear of reprisal. All of the ranch owners would simply look away from the hangout as they drove past because direct eye contact would render the ranch owners to turn into stone much faster than peering into Medusa's eyes. In fact, one of the neighbors had witnessed one of the other neighbor's demise when his dog got loose in the bikers' yard. The man caught his dog and picked it up and then came face-to-face with a biker when he stood up with the dog. Rumor has it, the man's stone carcass was mounted over in the entryway and the bikers cooked and ate the dog.

With all of the bad press constantly circulating around the bikers and their hangout, Charlie felt it was his duty to run them out of town. He envisioned the local neighborhood celebrating his great feat by throwing the town a party, along with putting together a parade with at least three or four floats and a band, changing the town name to Charlieville, and retiring the date from the calendar as a sacred national holiday, or at least a state holiday. His enthusiasm grew, so he invited his closest friends to join him on his quest. Most of those invited declined, as they knew this idea was not one of Charlie's best.

Many of the ranches in the area had egg-laying chickens. If you've ever been around chickens, you know that the average family has to eat roughly forty-three eggs daily to keep ahead of the egg production. If the families get behind the egg count and don't keep consumption at peak usage, then they will either end up owning four hundred new chickens each year from the hatchings or they'll end up throwing away a lot of uneaten eggs. You simply can't give away enough eggs because when your neighbors also all have chickens, they don't want your eggs either.

Charlie's strategy included collecting eggs over the next several weeks and leaving them in the hot sun to *ripen* in preparation for the upcoming Annual Rock Band Fest at the biker hangout. A slightly steep hill was perched roughly one hundred yards from the side of the hangout. The side of the hill was completely covered with the healthiest patch of the sharpest, nastiest, most infectious, and tallest thistle weeds known to man. The needle points on these thistles were six inches long on the smallest plants and twelve inches long on the bigger ones. One of Charlie's friends swore a man traversed the hill weekly to hand sharpen every thistle just to make sure they would cause significant damage to anyone crossing their paths. If you were unlucky enough to get within the reach of one of the thistles and were scraped or poked by one of the thistle needle's points, you would immediately swell up and start scratching at your skin madly.

Timmy Jenkins, who lived down the street from the thistles with his elderly grandparents, once lost a ball in the thistles. When he tried to retrieve the ball, he met with several of the needles and instantly swelled up to four times his normal size to the point where all of his clothes burst off with the exception of his underwear briefs. The problem with his underwear briefs being left on made things much worse for Timmy. With his swollen body, he actually looked like a sumo wrestler who had gotten lost in the neighborhood.

Timmy's elderly grandfather suffered from poor eyesight. He thought Timmy was a bear that was after his animals and shot several rounds of buckshot into Timmy's behind before realizing it was Timmy. That was the last time any of Charlie or his friends had heard of anyone getting close to those frightful plants.

The thistles were so dense that no animals would ever chance walking through them. The hill was just steep enough to keep the rancher who owned the hill from ever plowing the field under, so this plot of land had never been changed by man. Topography maps have proven that this piece of land exists today the same way it had during the time of the dinosaurs, and there was quite a bit of speculation that this single plot of land may have, in fact, been responsible for the demise of the dinosaurs.

The annual get-together was the bikers' largest event each year, attracting several hundred bikers, a dozen bands, 800,000 gallons of Budweiser, and 450 pounds of marijuana, 1,000 bags of Doritos, 3,000 condoms, and one bar of soap in the bathroom. No one ever figured out what they did with the soap because they always smelled awful.

Charlie's plan was a simple one. Over the next few weeks, he would sneak in a hundred or so sun-ripened eggs into a small open space dead in the middle of the thistle patch. This open space was approximately twelve feet by twelve feet and would allot him the necessary space needed for throwing the weapons of mass destruction. The challenge would be getting him and his friends into position under the cover of darkness on the night of attack. This would prove to be a challenge, as a wrong move could create thistle pains for months to come. Because it would be dark at the time of the attack, the small group of militants had better have their path memorized. Over the next couple of weeks, they loaded up the piles of eggs and attempted many evening practice runs into the thistles, each time losing one or two of their soldiers in their mock attempt.

Finally, the date of infamy was upon them. That evening they could hear the bikes rolling up the street seemingly for hours and the bands blaring away. The bands actually sounded pretty good, so in some respect, it was a shame what was about to happen. Darkness overtook Charlie and his comrades' position, and the only visible lights were those from the party. Charlie, having the best pitching arm, stood and took aim and threw the eggs as far as he could.

The eggs disappeared blindly into the darkness and would reemerge out of the darkness for a split second into the lights of the clubhouse before exploding onto the party goers. You could hear the screams and yells of those receiving direct hits from the eggs. After unloading half of the eggs onto the unsuspecting crowd, the kids retreated to the ground. The bands stopped playing. The crowd was going crazy throwing out colorful and descriptive threats and words, and everyone was milling around in circles like ants on an ant hill. Charlie and his friends sat quietly as the crowd widened beyond its original boundaries. Just when everyone started to resemble their original semblance, thinking no more eggs would be coming in, Charlie stood up again and resumed launching the remaining eggs.

Once again, the crowd came apart at its seams, yelling threats and saying they were going to do impossible acts to the kids when they found them and their families when they caught them. It was easy to see the smell of the rotten eggs was working its magic. Many started to evacuate the party, while others went in search of the unknown assailants. Many of the now victimized partygoers intuitively guessed Charlie and his gang were somehow located in the thistles but dared not enter. Those who did try to enter were immediately turned back by the painful greeting program of the thistle jungle.

The kids had to keep from laughing as they heard the anguish of the interlopers as they dared to enter the forbidden garden. "Son of a bitch. Dammit, these things are sharp. Ow, dammit!"

Just to make sure no one entered the hideout, the kids added quite a few cow patties to the entrance area of the thistle garden. If someone didn't see the patties and didn't know to jump over them, that person would definitely proceed no farther.

Again, their remarks continued to fly. "What the hell is that smell? I'm not going in there."

Charlie's friends lay perfectly still to avoid giving away their location. Also, because the party's posse had drifted toward the hidden encampment of kids in the darkness, Charlie's friends were quite nervous that they were going to be dead very soon. Situations like this never really bothered Charlie too much. He could see people's auras even in the darkness and knew they would all be fine. After a while, the bikers grew tired of getting poked by the thistles and stepping in cow pies while trying to find them and eventually left.

Of all of the pranks Charlie pulled when he was a kid, nothing compared to this one. Pranks like laying his sisters dolls around his brother while he was asleep and then taking photos or placing a couple of garbage cans in the neighborhood streets and egging the drivers as they got out of their cars to move the cans were all just fun and games compared to this monster of a prank.

In the end, Charlie, his friends, and the victims all survived the pranks. Many of his pranks even proved helpful in the end, as was the case with the bikers who eventually moved away to find safer domain. With that, Charlie felt he had accomplished a good deed and God probably chuckled about it along with him.

As Charlie's thoughts deepened beyond the fun memories and thrills he had as a result of these childish antics, he still couldn't figure out the bigger question as to why the CIA was continuing to bother with him.

Surely, Charlie thought, *these simple pranks can't be why the CIA and these other governments are interested.* Frustrated at not finding an answer worthy of his question, Charlie snapped allowed. "Dammit already." He then smacked his fists on top of his desk as he stood up and walked out of his house to get some fresh air and clear his mind.

14

Demarcation French and English Divided

Charlie once again found himself mired in several books trying to find answers to his questions. He was becoming a stranger to his friends and family, as he spent most of his time at the library possessed by his quest.

After hiring several lineage experts who were extremely successful at detailing the gaps that existed with Charlie's own research of his family's past, he learned that he indeed had quite a few monarch family relations all over western Europe. And so, his reading interest turned to that of French and English history.

Charlie couldn't help but feel the political landscape that must have been quite confusing for the people who lived during the middle of the twelfth century. The countries of England, Normandy, and France were all being led in one fashion or another by relatives from the related Houses of Capet, Normandy, and Blois, yet instead of operating in one united direction, the countries were all being led by very different points of view from the different family member goals.

It must have appeared to the commoners as a feud similar to the Hatfields and McCoys of the nineteenth century. To understand just how divided this separation was, one must understand that even among families there can become acceptable and unacceptable bloodlines once the family becomes too large and points of view become too different or too fractured from those of the primary patriarchs and matriarchs. Direct relatives quickly become direct enemies as family size grows and wealth and power divides.

Charlie learned why demarcation was used when royal families became so large that more and more branches of brothers and sisters, cousins, nieces and nephews, in-laws, children, and great-grandchildren emerge and all want to be the ruler. Charlie also learned that demarcation can be used to cover up past truths in order to create a new future for rulers who have no real rights to head a monarchy.

The House of Capets, also known as the House of France, were decedents of the medieval Frankish families and direct descendants from the Merovingian kingdom led by Clovis I after his conquest of the Meuse, Middle Rhine, and Moselle rivers from the Romans during the time of Gaul, now northern France. The Capet Dynasty started ruling in 987.

The House of Normandy, headed up by the Count of Rouen, Rollo in 911, were the descendants of the Vikings. Rollo was the king of England and Normandy and grandfather to the illegitimate William the Conqueror.

Matilda I, or Maud as she was more commonly called, was born in 1105 and was the countess of Boulogne. She was also queen of England being the wife of King Stephen. Queen Matilda was born in Boulogne, France, the daughter of the count of Boulogne and granddaughter of the king of Scotland. Queen Matilda was also the first cousin of her husband's arch rival, Empress Matilda, who was also King Stephen's cousin. Queen Matilda's direct lineage from the preconquest English kings would help her understand and properly fight future family disagreements.

All of these families were very intertwined with one another but would never be codependents of each other. In fact, to the contrary, most of these people, including brothers and sisters, parents and children, and cousins, genuinely hated and despised each other over their fight for power, wealth, and control. Probably the best example of this lay with the story of King Stephen and his cousin Empress Matilda.

Matilda of Boulogne and Stephen of Blois married in 1125. When Matilda's father died, Matilda and Stephen became joint rulers of Boulogne. They had several children together. Upon the death of King Henry I, Empress Matilda's (not to be confused with the wife of Stephen, also named Matilda) cousin Stephen was crowned king in 1135. His wife, Matilda, was crowned queen the following Easter in 1136.

Queen Matilda was a supporter of the Knights Templar and had a strong relationship with the Holy Trinity Priory at Aldgate. She proved to be her husband's strongest supporter. When England was invaded in 1138, she collected her husband's troops and troops from the neighboring allies and formed treaties. After her husband's capture at the Battle of Lincoln in 1141, she raised an army with the help of allies and rescued her husband, thus squashing the rival Empress Matilda's dreams of coronation.

King Stephen, with his wife, Queen Matilda, at his side, would never again be without continuous attacks from his cousin, Empress Matilda, over control of the throne. This drive to keep control of the power and wealth not only consumed the lives of these individuals while they were alive, but they also wanted to keep control in some form or fashion after their mortal passing.

Like all families, there would be ample offspring resulting in a healthy drive to cause future dilutions of bloodline. The Capets would never recognize the Norman House bloodlines after William the Conqueror's reign due to the illegitimacy of King William's birth and would always try to retake lost control and power of the lost lands. It is important to note the simplicity of the term *illegitimate* used during these frays. The child in question still had a real father and a real mother with real bloodlines. Illegitimacy is clearly a human term derived purely to eliminate others by using dissolution to discriminate and ultimately disavow someone of his blood rights.

The Frankish Capets never felt William the Conqueror, also known as William the Bastard, had any rights to the western kingdoms due to his illegitimacy. After William's death and during William's son's poor efforts at leadership, battling constant infighting among the other siblings, the Capets worked to take back the western kingdoms until Phillip II was finally successful in 1190. This enabled Phillip to change his title from the king of the Franks to become the first in his royal bloodline to hold the moniker as the king of France.

Prior to controlling all of France, the family of King Phillip II had to remove any possible challenges from William the Conqueror's lineage to prevent all future claims to the Norman territories of western France. This task would fall on Louis VII, king of the Franks and father of King Phillip II. King Louis VII had a sister, Constance Capet, countess of Boulogne, France, who had married Eustace IV, count of Boulogne and son of King Stephen, who was also of Frankish nobility under the House of Blois, which dated back to 906. As the grandson of William the Conqueror via William's daughter Adela, King Stephen was both a member of the House of Blois and the last Anglo-Norman king.

King Stephen's oldest son Eustace was described as a child with a happy disposition, full of life and joy. As the child grew, he demonstrated generosity and courtesies toward all others. As he learned his lessons and manners, those around him described him as having a personality similar to his father's. His early lessons as a warrior showed great promise, as well as coordination and raw courage. As a young man, the king celebrated his son's success by holding grand royal celebrations that were always held in front of other monarchs and contemporary leaders. He knighted his son, gave him large swaths of land, presented him with his own team of knights, and made him an earl all before he turned twenty years of age.

Although Prince Eustace was mainly described as an easygoing and friendly child, he was also reported to have an evil side to his personality when left to his own devices. Scholars debate where the boy's inner anger came from, but most agree that it was primarily driven by a constant need for attention from his father. When Eustace's anger appeared, it was usually unexpected and unprovoked. He would become aggressive and warlike against his own people, usually to prove a point that didn't need to be proven. He levied higher taxes than his people could pay. When the taxes weren't paid, he would take their land or burn their homes to the ground. His own soldiers described him as purposeless and only interested in demonstrating his wrath.

As a young boy, Eustace had been contracted in an arranged marriage with a much older Constance Capet. Everything Eustace was his wife Constance Capet was not. She was a very warm, loving soul who cared for everyone and wanted the kingdom to succeed. People loved Constance Capet in the same fashion people loved modern-day Princess Diana.

King Stephen started to realize there would be several difficulties with his son getting the crown or relying on Eustace and Constance Capet to have heirs to continue the lineage. The fact that was not hidden from King Stephen was how far mentally Eustace and Constance Capet were from ever having children. There was simply no love in the relationship. The age difference certainly created distance between the two, but more importantly, the two did not share any similar philosophies. Behind the scenes, Eustace's true personality would show itself. He was reckless and only cared about himself, while Constance Capet's humility and humbleness took center stage further angering the immature Eustace.

King Stephen had originally tried several times without success to get the arch bishop of Canterbury to crown and anoint Prince Eustace as an associate king, as he was the living heir. The king was hopeful that if he was successful with the promotion of his son, he would surely be granted the kingdom upon King Stephen's death. The pope surprised the king, as he forbade the crowning of Eustace due primarily to the Prince's poor behavior and young age.

Also working against King Stephen's goals for his heirs to continue in the line of power were the opposing views of his daughter-in-law's brother, King Louis VII. If the sister of King Louis VII had produced a child with Eustace, the Norman rule would have continued over western France, or at least it would have been much more difficult for the future Frankish kings to lay protected claims over the land.

Fortunately for King Louis VII, his sister had been in an arranged marriage with Eustace, and upon introduction, the two immediately and forever hated each other. The boy was twelve and the girl was nineteen when they married, and the age difference created a vast difference between the two. Eustice IV would grow to be a spiteful young man with a hollow soul and cold heart.

Over time, the countess never grew closer, but rather further from Eustace. King Steffen saw his time, options, and lineage disappearing from the kingdom forever. Eustace would disappear into the countryside for long periods, always drinking and fighting among the peasants, the monks, and his own soldiers. King Stephen and his wife, Matilda, often discussed different options and strategies to merge both bloodlines because they both felt that Eustace and Constance Capet would never come to terms.

King Stephen, Matilda, and Constance Capet always got along well, and the three discussed the situation often. Constance Capet and Eustice would never bare any children, so the story should have ended there, killing all hopes of creating one of the greatest bloodlines ever known. The special lineage would have died as well. But, did it?

As a member of the House of Capet and as a spouse within the ruling family of England and Normandy, Constance Capet found herself in a very odd, yet powerful position to not only mother the future King of Normandy and England but the Frankish kingdom as well. A royal bloodline such as this had never existed in the world before or since. This bloodline not only carried the royal DNA but the coveted Benjamin Tribe's DNA as well.

King Stephen had had a civil war with his cousin Empress Matilda. Empress Matilda felt that upon her father's death (King Henry I), the kingdom should have passed to his lineage. However, the king, being a quality judge of character and understanding the bloodline and the hope of keeping England and Normandy together, bequeathed the kingdom to his sister's son Stephen, thus starting a long-term family feud over the matter.

Years before Eustace's death, King Stephen had seen weeks of contrasting premonitions of a united continent, as well as visions of the united continent disappearing. The dreams of a broken continent included only one similarity; they always included visions of Eustace's survival. The contrasting visions of a united continent always excluded Eustace's presence.

King Stephen would awaken from his deep sleep soaked in sweat as he struggled with these dreams. King Stephen's wife also had similar dreams. When they discussed the dreams further, they came to the same conclusion, if the continent was to unite and create a grand monarchy through a royal bloodline. Eustace would have no future children with Constance Capet. The dreams further indicated that King Stephen and Constance Capet would have to create a child to carry on the line.

Because Eustace was still alive at this time and married to Constance Capet, the bloodline would have been of royal order and unchallengeable. This never came to be, as Eustace would be poisoned to death before any children were conceived. The infidelity of both King Stephen and Constance Capet that had to take place even prior to Eustace's death would create continuous attacks of illegitimacy, but if the birth of a child was successful, the bloodline could never be challenged. The three monarchs, King Stephen, Queen Matilda, and Constance Capet, weighed in and eliminated all other options before coming to final terms and eventually agreeing to the outcome under a secret bond. The baby of King Stephen and Constance Capet was so created.

As many good plans sometimes do, this plan met with unexpected challenges and risks. The biggest being that Constance Capet's older brother, King Louis VII, along with the Roman Catholic Church, had already started considering potential risks after watching Constance Capet's marriage with Eustace fall apart. Would Constance Capet remarry and have children and threaten King Louis VII's reining lineage? Once the king and the pope realized Constance Capet and Eustace would bear no children, the fear dissipated for the time being. However, even the king and pope couldn't ever have imagined the secret bond between King Stephen and his daughter-in-law Constance Capet that would take place and change things forever.

King Louis VII was at the height of his power at that exact time and heavily backed by the Roman Catholic Church under the current leadership of the highly controversial Pope Innocent II. Both were codependents for the power they possessed. The two men thought the threat was quickly disappearing upon continued news that Eustace and Constance Capet did not get along and were, in fact, living apart. Rumors started to circulate around late 1142 that Constance Capet was in hiding, avoiding the public and family gatherings. Further rumors progressed and by spring 1143 had turned into sightings of Constance Capet with a baby.

Rumors of a child also reached young Eustace who vowed to kill Constance Capet, the father, and the child if rumors were confirmed. As rumors reached King Louis VII about Constance Capet's child, Pope Innocent, in partnership with King Louis VII, conspired to find and kill the child.

The boy child was born in 1143. Due to the failing health of King Stephen and pressures exerted by King Louis VII and Eustace searching for the child, the mother placed the child in protective secrecy where he could not be found. The child was named Roger Benjamin. The family placed the last name Benjamin instead of using a standard royal traditional name of a territory on the child. This was the first real surname given to a royal child in several centuries. The name Benjamin was chosen to directly tie the child back to the royal lineage that had wandered as the last tribe of Israel a thousand years earlier.

It was thought the child would be introduced as king later in life as an adult when he was better prepared to defend himself. Before that could happen, King Stephen would become ill and die on Roger Benjamin's tenth birthday.

Constance Capet, King Stephen, and his wife, Matilda, felt the story and the child's real identity may as well be left untold for the time being to allow the boy to proceed through life ignorant of his true identity. This would also allow the survival of royal bloodline, which carried more than just a given namesake but also the real royal bloodline of the twelfth Tribe of Benjamin and the Norman gods as well. This child was the only child known to possess the bloodlines of Israel's rulers from the Benjamin lineage, Rome's rulers, the serpent gods that bred with the Merovingians, and the Viking gods. Those closest to him would forever keep this secret from him, but they would also allow the child to be trained and protected and to become humbled along the way in hopes that current secrets could be revealed once the world was ready to understand.

Eustace's desire to kill Constance Capet, the child, and the father quickly disappeared. The young man continued to destroy himself through drinking and bad actions until he would be found dead several years later in the countryside after being poisoned by his own men and the local monks. It was often said that Eustace did more harm than good for the kingdom, the parishes, and the lands, and he died because God himself actually struck him down,

Eustace died in early August 1153, struck down, as many described, by the wrath of God while plundering church lands near Bury St. Edmunds. King Louis VII and Pope Innocent would search for the child without luck by destroying people's lives while masking the real motivations and manipulating the Roman Catholic Church into participating in the Crusades. King Louis VII aligned his military with the church and gave power and order for the unnecessary killing under the false belief and name of religion. The soldiers focused their efforts primarily where Constance Capet was living under the belief that Constance Capet must have the child close in proximity to her. Because Constance Capet had long ago passed away but had been living in Toulouse, France, the French Kings believed she must have had her child living with the Cathar believers.

Attackers against the Cathars believed the actions would be easy to defend from a political standpoint, as the Cathars were thought of as neither pagan god believers nor true Christians because they did not believe in the Trinity. These people were really dualist and believed in the New Testament where it was taught as the good God and all things human as being of the bad God. Because the Cathar beliefs were not part of any mainstream religion, citizens of the day would feel justified in the Crusades.

Early attacks against the Cathars were savage and required the Cathars to denounce their religious beliefs or die by being burned alive. This period would be remembered through history, as the Abbot Arnaud Amaury gave the orders to a concerned soldier who had started questioning the practice of killing women and children who may or may not be true Cathars by commanding.

"Burn them all and let God sort them out later," he was told.

The soldiers under direct orders from the king and the church savagely attacked and killed the peaceful heretics of the Languedoc, Cathars of southern France, with viciousness and unimaginable arrogance in their righteousness.

The Cathars called themselves *pure ones* and believed the only way to reach heaven was by obtaining the status of perfect or pure, good Christians. The Cathars protested against the moral, political, and spiritual corruption of the Catholic Church and refused to participate in the Catholic Sacrament of the Eucharist, saying that it could not possibly be the body of Christ. They also didn't believe in baptism by water or in the Trinitarian of Jesus but rather thought Jesus was the human form of an angel and believed that man, like Jesus, would have to divest themselves of all human materialism. The primary reason the soldiers followed through on the mass murder of hundreds of thousands of Cathars was because of these alternative views about Jesus.

Political leaders by both the monarchy and the church had other additional reasons why they wanted to eliminate the Cathars along with the royal child. The Cathars claimed to hold the secret book of Mari (love), which is said to have been partially written by Jesus himself and given to John. The book became the foundation of the Cathar Church. It was transferred through time and commuted to and followed by the Cathars as well as the Knights Templar, who were a very powerful Catholic military order created to guard the true secrets of Christianity.

Both groups found themselves at the crossroads of the Crusades in the region of Languedoc, which means *illumination*, and the Cathars adopted it. The book was said to have been delivered to this region of France by Mary Magdalene herself after Jesus's death. It is said to possess the power to transform human blood into internal wisdom of the pure and holy blood of the Illuminati. It is written in the book that this is the true power obtained from drinking from the cup of the holy grail, and the power is held throughout the existence of the bloodline of those who drink from it. Its secrets revealed how to understand and control the forces of nature. This gift from God was believed to have been protected by the Cathars and was known to only a small number of Templars who rose above the political forces of the time to help protect these secrets.

From the book of Mari, the Cathars learned what the word *light* meant to Jesus. The body was seen by Jesus as a vessel for either good or bad. The greater the good one performed, the closer he was able to get to pure light. Jesus taught that only those closest to good would be able to see God's energy. Some people feel the wind; people in the light are able to see the wind. Some people feel energy; others close to the light see the energy. The Holy Grail is not an actual cup but a metaphorical cup. Jesus wanted everyone to drink from the cup metaphorically, which meant he was teaching others to believe in the powers of good so they could live inside their human vessel and live in the light.

The Cathars' Jesus code offered salvation to the world by offering love to all. Jesus taught that the same energy surrounds everyone, and if you are Buddhist, Daoist, Shintoist, Jewish, Egyptian, Islamic, Christian, or follow ancient occult beliefs such as Hermetic or Gnostic tradition, your body can be *clear* (perfect as the Cathars defined it) and can see energy as long as you possess true love in your heart. This energy, or light, is pure and enables the possessor to see clearly in the dark, or as a blind person, the possessor would hunger for nothing, walk without legs, speak without a tongue. This power is a threat to all who attach it to their wants of the human vessel and devastating to those who preach a false way or those who follow human values. Only those who see the illumination will feel the mysterious light and have the true secrets of the world revealed to them in the new enlightenment. Understanding the language of the Cathars can reveal the meaning of life.

Scholars have pointed out that the symbol of the Oc directly resembles not only the fish of Jesus but also the Egyptian bird of light, is the base for the number 8, and symbolizes the mathematical symbol of infinity. Jesus taught this through the book to his followers to understand the future.

The power of the book of Mari is unmatched in world history and is the very basis for the saying "information is power." This power would be purged throughout mankind's history and on into its future. There are times when this power is sought silently and other times when it seems the world is turned upside down and simply out of control. You may not understand what's happening at the time but understand that this is probably what is taking place.

To understand the differences between human power and the true power of the light, simply review some of history's greatest conflicts. When you review these times, you will notice the theme of events where one party in charge is trying to protect or control their events by controlling or destroying those around them, usually when the controlling person is physically or morally taking a stance against love or the light.

After Jesus's teachings started taking hold, political leaders knew they had to act. Jesus's followers no longer believed they had someone standing between themselves and God. As a result, they no longer had the need to pay money to a place of worship, and they no longer had to be directed by a priest or a rabbi. These people were independent with their God. In the same way, the Cathars believed mankind simply needed to understand and mirror good deeds to see the light and avoid demons of the human body. These views also created a society of unregulated, non-tithing citizens who did not and could not support the government or the church's financial needs.

Not only were the Crusades and their military strengths used by the political powers of the time to destroy opposition against outsiders, but they were used to destroy opposition from within. Once a leading monarchy's group of heirs become too large for a king's comfort or greed or other nefarious or selfish reasons, the monarchy would inevitably dissemble or destroy powers they deemed to be unnecessary or that might become too interested and ultimately a threat to power now or in the future. This fear was strong for some of history's greatest figures.

The Cathars' way of life and how they communicated with God independent of a church leader's mediation was in direct conflict with the Roman Catholic Church. It reduced pay for both the church and government, so they had many reasons to find the book, stop the Cathars from spreading their message, and find and kill the royal child.

The book was finally revealed early in the twelfth century after the Catholic Church subjected both the Cathars and Templars to extreme torture to disclose its location.

In the middle of the sixteenth century, King Henry VIII was given the power to disband and sell off assets under the Act of Supremacy called the Dissolution of the Monasteries. The act was passed by Parliament, which was bullied by the king and gave the king uncontested authority of the Church of England, thus separating England from the pope's control. During this time, the king disbanded and sold off any and all assets he wanted, including priories, monasteries, convents, and friaries, without contest. All of the proceeds from sales under this act would be controlled by the king.

A secondary reason for the use of dissolution of monasteries was erasure of historical lineage relations to the throne itself. Without proof, there could be no claims. Almost all records of those periods were kept within religious walls. During these periods, the people and records would be removed and the records would be burned, leaving zero trace into history.

Future periods of challenges for the throne, such as during the time of Henry VIII when rumors of a possible rightful lineage bloodline would possibly reclaim the throne, led to similar instances of demarcation in later years. King Henry's actions would be short-lived but would cause major implications for the world. The dissolution performed by the king was not regarded by the majority of the population as a bad thing because they seldom understood the king's true motivations. Also, due to centuries of financial and physical abuses by the powerful and wealthy ecclesiastical organizations of the Roman Catholic Church against commoners and the weaker society, the king's changes were generally welcome. Resulting from the years of abuse from the church, there was already a wave of movement due to the adoption of Lutherans' teachings, and the Reformation period had already taken deep hold during the sixteenth century.

During King Henry's separation from the Catholic Church for selfish reasons, people's eyes were opened and they started to challenge the Roman Catholic Church and its ways of thinking throughout Europe. Scandinavia, Sweden, Denmark, Basel, Zurich, and Geneva all followed suit and confiscated the religious orders in their countries and started contributing the new wealth to their poor people in the form of education and training. Other countries, such as France or Scotland, started the process of commendam to transfer the controls to the custody of a trusted individual.

People seeking religious freedoms would start thinking about traveling to the New World armed with the enlightenment of Martin Luther and other free thinkers of the day during the Protestant Reformation.

As good people's thoughts around religion and interaction with God developed as a result of the changes, there would be many others throughout history who would learn just how powerful religious dominance could be if wicked people controlled it. In a similar way further in the future, the Nazis would clearly understand this power. Their Arian manipulations would be used to justify the execution of six million innocent lives with clear conscience for their differences of beliefs during World War II. Remember the root *Ari* is the root word for Arian. During the original meetings in Nicaea, it was believed Jesus was not God, and they didn't believe in the Trinity. Due to this understanding, and compounded by poor economics that still hung over Germany from World War I, the radical beliefs by Arians (Nazis) issued propaganda outlining themselves as the superior race under the use of Ari, as in the name Arian. There was no mistake why the Nazis had such an incredible determination to try to find the hidden secrets of the Cathars and the protected bloodlines of the Holy Grail.

The word *Arian* has several meanings and is also used in the name Cathar, as they also do not believe in the Trinity. They are still considered to this day to have many secrets to get to the light properly. There were many misunderstandings during the meetings in Nicaea where the Roman Emperor Constantine himself may have made a mistake due to little knowledge of the time and should have picked Arian Christianity verses the Homousian Christianity that was adopted by a very thin margin. Although the Nazis manipulated the Ari as in both Arian and Cathars, the Nazis used it for nefarious reasons, while the Cathars used it and continue to use it in secrecy as the true understanding of Jesus and God's energy as outlined in the book of Mari (love).

Whether during King Stephen's, King Henry's, or even the Nazi's period of rule, everything always sorts itself out over time. As was the case following King Stephen's period, the throne would return to the direct lineage of Henry I via his eldest daughter Empress Matilda and ultimately to her son Henry II, who would once again lose the throne to illegitimacy. As Roger Benjamin's fate would have it, his parents never introduced the boy to the world, and the legitimate king and his bloodline with God's covenant would exist only in the shadows of the world, only surfacing when necessary.

Charlie's conclusions started to materialize as he studied the information provided by the genealogist's data and the historical evidence that he had discovered from all of the books he'd read. Were the rightful monarchs removed from the throne in England by an act of demarcation after failing to locate the true heir to the royal bloodline? Who were the rightful monarchs? Were the monarchs of former times leaders of man or leaders of God? King Henry's father had taken the rightful heir and subsequent lineage out of the kingdom through battle. So, had King Henry VIII learned the true history of the bloodline while attending the same private school as Roger Benjamin (a child Charlie had started reading about) and then decided he needed to cover up the information by using demarcation? Who was this Roger Benjamin? Where did he come from, and what did he have to do with Charlie? Were the stories of Poseidon and Argotta, the Merovingian Queen, true? Was Charlie somehow tied into all of these monarchs and their kingdoms?

Charlie looked down at his webbed toes and swallowed hard, as he now knew he was somehow intertwined in all of this. The governments who sought his skills somehow knew some of this information, but how much? The hardest fact that Charlie now understood was why he always spoke directly to God and God spoke to him without interference. In fact, anytime a church person ever tried to interfere or interpret any of these conversations, things only became confusing or the information turned out to be simply wrong. Charlie's intuitive capabilities were becoming extremely strong as he was starting to realize who, in fact, Charlie Benjamin really was.

Benjamin Name Reestablished—
Roger Benjamin, 1143

Charlie continued reading the genealogy reports he had received and kept running into two tails of a similar story. His lineage included a story about a couple named John and Abigail Benjamin who ultimately came to America in the early sixteen hundreds. The interesting fact about both of their lineages was Abigail's traced directly through the English and Norman monarchies going back several hundred years. John's lineage appeared to do the same, but there were some dark passages around King Stephen and his daughter-in-law Constance Capet of France, as well as a child of obscure information named Roger Benjamin.

John and Abigail were a power couple in early American history, as both were from wealthy families and directly related to royalty. Where Abigail's lineage cannot be argued, John's could. Both, however, if the lineage stands correct, shared the same lineage, which reconnected during William the Conqueror's time.

Charlie continued reading from the volumes of materials he researched, hoping to find the answers that started from a family dispute over power almost a thousand years earlier after several significant family members and their heirs had passed away.

The dispute started when King Henry I, William the Conqueror's fourth son, lie dying in Lyons, France, on December 1, 1135. Despite common perception, the English throne rarely passed from father to son during this time period. King Henry I and Matilda of Scotland would have a daughter named Matilda, who would go on to become the Holy Roman Empress, and a son named William Adelin. Matilda and Adelin were the only legitimate children of King Henry I and Matilda of Scotland. William was in line to become heir to the throne; sadly, he was killed at a young age in a boating accident called the White Ship Tragedy two years after his mother's death, thus passing the heir trail to his only legitimate sister, Empress Matilda.

Prior to Henry's death, he secretly named his daughter Empress Matilda heir to his throne in the witness of his barons, making them swear allegiance to her. The very pregnant Matilda went off to have her baby. Unfortunately, her father passed away during the last months of her pregnancy. This disabled her from traveling to the kingdom and take the throne, leaving an opportunity for her cousin Prince Stephen to step in and assume the role. The barons would not back the oath with Matilda, and the throne passed to Stephen.

When King Henry passed away, Stephen's speedy arrival may have beaten the empress to the throne, enabling him to be crowned first, but King Stephen had a weaker claim. Matilda and Stephen were both William the Conqueror's grandchildren; however, Matilda was the sole legitimate child of King Henry I, while Stephen had to be ordained when he was crowned.

The coronation of King Stephen was never forgiven by Empress Matilda, who would wage war against him throughout his nineteen-year rule. Empress Matilda maintained she was the rightful heir and waged endless war for her rights. Unfortunately for both, neither had enough individual power to overthrow the other, so the country remained in a prolonged family feud.

The empress most likely would have had better results had she been friendlier to her people, as she had the claim to the throne, but no one wanted to support her efforts because they did not like or trust her. On the other hand, King Stephen was a warm and friendly leader. Initially, he enjoyed the backing of his barons and his people and appreciated their continued pushback against his cousin.

Lineage is often odd. Looking at it from the twenty-first century when governments are less concerned about being on the side of monarchies who would or could grant power and safety to their followers, it is hard to understand the mindset that existed in the early years of the eleventh and twelfth centuries when loyalty often meant the difference between life and death for you and your family.

Knowing the difference in personalities and attitudes, the pushback he was receiving from the church, and the constant battles that ensued with his cousin Matilda, King Stephen had decided to follow his premonitions to ensure any hopes of securing power for the royal bloodline and created a child with his daughter-in-law, Constance Capet. Thus, he created a grand monarchy and united Great Britain, France, Normandy, Germany, and even Jerusalem.

This is where the story of the Benjamin line becomes very interesting and difficult to believe, while at the same time being impossible to deny. This is also where the story truly begins.

It was an early fall morning in 1143 on the coast of Calais, France. Soldiers mounted in full uniform on their majestic chargers emerged through the light fog unknown to all except for the gulls that announced their arrival upon the open beach. It was beautiful and picturesque, and the smell of the sea air was heavy as the waves gently lapped upon the shore. It was seemingly a wonderful slice of the world shared by a small handful of soldiers and Constance Capet and a newborn child. The countess wore a burgundy dress with brown waist and wrist ties and a white headdress. Although the ensemble was fashioned out of the finest silks common to the area, the outfit somewhat hid the countess's identity. The baby boy held tightly in her arms wore a gold wrap highlighted by white piping, golden wool booties, and a white head wrap all finished in a lace blanket with the name Roger Benjamin embroidered upon it.

As the soldier-led woman and child approached the cog ship that emerged from the sea, there was simply silence from everyone. No one spoke; no one asked questions. The ramp from the cog emerged, and two soldiers emerged wearing full royal English attire. The countess hugged the child one last time as she shed a slight tear. It was certain the young countess loved this child but knew not to allow her emotions to show today but rather release them later in her privacy.

Upon taking the baby, the soldiers loaded back onto the beautiful oak cog and made their twenty-mile journey back home to Dover, England, where they were instructed to leave the young boy with the monks at the Saint Mary the Virgin Priory. While journeying back to England, the crew took great care of the child and actually enjoyed his quiet character. Never before had this crew been assigned a child to transport, and the boy's gentleness was refreshing and offered the men a new point of view.

Before the arrival of the young boy, Archbishop Theobald was commissioned by the king to complete necessary buildings and improvements at St. Augustine's Abbey, which were finalized in 1143. The abbey was originally a Benedictine monastery that stood in Canterbury Kent, England, from 598 until 1538. That was when King Henry VIII, who grew up in the same location, attempted to have its contents destroyed in an effort to hide certain facts that had taken place here, forever erasing any traces of history or evidence that now lay silent in the halls. Some people say these facts are mere coincidences. You decide.

King Stephen would visit the priory often, leaving those close to him and members of the priory to wonder why the king took such homage on the small child. The king never spoke of his reasons, and certainly, no one ever asked him. Rumors circulated as the child grew older and the two started to share resemblances. The king was a tough man intent on the child receiving the best education and complete respect from those around. Their questions grew even wider after the death of the king; while staying at the priory, he asked that only the young Benjamin boy join him as he lay dying in 1154.

While no one knew the boy's true identity, everyone knew this child had significance. He would be checked upon thoroughly by the king's court as well as the king himself who made regular visits throughout his lifetime. The monks were told to ensure the child learned his lessons and understood royal table manners, greetings, and proper attire. It was like this child was privileged but without a kingdom.

The child was well liked and seemed to have an amazing karma and charisma. He never treated any of the children differently but loved the poor children as well as the wealthy children. He never seemed to cry even when sad. He had amazing vision, both physical and spiritual. He just seemed especially insightful and intelligent. He loved Dover and the surrounding Kent. And he never seemed to rest, always being able to be found outside enjoying the morning dew and only to return as the last to bed after closing down the evening with a gaze upon the stars, listening one last time to the nightingales, blackbirds, and blackcap birds signing good night.

Further details of Roger Benjamin have escaped history except those held and passed through direct heirs and the vicars who served him and kept diaries. In 1538 upon King Henry's dissolution of priories, all records were ordered to be destroyed and all of the buildings and artifacts to be removed by the locals in order to remove all possible relatives from future claims to the throne. Following the destruction of materials located within the priory, King Henry himself made a rare visit to confirm complete destruction. What was his fear? Would this information have cost him the throne had it ever been released to the people? Did Henry VIII use dissolutions the same way Louis VII used the Crusades?

Young Roger's start was interesting for sure, but his real history was even more interesting because of the rare lineage he possessed. As an heir to the Roman, Norman, and Benjamin Tribe lineages, he possessed not just everyday human insight but also the godlike abilities that flowed through his bloodlines and gave him vision, authoritative focus, command, and heavenly compassion. The boy's powers included instinctual knowledge that seemed to tie Roman insight to the ancient world of both the Mediterranean and Asian areas. He understood the powers of the sea, which possibly also ran through his veins according to stories that he had originally believed to be fabled. These stories told of the conquest of his great-grandmother Argotta, Queen of the Franks, by Poseidon and the spiritual lineage of the biblical Abraham.

Many would ask, "Why such secrecy around this child?" The answer is actually quite simple. With great power comes great responsibility. Young Roger's lineage placed not only himself at great risk from his birth but his future lineage as well. His parents understood this and decided to protect the boy and allow attitudes to catch up to his in a future, hopefully gentler era.

To better understand this thought, think about times when your own beliefs have been challenged. Beliefs such as religion are very tough to change, and if someone's beliefs are changed, there is a hollow openness left in the void for a short period until it can be refilled with new beliefs. If someone is associated with great wealth or powers, either of their own or those possessed supernaturally, then other people who are void of these abilities will search out and befriend them in hope of taking control of the person's unending power and wealth. Some people do horrible things and will stop at nothing to get to power and wealth.

Unfortunately, religious persecution has been used as a tool over the centuries to control wealth due to its purity and depth of belief within people. In other words, people who would not ordinarily kill others will kill in the name of religion if their beliefs are being challenged, even in the face of the Ten Commandments. Truly spiritual and intelligent people would never kill for a religious belief because they understand religion to be man-made, while covenants are made with God.

When a religious person hears another person say he is not religious, that person often becomes upset, especially when the two are close relations. However, the religious person should step back a moment and try to empathize. There have been many instances over the course of history when religious persecution has actually driven people away rather than toward religious beliefs.

A person could start from the time of Jesus when an individual was condemned because of beliefs that threatened the religious and political order of the day in Israel. In another example, hundreds of years later, Constantine and the Roman political leaders used religious doctrines to control southern Europe and the Middle East. The Romans created the Catholic Church in order to rule politically through the fear of the unknown in the name of their God. There were Crusades throughout history, and they continue to exist today due to differences of beliefs.

Centuries ago, a continent yet to be discovered by Europeans would encompass a future country called the United States of America and would go on to become the most powerful country the world has ever known. The country would be formed out of the desire for religious freedoms not available in other regions of the world. Eventually, the United States would adopt the motto "in God we trust." But even in this free country, citizens would blame the God they trusted by selfishly turning their backs on his messages taught in their Bibles. Once again, for religious disagreements, this new country acted in the same fashion as Europe and tried, convicted, and crucified people for not being able to prove their love for their God in the same way as the majority around them.

The most obvious example exists in American history during the Salem witch trials. People were burned alive, but accusations were later proven to have been false. Accusations were made by people for nefarious reasons. Generally, one individual was after a widow's wealth or land, and religious beliefs at the time allowed for a man to accuse a woman of witchcraft. The woman would subsequently be burned alive. If she truly held magic, she could have escaped, but if she didn't possess magic … Well, everyone knows the rest of the story.

This is exactly what happened throughout Europe and the Middle East during the Crusades. Medieval times saw the Crusades as a way for the Latin world to take back holy lands from the Muslims. Later, Crusades sanctioned by the Catholic Church under the name of monotheism and the end of paganism's multi-god beliefs would be the reason for these wars. The reality was political power; a land grab and wealth were what was at stake. The grandest horrific manipulation of the Bible took place during the third and ultimately the forth Crusades that resulted from Christian loss of power in the Middle East to Islamic rule, the failure of Europe's monarchs, and forced tithings imposed by King Henry II of England to pay for the wars and ultimately eliminate one of the world's tamest religious orders: the Cathars.

When one tries too hard to understand history, it's important to try and laugh sarcastically at the reported facts and step back before you place yourself back in time trying to understand the mindset.

Were King Stephen's premonitions correct? Would his kingdom and royal bloodline have been omitted from the grand plan if he had relied on Eustace?

Around August 10, 1153, Eustace brought his army to what was one of the greatest monasteries in England: Bury St. Edmunds. The monks welcomed him with great splendor and held a fine dinner for him. Prince Eustace, however, needed money to pay his soldiers. When the monks refused to hand over the sum he demanded, Eustace ordered his men to loot the monastery and lay waste to its lands.

A job well done, from his point of view, Prince Eustace returned to Cambridge Castle and sat down to eat the food he had stolen from the monks. Immediately after he started eating, the young Prince began to convulse, gaging and coughing as he fell to the floor. Some records state he survived in pain for several days before succumbing to the poisons. The monks named a vengeful Saint Edmund as having killed Eustace because of his evil actions in defense of the monks who had been tormented by the prince. Other accounts blame Eustace's own personal soldiers for his death after conspiring against him due to his bad behavior against his own people. While there may be disagreement on how Eustace died, you'll find full agreement that no one was sad about his death.

The accounts of Prince Eustace's death vary. Some suspect poison. Some said Eustace died from grief (not choking or poison) as a result of his father's betrayal when he began treating Duke Henry as a son. No doubt, however, the church saw it as divine approval when, on the day Eustace died, Duke Henry's first legitimate heir was born. Regardless of the cause of death, some historians have argued that if Eustace hadn't died, peace would never have been possible.

Thank goodness King Stephen listened to the energy that sent him the visions prior to Eustace's death. What are the odds in nature where two people can create a grand monarch capable of running a complete empire with simply the birth of one child bringing together multiple royal bloodlines.

After Queen Matilda's sudden death in May 1152, Eustace's death in August 1153, and, finally, King Stephen's death in October 1154, Constance Capet was faced with inner thoughts and decisions of her own.

Quickly, the only daughter of France's King Louis VII was not only the mother of France's rightful heir but also the illegitimate heir to Great Britain, Normandy, and Jerusalem. The child, Roger Benjamin who was being raised indiscriminately for the future greater good of the world was now being raised without family guidance and was removed from all knowledge of his true identity. Following the death of King Stephen in 1154, Roger, who should have been known to the world as Roger Boulouse, would be raised under the name of Roger Benjamin unbeknownst to him or to those around him.

The name Benjamin would tie him into the true family lineage of the Benjamin Tribe. His wealth would not be made up of gold and castles but of the value of the bloodline of the man.

Roger's mother, Constance Capet Countess Boulogne of France, was remarried in 1154 to Raymond V, Count of Toulouse, after being widowed from Eustace for a year. Only a true mother's love could have left her child in the throes of the world with the understanding that if Roger survived to better the world, it would be because of the lineage covenant with God.

Upon the countess's arrival to the Toulouse area, the Crusades against the Cathars exploded on the scene, seeming to eliminate heresy from the religious sect. However, many believed the Crusade was nothing more than a termination process to find and eliminate the boy, Roger Benjamin, from returning and taking over his rightful throne. It would not be necessary for King Louis VII to kill his sister, as she could not assail past him and his children to the throne, but Roger could claim it. Unknown to the king, Roger would not be found and would not be killed because he was living five hundred miles away under a shroud of secrecy.

In the end, Roger went on to live a very normal and peaceful life in Norfolk, England, before he died in 1175. Roger would eventually be buried next to King Stephen in an unmarked grave on the king's right side at Farversham Abbey in Kent England. Two internment objects were included in his tomb, a shield with the Blois coat of arms and a king of England shield as a reference.

The surname Benjamin never existed in England prior to Roger Benjamin—Jewish, English, and French from the Hebrew male personal name *Binyamin*, or son of the south. In the book of Genesis, it is treated as meaning son of the right hand. Benjamin was the youngest and favorite son of Jacob and supposed progenitor of one of the twelve tribes of Israel (Gen. 35:16–18; 42:4). The name was very uncommon in Great Britain, Normandy, and France at that time. The first time the name Benjamin showed up in English history was in Norfolk, England, in 1161 when Roger Benjamin was recorded when his son Hugh was born.

Years later all of the tombs and most of the records were destroyed during the dissolution of the monasteries by King Henry VIII. Sometimes referred to as the suppression of the monasteries, this was a series of destruction of records kept in the monasteries, priories, and abbeys under the name of religion between 1536 and 1541.

Charlie completed his research with more questions than he started with. Was King Henry VIII trying to hide important facts to protect his power? Why would King Stephen take such an interest in a little-known child named Roger Benjamin? Why would Roger's body be found buried years later under the royal shields? If King Henry VIII wasn't the proper heir to the crown, then would the current royal family also not be the proper heirs to the throne?

16

Battle of Shrewsbury— Backing the Family Again

With Charlie's questions about Roger Benjamin going unanswered, his sense of wonder only became more intense as he read about the Battle of Shrewsbury. This battle represents a significant period of English history. It was the first time English royalty opposing English monarchs fought on English soil for control of the throne. At the conclusion of the battle, one of Charlie's ancestors, Richard Benjamin, would be knighted by King Henry to become Sir Richard Benjamin.

Being knighted was an honor given to those who showed great bravery and loyalty to the king in times of battle. Knighthood was also generally given to individuals who represented great wealth and standing. So how was it that someone in Charlie's lineage had accomplished this opportunity? He continued to read about the battle in hopes of finding more answers to these questions as well as hopefully finding out more about why governments were becoming more and more aggressive with what Charlie knew about himself and what he continued to learn.

The long culmination of verbal attacks, hollow accusations, and a generation of treason by the hopeful interloper and rebel Henry "Hotspur" Percy against the rightful King Henry (Bolingbroke) IV would finally have its long-awaited justice, which would be decided by the court of battle. It was July 21, 1403, and after many minor skirmishes by seemingly anyone who was living in what we call Great Britain today seemed to be at odds with who should ultimately run these lands.

Through the decades, the English had fought the French, the Welch, the Romans, and the Normans, but now they would fight each other for control of the English throne. This day would start as it had each day since the dawn of time for the quiet lands of Shrewsbury as the sun crested the horizon. It would be warm this day as the summer sun stretched out its long rays. The area around Shrewsbury is laid pleasantly with good bottom soil that lies softly among smooth rolling hills and is surrounded by the River Severn in England, just beyond eastern Wales. As with most warm summer mornings, this day's meandering river would create an early morning fog through the valley that would dissipate as the rays of light made direct contact with the land. The falcons and waxing birds could be heard in the distance, calling out as they focused on their morning hunts.

As the day continued to break out, the sounds of the night herons and river toads softened toward silence with their calls being replaced by the sounds of the grass blades lifting themselves toward the sky and shedding their morning dew. The west winds were light and refreshing. If it were not for the fact that several hours from now, just before dusk, one of the bloodiest fights to ever be waged on this soil would take place, no one would ever have realized that this day would break Shrewsbury's lifetime history of peaceful tranquility. In fact, if it wasn't for this day, many in the world would never have heard of Shrewsbury, and it would still be sitting nestled in its quiet world. History had other plans, though, as would soon be realized in the violent events.

What led to the Battle of Shrewsbury was Lancastrian King Henry IV and the Northumberland earl's oldest son, Henry "Harry Hotspur" Percy, who through different manipulations by their forefathers had created their contention for each other as they competed for the rightful ascension to the throne. Scholars who have studied the rise surrounding the cause of the discord actually place much of the blame on Hotspur's uncle, Thomas, who purposely created an angry environment that, once energized, could not be turned off. Hotspur was a proven admiral and considered a top lieutenant in Prince Henry's army and was extremely trusted by Prince Henry. At one point prior to the Battle of Shrewsbury before all of the unrest, the king, just six months earlier, actually entrusted Hotspur to deliver the king's wife to him.

Between the time of the delivery of the king's wife and the Battle at Shrewsbury, Hotspur had been demoted from his military position and had created open rebellion against the crown that had to be put down.

Upon confirmation from Parliament as to King Henry's proper seat and head of the throne, Sir Percy, or Hotspur as he was commonly known, would never concede to these facts, and his life would be spent on this quest up until his death as a result.

Hotspur's House of Percy had previously supported Henry IV to put down earlier rebellions and conflicts against Dŵr and Scotland and in the war against King Richard II of England, which ended in 1399 when Henry IV took the throne.

King Henry IV had been supported by a number of wealthy landowners to whom he had promised land, money, and royal favor in return for their continued support. When the war ended, lands in and around the kingdom were given not to the promised loyalists who had fought and won for the king but rather to their rivals. Payment for their services was also not made as promised. This led to obvious uprisings, and the loyalists soon became less enamored and renounced and revolted against King Henry IV. The king also broke promises and charged taxes against the church, disallowed free Parliamentary elections, and imprisoned and murdered King Richard II. This caused Percy to publicly renounce his onetime friend King Henry IV and revolt.

Henry Percy marched his way south from Northumberland to a rendezvous with his uncle Thomas Percy and a confrontation with his old friend, now enemy, King Henry IV, with a small group of initial followers. As they traveled toward the king, they had collected into their ranks several powerful noblemen and their much-needed men. His most successful recruitment came from Cheshire where he successfully picked up the well-trained Cheshire Army soldiers and their team of famous archers. Some of these men had been the personal guards to King Richard II. These men saw King Henry as a traitor and murderer for his treatment against King Richard.

Hotspur would also hope to secure the reinforcements from Owain Glyn Dŵr, the self-proclaimed prince of Wales. Dŵr was a champion of the people and a masterful military leader of his day. His services with Percy could have changed English history, but it was not to be as he and his army were still a few days away from Shrewsbury fighting an unrelated battle at the time.

As the morning fog lifted on July 21, 1403, it would become apparent that Hotspur, even though he had a smaller army this day of roughly ten thousand men verses the king's fourteen thousand, held a military advantage. Hotspur's troops were leveraged by their position upon one of the hills overlooking King Henry's militia. Another advantage Hotspur had were the Cheshire archers he had recruited. On the other hand, the king's troops were better trained, more seasoned, and more experienced fighters, so the battle would be fair.

July 21 was a Saturday, and as was customary for the Church of England at that time, no fighting could take place after sunset Saturday until daylight Monday in respect for the Lord.

This battle would have no favorites from the people, as most towns, parishes, and castles were continuously burned and laid to ruin as different leaders would put together a chevauchée to leave fear in their citizens' minds. Most of these people were innocents who included farm wives and children. They couldn't choose sides, as the wrong pick usually meant treason and instant death. Even sadder is the fact that even if they chose the correct side, they would still be killed, as a paranoid leader would not believe their claims. If the attacking army needed new soldiers, who were scarce at the time, the invader would simply take the men or older boys with them and leave their families to fend for themselves.

At the time of the battle, soldiers were picked by the local sheriffs, and the soldiers had to pack and carry their own weapons, armory, and food. If they were poor and untrained for battle, as most were, odds were they would not survive. Because of this fact, roughly 50 percent would become AWOL and escape before the battles. If the men and boys came from wealthy families, the sheriffs were generally paid to recruit men from other families.

The armies were rarely paid consistently and fed even less frequently unless they were knights or part of the inner circle. At the end of the day, men would be fighting for a battle they didn't understand and a crown they did not follow for no money or food.

King Henry IV became aware of the Hotspur rebellion roughly a week prior while marching to help Percy on the northern lines. After receiving word that Percy was heading toward Shrewsbury, the king changed his plans from the north and headed west to the point of confrontation. Both sides ended up at Shrewsbury on July 20, 1403, setting up their respective camps on both sides of the Severn River, which wraps around the town. Hotspur was on the town side of the river, while the king encamped on the outer banks.

For this particular battle, both sides came together on Saturday, July 21, and King Henry and Hotspur knew they didn't want to keep their soldiers through Monday as required by the church. Both leaders wanted the fight or surrender to take place that day. King Henry also knew that if the battle delayed for a day or two, his larger and more formidable foe, Owain Glyn Dŵr, may find his way into this fight. Because Dŵr was considered to be masterful in his military achievements the king wanted to avoid an introduction.

Side note: Dŵr was so well loved and respected by his people of Nottingham, England, that upon his eventful death, stories of his spirit's triumphant return found its way into lore as they would pass along one of the world's first historical fiction stories, which later became the story of King Arthur and the fabled Knights of the Round Table.

King Henry wanted this meeting between his army and Hotspur's army to end peacefully, as the two leaders had a history of fighting alongside one another to subdue a previous bad-acting king and other invaders. This day, though, the king would not get his wish.

The two sides negotiated for most of the morning, using the local abbots to present their terms. At first, Hotspur declined all terms and sent his uncle to speak with the king.

The discussions became hostile, and the two argued and exchanged insults. Before the negotiations concluded, Hotspur was close to accepting the king's terms, but his uncle wouldn't budge from his position. And so the stage was set for the battle. Even though Hotspur was somewhat inclined toward accepting the king's position, his uncle Thomas Percy was not, so negotiations ended near midday, and the two forces advanced closer for the fight.

Several soldiers, including one rebel who was later pardoned, went over to the royal army, and the king knighted several of his followers on the day of battle, including twenty-year-old Sir Richard Benjamin.

About two hours before dusk, King Henry IV raised his sword, giving the signal to start the battle. Within seconds, a massive barrage of tens of thousands of arrows from the longbows rained down upon both armies. Scores on both sides were injured or killed. The poorest of soldiers who owned no shields could only pray for protection. Because most had no formal training, their test of skill would reveal itself as the two sides came together in close confrontation using hand-to-hand strength. The sky remained darkened by thousands of arrows for only a few minutes but seemed to last for hours.

During the next few minutes, the field turned bloody. Many prayed they would survive; after being struck, some prayed for death. The smell of sweat from high levels of nervous perspiration filled the air. Arrows, daggers, and swords all thrust together in hopes of finding and piercing the enemy's flesh. Heavy horses stepped solidly upon the bodies of fallen combatants with the identifiable sounds of bones crushing and guts tearing beneath their steps. Screams of dying solders were replaced by deep gurgles of blood as it filled their lungs.

As the battle continued, Hotspur made a last-attempt charge where he wanted to kill the king himself. The newly knighted Sir Richard Benjamin was fighting on the king's weak flank on the right side when Hotspur came charging in. Hotspur had the king in his sights, and thinking a direct kill was eminent, he lifted his visor during the attack. Suddenly, a swarm of arrows coming from the weak side hit Hotspur in the face, killing him dead before he even hit the ground.

At the same time, the king was hit in the face with an arrow and fell from his black steed, wounded. Both sides yelled victory and called out to the leaders as was customary. Percy never responded, but the king did, giving him the victory. Due to the skill and proper treatment of his physician, the king would recover but would be left with a permanent scar. Opponents trying to escape were cut off and killed where they stood.

After the close of the battle, several leaders from the rebel side, including Thomas Percy, were hanged and beheaded. Their heads were then displayed on the Tower Bridge in London. Rumors also spread that Percy had lived and taken the kingdom, so King Henry had the body disinterred, salted, and set up in Shrewsbury impaled on a spear, later to be quartered between two millstones in the marketplace pillory with an armed guard to protect against removal. His body was then put on display in Chester, London, Bristol, and Newcastle. His head was sent to York and impaled on the north gate, looking toward his own lands.

The Benjamins Come to America

As noted earlier, the information provided by the genealogists and the books Charlie researched about John and Abigail Benjamin's lineage detailed vast amounts of information. Charlie had also uncovered detailed personal information from churches the couple had attended during their lives. Charlie was fascinated as he uncovered personal data recorded by church vicars, as well as copies of notes and entries into church and family logs from the couple themselves.

John Benjamin was born in Heathfield, Sussex, England, in 1585 to a wealthy merchant named John Richard Benjamin and Joane Hookes. John wrestled with his understanding of his religious beliefs, who he was as a person, and his family origins. Like other children of his time, he struggled with the religious beliefs taught to him and what he was raised to believe about his God and his understanding of the world around him.

John spent long days working in the shadows of his father's business where he was taught the necessary rules on how to be a successful businessman. He studied hard and read everything his curious mind could find. John, like his father, would grow to be a very successful businessman and would create great wealth for his family. So much so that upon John's death, he would leave an estate worth $13 million in twenty-first-century dollars. He would also leave land, literature, and books from his personal library to form Harvard University.

John's family was very religious. They constantly read the Bible and pulled information between the Jewish, Christian, and Cathar teachings. This suited young John very well, as he loved his family and all the success that found him, but his quest in life was not material. Rather, he sought the truth and meaning about life.

As the child of a well-to-do business leader, John was shipped off to Cambridge University in England with the hopes of fulfilling the goals of his family and the monarchs of the time to become a solid leader himself for his community's future. During the seventeenth century, young men didn't attend Cambridge for an eventual degree but rather to obtain valuable contacts with other successful families. An original reference to the phrase, "It's not what you know, but rather who you know."

Young men from wealthy and royal families would become members of the Inns of Court of London before assembling on the Cambridge campus. While at school, John would focus on his studies such as Hebrew, Greek, divinity, philosophy, civil law, and physics. He would also continue his skills up to the level of masters in fencing, tennis, and riding. Most of John's day-to-day concerns were cared for by his servants giving him time to focus on the climate of religious persecutions that were currently taking place. He would make many friends as his procession of servants would cook, clean, and tailor for him while he was at the university.

The search for answers and understanding relating to spirituality and religion never left John. During his time at Cambridge, young gentlemen would gather to discuss religious issues, as it was the current hot topic during his tenure. This brought John Benjamin to his friendship with John Winthrop, a leading figure during the great Puritan migration to America. While at Cambridge, the two men would become lifetime friends. They shared deep philosophical thoughts about religion. Others would describe them as having unique powers or abilities to translate detailed and difficult subject matter between God and humans.

The seventeenth century in England featured the effects from the church reform by King Henry VIII a century earlier. As Cambridge was a hotbed of wealth and because the country was still trying to identify religious tolerances, the university became ground zero for idealism and youthful energy. As fate would have it, the Benjamin lineage would once again find themselves right in the middle of the largest concentration of the world's religious movement. As a result, the Puritan movement exploded on the scene, taking John and Abigail Benjamin right along with it as they left England in search of religious freedom in America.

John and Abigail sailed together from Plymouth, England, on June 22, 1632, aboard the ship *Lyon*, led by Captain William Pierce. As fate would have it, this was to be the *Lyon*'s last successful voyage, as it would crash upon the rocks and sink the next launch out at sea. John took the oath of allegiance to the king and government of England before he embarked.

This group of Puritans were members of Thomas Hooker's Braintree Company. After being at sea for twelve weeks, they landed in Boston Harbor on Sunday evening, September 16, 1632. They brought with them their children John, Abigail, Samuel, and Mary. The *Lyon* carried 123 passengers, with 50 being children. To understand the value of the human cargo on this passage is very important. When most people think of Puritans during this time, they visualize meek or people close to poverty living close to the land. The group on this passage was actually the opposite. They were well educated, and most were from very wealthy families of Freemen, which is why this was the first crossing that suffered no deaths during the voyage.

Winthrop would become one of the first governors of Massachusetts, and Benjamin would become one the first constables of Massachusetts when he followed Winthrop two years later. The position of constable during colonial days was the same as being the main executive in charge of the town or parish. Both would become primary founders of the Massachusetts Bay Colony, a powerful leadership organization of its time.

Abigail Eddye, who would later become John Benjamin's wife in 1619, was born in 1601 in Cranbrook, Kent Co., England. She was the daughter of Rev. William Eddye, vicar of Saint Duntan's Church in Cranbrook, and his wife, Mary Fosten. A vital fact that made this union so unique is that it regrouped the Benjamin lineage back to Abigail's royal ancestry. In fact, they shared the same grandparents five hundred years earlier. Whereas John Benjamin's royal bloodline is sometimes challenged with assumptions as to who was the real father of Roger Benjamin (John Benjamin's namesake), there is no argument regarding the royal lineage of John's wife, Abigail Eddye.

Abigail's father's lineage included knights of the highest orders, such as the Order of the Garter, as well as dukes and princes. Following Abigail's mother's direct lineage would trace through an incredible journey, as it included the Saxbies, Sir John Danvers, Sir John Bruley of Bonkroft Castle, the knighted de Grey's of Rotherfield, Matilda Maud, countess of Huntingdon, queen of Scotland, Adelaide of Normandy, countess of Aumale, sister of William the Conqueror, daughter of Robert I the Magnificent, granddaughter of Richard II the Good, and King Rollo (a Viking and the first ruler of Normandy). Abigail's documented lineage continues all the way back to AD 189.

The importance of this is that John Benjamin's heritage may never be fully confirmed due the controversies surrounding his ancestor, Roger Benjamin, or specifically Roger's lineage. While Roger's lineage can be argued, it is important to note that the original royal bloodline of Abigail cannot be denied due to the ample and detailed documentation.

Through Abigail, the royal bloodline made its way back into the Benjamin bloodline with the children of John and Abigail Benjamin and finally onto American shores in 1632 with their arrival on the ship the *Lyon*. This is extremely important when determining original descent from the Benjamin Tribe. As cultural historical events such as paths of monotheism changed over time, equality among all individuals associated with the Benjamin Tribe, specific lineage customs represented by both men and women, unending lineage, and unmatched bravery were all traits carried with both of these two people's ancestors throughout history.

The Benjamins soon settled in Newtowne, Massachusetts (present-day Cambridge). On November 6, 1632, John became a Freeman. A Freeman had the right of suffrage and enjoyed advantages in the division of land, and before the representative system started, Freemen were members of the general court. These privileges were appointed through the church and support the characterization that he was held in very high regard. John Benjamin held the status of Freeman very early upon his arrival to Boston. He received the title less than two months after his arrival, which was extremely uncommon.

On May 30, 1633, John Benjamin was appointed constable of Newtowne by the General Court. The constable in England and in the colonies was the chief executive officer of the parish or town. Hence, it was an office of honor and organizational importance.

On six acres of land the couple purchased in Newtowne, Benjamin built what Gov. John Winthrop described as a "mansion ... unsurpassed in elegance and comfort by all in the vicinity." It was also a mansion of religion and hospitality, visited by the clergy of all denominations and by the literate at home and abroad. It's an easy conclusion to understand that John was a very wealthy, educated, and powerful leader of his time and certainly well respected as governor. Winthrop referred to him as Mr. Benjamin, a title indicating prominence and used rarely. He described Benjamin's home and library collection as being highly desirable and the grandest in all of Massachusetts.

The date April 7, 1636, marked an unusual milestone in the Benjamin family history. It started from a horrible event when the Benjamin home in Newtowne was damaged badly by fire. Its loss was valued at more than one hundred pounds. John was said to have had a very large library. Many of his books were lost in the fire. In combination with the fire and the recent passing of his friend and community leader John Harvard, the two tragedies would turn into a historical American fortune.

In 1636, John Harvard, a wealthy clergyman, bequeathed the greater part of his fortune and library to the creation of Harvard College, which would go on to become Harvard University. Harvard's gift to the foundation of the first college in America was expected, as he was without heirs. In that same year, Constable John Benjamin, John Harvard's friend and college mate from Cambridge University, had his home and library partially destroyed by fire. The Benjamins' surviving structures, books, and property would be combined with Harvard's estate and gifted to create the college. Benjamin's property included lots fifty-two, fifty-three, and fifty-four and were the closest to the shores of the Charles River. This gift would forever align the Benjamin lineage with a gift in perpetuity.

Was this a gift or God's design or simply the luck of being in the right place at the right time? We will never know. However, what is known is that John Benjamin's gift would go on to play a major role in designing the institutional foundation of one of the most successful universities the world has ever seen. Harvard would go on to attract some of the brightest minds to the area, which would forever foster thought and discussion and change the world.

George Washington would use the Market Place Square, which is now part of Harvard, to create the Continental Army. Harvard would create the first and oldest operating law school, which would go on to educate some of America's founding fathers, presidents, and US Supreme Court justices. The university would also inspire use of the first printing press in America, enabling young leaders to take the knowledge they learned from the Harvard community back to their countries in lands far away.

Later in 1637, John moved his family to Watertown, Massachusetts. Watertown records of 1642 say that he owned the largest homestead in the town at that time. This lot was bought from the Oldham family, and much of his land became the current site of the Perkins School for the Blind, America's oldest and largest school for the blind. John Oldham had been killed the year earlier at the hands of the Pequot Indians, which led to the Indian wars. The homestead in Watertown was sixty acres and was situated east of Dorchester Field and bound on the south by the Charles River.

As history often does, lineage documentation focused on the male surname and direct line. There is no doubt history would follow John Benjamin as his events and successes were worthy of notoriety. However, his wife, Abigail, had significant lineage events, her property dowry, and documentation relating to ancestral achievements that were at least equal to those of John Benjamin. To make things odder, both John and Abigail even had noted mythical forefathers in respective histories who ruled lands as both humans and gods.

Where John Benjamin's lineage can be traced using diaries, family Bibles, and parish entry data, it does suffer from some discrepancies. Although conclusions can be made with relative certainty, these gaps make it impossible to guarantee the lineage 100 percent. John's is murky around who Roger Benjamin was and how he came to be the very first recorded Benjamin Tribe descendant recorded in England. Was he the son of royalty? Was he Constance Capet's child from King Stephen who had hopes of keeping the family bloodline in power and out of the hands of his enemy and cousin Matilda? Because of the demarcation processes ordered by Henry VIII, we may never know the answers to these questions.

Abigail's heritage, however, is completely clear and well documented. These recorded pieces of evidence have even survived several periods of demarcation when kingdoms tried to eliminate history in order to remove competing heirs' claims and future insurrections by other royal relatives. King Henry VIII understood this and seemingly made demarcation an ongoing event, continually misshaping history. The current royal family in England has often been challenged publicly for not being the rightful heirs to the crown as facts that survived demarcation periods have become known.

To better understand John and Abigail's family history, one has to step back through their history. Their interesting point of crossover history starts during the 1020s as Robert I the Magnificent and his wife, Harlette De Falaise, had children. Robert I had a son with a mistress. This illegitimate child, named Guillaume Ier de Normandie, would grow up to become the French-speaking king of England who was better known as William the Conqueror.

His lineage would continue to rule all of Normandy until the murkiness of King Stephen, Eustace, and Constance Capet Countess of Boulogne, France. Constance Capet's brother, King Louis VII, wanted all of France, including those lands under King Stephen's control, which led to the real reason behind the Crusades. The child of either King Stephen or Eustace and King Louis's sister Constance Capet had to be destroyed. The discovery and acknowledgement of this child by the world would have eliminated the family reign of King Louis VII, which also would have severely threatened the power of the Catholic Church. The Crusades had to be crafted to find and destroy the child who became Roger Benjamin. The existence of this child was also why crusading soldiers were ordered to attack the Cathars under false pretenses.

Where murkiness surrounded John Benjamin's lineage, perfect clarity surrounded the lineage of Abigail Eddye Benjamin. Robert I had a child not with his mistress, but rather with his wife, Arlette Falaise. They had a daughter, Adelaide of Normandy, Countess of Aumale. She was a half-sister to William the Conqueror and would be the great-grandmother to Abigail (Eddye) Benjamin centuries later, thus keeping a clear line to follow.

John Benjamin was a great mind, innovator, and achiever for setting up the foundations that would forever solidify the American experiment and his wife, Abigail, played an obvious role in this relationship that is quite detailed even at a time when women's history was not recorded. Upon their deaths, John and Abigail would leave an estate valued at $13 million in twenty-first-century equivalent value, as well as a great deal of literature and documentation.

John Benjamin participated in religious and legal study and discussions that were the beginnings of a movement that formed fundamental language later written into the Declaration of Independence. Those early discussions would also leave rules to act and govern communities. The family land and books started one of the greatest universities the world has known. John and Abigail raised offspring who would continue to be fruitful in their desire to improve the country they were creating and defending it at all costs, as would be seen in the actions of members of the Benjamin family for generations to come. Sadly, John Benjamin would die on February 13, 1645. Abigail would pass away on May 20, 1687, more than forty years later. Thankfully for America, the couple breached her shores, forever changing her thoughts and discussions for the good.

18

The Shaping of America

As Charlie continued studying his ancestors throughout history, he started becoming overwhelmed by the volumes of information discovered as he moved closer to more recent dates. He was amused as he learned so many of his relatives weren't merely involved in key historical events but had actually caused some of these events beginning in their early days after coming to America. Never being one to ignore a good fight, Charlie now understood the source of his attitude was his DNA.

As the Benjamin Tribe descendants started stepping on American soil from its earliest days, they adopted the new land as their home and immediately started to contribute to her values by becoming entrepreneurs, governors, constables, sheriffs, landowners, teachers, and church leaders. They would amass great wealth and property and share it with their communities. Going back to the original settlers in American history, Charlie realized his ancestors were among the very first group to arrive. His ancestors were not only present during all notable events, but they were, in fact, key participants. Their actions were often described and highlighted in records, and they were personally named and recognized for their contributions and actions. Many of the Benjamins fought for the new country, and some died for it.

Mayflower Descendant, 1620 (John Cooke, Great-Grandfather of Obediah Benjamin via His Mother)

One of the first relatives Charlie found to have made it to the new world showed up even prior to John and Abigail. In a ship called the *Mayflower*, roughly one hundred individuals traveled from the streets of London, one of the most advanced cities in the world, to those of a crude and undeveloped land called Plymouth, Massachusetts. In an effort to escape religious persecution and find a world where they could practice and pray without restriction, these individuals, known as the Pilgrims, would sign an original agreement called the Mayflower Compact, which included words and legal concepts that would lay the framework to the new democracy.

The *Mayflower* set sail in July 1620 from its home port of Rotherhithe, Surrey. The small vessel would sail down the River Thames into the English Channel, ultimately anchoring along the south English port of

Southampton Water where it would rendezvous with the *Mayflower*'s sister ship the *Speedwell*. The *Speedwell* carried roughly sixty-five English separatist Puritans from Holland. This group was from the Leiden Congregation and was fleeing religious persecution. After meeting up and transferring some of the passengers to the *Mayflower*, the two ships finally set sail for the new world and new freedom on August 5, 1620.

The *Speedwell* started the voyage with leaks, causing both ships to have to return back to England for repairs. Unfortunately, the repairs would not be permanent, and the ship's troubles would ultimately force the *Speedwell* out of the journey. The two ships returned to port and determined which passengers would make the voyage to America and which passengers would be returned to Holland.

Finally, the *Mayflower* set sail for America on September 6, 1620, from Plymouth, England, with roughly one hundred passengers and thirty crew members. One of these passengers, John Cooke, was only thirteen years old. John's education was superior compared with other children of his time, and his knowledge would prove invaluable in the new world. Although John would initially travel only with his father and be reunited with his mother and other siblings three years later, he would prove his value to the community's survival and success. John, at age eighty-five, would be the oldest surviving member of the first *Mayflower* journey.

Late fall winds make sailing across the North Atlantic very risky, and because the ultimate journey took place after so many delays, the provisions, patience, and energy of the Puritans were running low from the start.

Although their initial winds were prosperous and gave hope, the passage was miserable. The ship took on constant direct hits by strong waves, leaving the top deck constantly wet and cold. Through it all, the tiny vessel held strong until a crushing wave fractured one of the key structural timbers. Although everyone was already tired, hungry, wet, and cold, the crew and passengers worked together against all odds to repair the beam and continued on the ship's course. On November 9, 1620, they finally sighted present-day Cape Cod. After several days of trying to navigate the strong winds with the hopes of landing at the colony of Virginia, the *Mayflower* was forced to return to the harbor at Cape Cod Hook on November 11, 1620. The new pioneers signed the Mayflower Compact, dropping anchor and forever starting the new democracy.

Upon landing in the New World, the Pilgrims offloaded the essentials necessary to investigate the surroundings. The settlers quickly found a deserted native village, now called Corn Hill, in Truro due to the early findings of Indian corn supplies. The snow-covered lands were an initial challenge these settlers were not properly prepared for, as it was much colder and wetter than back home.

The *Mayflower* remained during the first winter, and half of the crew and passengers died as a result of scurvy, tuberculosis, or pneumonia. The Pilgrims were finally able to disembark fully and start on their new village on March 21, 1621, using the provisions and fortifications they had brought to create a properly defended community.

Following their relatives and fellow Puritans to America in June 1632, John and Abigail Benjamin quickly took to the opportunities the New World offered. Because he landed in America armed with great knowledge, John Benjamin, along with his partner John Winthrope, would legislate and create law and order he and the new community would enjoy, working together in cooperative fashion.

As should be expected, the creation of a new country would have many challenges big and small along the way. The Benjamins would be part of these challenges and the solutions as is now historically recorded throughout the early records that ultimately formed what is now the United States of America.

Pequot War, 1636–1638 (John Benjamin)

To truly understand the events that led to the Pequot War, the first task is understanding there were native people living in ancient lands being inundated by people from a far-off land. This migration was also being financially backed by the well-developed English community. Conflict would be immediate, and the victors would be with the wealthy, well-fortified people.

These conflicts lasted from 1636 to 1638 between the New England colonists and the Pequot Tribe. The Pequot Tribe was decimated in the process, and the prisoners were sold as slaves in the West Indies.

Some people would have seen this as a well-armed European conquest over the naïve native people. But actually, these wars were primarily between two current tribes, the Pequot and the Mohegan, which had separated over the centuries from one original tribe.

During the 1630s, the Pequot Tribe was aggressively extending their lands and political power over all of their neighboring tribes because they wanted to control the fur trade with the Europeans, which was creating great wealth with the natives. Finally, the native tribe of the Mohegans pushed back in response, creating great turmoil in the Connecticut River Valley.

In addition to the Indian unrest, there were also several years of disease that killed off many of the Indian populations, leaving an opening for the European settlers to invade and take advantage of the new trades taking place from the resources of the lush new lands.

John Benjamin arrived in Newtowne (modern-day Cambridge, Massachusetts) and was the acting constable for the area. He arrived just in time to find himself in the epicenter the upheaval between all of the parties involved. The Dutch and English were competing for goods, and by 1636, the Dutch and the English had built several trading forts in the area.

Due to political differences, the Pequots aligned themselves with the Dutch, and the Mohegans partnered with the English. The two sides came up with several rules designed to bring a truce to recent skirmishes, but peace did not result between the Dutch and Pequos who continued infighting. The Pequos had controlled wampum (Indian beads used as money) until the English Massac Hettes Bay Colony took over this control.

After ongoing murders, abductions, skirmishes, and attacks, the truce was at great risk. Then, on July 20, 1636, John Oldham, a respected trader, along with his crew was attacked and killed by the Pequot Indians during a trading voyage to Block Island. The Indians had hoped to discourage future English trading with their Pequot rivals. Those responsible for the murderers had been allowed to escape to and blend in to the sanctuary of the Pequots.

Oldman's death was the wick that ignited the fire under John Benjamin and other Massachusetts Bay Colony members to seek out those responsible. When the Pequots stalled giving up the perpetrators, the Bay Colony attacked, burned, and destroyed the Pequots' villages.

In the aftermath, the English of the Connecticut Colony had to deal with the anger of the Pequots who were trying to get the other tribes in the area to join their cause, but the other tribes sided with the English instead.

After ongoing unprovoked attacks by the Pequots against the English, the English had had enough and raised a militia of roughly ninety English in cooperation with 275 Indians. The group made its way to the main populated and fortified Pequot Village of Mistick. Heavy fighting took place on May 26, 1637, killing all but roughly a dozen of the five hundred Pequot men, women, and children and leading to the name The Mystic Massacre.

By midsummer 1637, other Pequot members not present at the Mystic Massacre and led by Sassacus unsuccessfully tried to take refuge with the Mohawks in modern-day New York. Instead, Sassacus was caught, beheaded, and had his hands cut off and sent to Hartford for unknown reasons, thus ending the Pequot War.

This war forever molded the differences in fighting techniques, attitudes, and forfeitures and set the stage on how the Europeans and natives would treat and fight each other throughout American history.

King Philip's War, 1675–1678 (Joseph Benjamin Sr.)

King Philip's War is commonly called the First Indian War, although it was fought forty years following the Pequot Indian Wars. The name recognizes the vast impact left upon the colonies after the war, as more than 10 percent of the colonists would die as a result.

This war took place from 1675 to 1678 between New England colonists and their Indian allies verses other Indians in the region. The war's name comes from Chief Metacomet from the Wampanoag Tribe who adopted the name Philip in respect for his father's (Chief Massasoit) relationship with the Pilgrims.

Massasoit had maintained peaceful longevity with the Wampanoag Tribe and colonists, but following Massasoit's death and transfer of power to his son Metacom this peace would not be maintained. When the first Pilgrims arrived, they worked very hard to make peace with the Wampanoag Tribe, but now attacks such as Metacom's were becoming more and more common throughout the region. As the European settlers continued to push farther and farther into Indian lands where natural resources were being reduced as a result, religious differences were also creating frictions. Selfish partisan viewpoints were killing much of the original goodwill.

During this expansion period, the settlers established a few new towns in the interior lands between Boston and the Connecticut River towns. This was done under the treaty between the Wampanoags and the colonists. The Wampanoags understood the treaty to mean the colonists would provide protection against other the tribes that both the Wampanoags and the colonists skirmished against together. However, the colonists did not believe the treaty prevented them from occupying Wampanoag lands. This resulted in the Wampanoags siding against the English colonists and helping the Dutch settlers by selling them land and negotiating with other tribes to assist in attacking the English. The English colonists passed laws making it illegal transact commerce with the Wampanoags. Relations became very tense.

The final straw presented itself through an unusual situation. Resulting from the Long Parliament's passing of the ordination allowing Indians to be converted to Christianity and change their names to more traditional European names, one Indian would change his name to John Sassamon. Sassamon was an original convert and would later be called Praying Indian.

Joseph Benjamin converted the Indian John Sassamon. Sassamon went on to act as a mediator, negotiating between the Indians and the colonists. During this period, Sassamon's body would be found in a frozen pond, and three of Metacom's Wampanoags would be tried for Sassamon's murder by a jury of Indian elders and hanged. Unfortunately for Metacom, as the war closed to its end, his alliance soon fell apart, and he was captured and killed by the English colonists.

The war continued until the signing of the Treaty of Casco Bay in April 1678 and left both horrible and amazing results for the new American colonies. For a causality count based on percentage of population, this was one of the deadliest wars in American history. More than half of all the towns in New England were involved at one time or another. Many of the towns and their people were destroyed and burned to the ground. The economies were destroyed, and roughly 10 percent of their population was dead. This war also created the fact that the English American colonists were truly independent, as they fought this enemy without any support from an outside government or their military, once and for all separating their identity from England. The foundation of America as an independent country is often said to have started on April 12, 1678, with the Treaty of Casco, which was signed by Joseph Benjamin and other Massachusetts Bay Colony members and the Penobscot chiefs.

King William's War, 1689–1697 (Joseph Benjamin Sr.)

Just a few years after the Treaty of Casco ended the King Philip's War, Joseph Benjamin and other colonists would once again be fighting with the Indians. King William's War, also called the Second Indian War or the French and Indian War, was somewhat of an extension of the King Philip's War and an extension of European aggressions between England and France. Past signed treaties were not being honored.

Secondarily, there were tensions taking place between France and England back in Europe, as well as in the new colonies. The European kingdoms back home were busy enough and didn't see the point in also fighting the disagreements between the colonists, so they let them sort their own conclusions. The French controlled the fur trade around New York and the Great Lakes region and were creating hostilities against the Iroquois Indians, and the British were trying to take the control away.

The English armed the Iroquois Indians to push out the French and improve the English–Indian trade in the region. During the fighting, the French proved very cunning combatants but were outnumbered ten to one by the English. After years of skirmishes, massacres, and failed treaties finally ending further uprisings, the English, French, and Indians finally came to terms. Many scholars believe this war never really ended even though the Treaty of Ryswick had been signed in September 1697. This war was the tipping point that established English as the dominate language in the colonies.

Another subject matter that held top news conversations of the day that has been debated over the decades by scholars is the role this war played in creating the Salem Witch Trials of 1692. America was still being settled by people looking to escape Europe for religious and political freedom. At this time and place, there were also many displaced people in the area because of the ongoing conflicts between the French and Indians. Many women were said to have been accosted and taught black magic ways to survive.

Most colonists of the time associated the devil with Indians and magic. During the years 1692 and 1693, New England witnessed primarily young women being falsely accused and hung or burned alive by Puritan leaders. This burning of people alive under religious persecution had biblical historical connections with the Christians due to events that happened during the Crusades. This course of action was so rough and ugly that it changed the minds of Puritans and led them to understand and accept other religious beliefs and is considered a cornerstone event that changed America's religious view permanently.

Back home in Cambridge, Massachusetts, in 1697, Joseph Benjamin Sr. was trying to establish life with his family in the new and developing world, which teetered between native and English practices and attitudes. The daily activities consisted of the men going off to hunt or work in the fields, while the women would stay back and manage the home and children. They also had the direct responsibility to educate the children of the time. Every once in a while, the settlers would be faced with fights between the French or Indians. Massachusetts was very much an English-based territory. The surrounding territories were interesting during trading events, as they encompassed Germans, Dutch, Irish, English, Spanish, and Indians. Settlers never really knew what their language or background experiences would be.

Joseph Benjamin Sr. learned the true pains of these ongoing skirmishes, as he was severely injured by a French and Indian attack when he was present at Fort William Henry. Joseph was a participant in some, if not all, of the events surrounding Fort William Henry. A pension petition that Joseph had directed to the General Court in Boston on March 13, 1699, gives Joseph's actual account of an event of which he was the sole survivor.

"Being a soldier under Capt. Goram was Impressed into his majesty service some time in ye month February about five years ago to serve under Major March at Pemmaquid. And in the month August next following I was sorely wounded, on one of my hands & ye other Arm, by the Indian Enemy. And by reason of ye wounds then received I have been Ever since disabled to Labour for my Living and I Being a married man & have a chargeable family am incapassitated to provide for them as I should."

During his service at the Fort, Joseph was also a witness to several of his friends being cut down by French soldiers during unprovoked attacks bent on open murder. Joseph's notes and account are fully supported by observations and postmortem data collected by military investigators of the time. After Joseph's death, his family would eventually be rewarded with several parcels of land for his service.

King George's War, 1744–1748 (Obediah Benjamin)

Most of Connecticut was made up of Dutch emigrants and native Indians. The English emigrants in the area were Puritans, descendants from the Massachusetts Bay Colony. Obediah was living with his family in Hartford Connecticut in 1744 when King George's War broke out. At the time, Hartford was still a small fledgling community entrenched in farming and shipping goods throughout Europe and the West Indies. Women usually married by fifteen and were considered their husbands' property. If they ran off, they would be considered thieves for stealing the clothes they wore.

Most families owned slaves who worked in the fields and with the wife doing chores. The slave trade was high with roughly 10 percent of the population being slaves. Trade was high with the settlers trading metal goods for furs that would be shipped to Europe. Life was harsh for most colonists who managed to survive. Winters were much colder than what the colonist were used to in Europe. Colonists raised crops and cattle on the farms, built ships, fished, and whaled along the coast. They also wove their own fabrics.

As the settlers grew in numbers, the Indians felt crowded. Many battles, skirmishes, or outright wars would take place as America sorted herself out. From the time when the first Benjamin lineage appeared to until the middle of the seventeenth century, the Benjamins would continue the fight for America and her newfound freedoms. From 1744 to 1748, Obediah Benjamin found himself fighting during the King George's War, although one probably can't determine whether Obediah or others of his time were fighting on behalf of England or the fledgling new America.

The war was actually created thousands of miles away back in Central Europe due to the challenge against the legitimacy of the ascension to the Austrian throne by Maria Theresa of the House of Habsburg. England was an ally of Austria; France and Prussia were opponents. As the motherland in Europe fought, so did the English and French colonists in America.

The Treaty of Aix-la-Chapelle ended the war on October 18, 1748, and restored Louisbourg to France but failed to resolve any other outstanding territorial issues. As a result, festering wounds would once again turn into skirmishes for many years and would ultimately cause the French and

Indian War to break out in 1754. This war would have a reverse trend. It started in North America and spread to Europe and would become known as the Seven Years' War.

These wars never seemed to solve much and simply gave the appearance of people fighting for the same seat on a crowded bench. A lot of shuffling around would take place until finally everyone fit in together.

The Benjamins' personal beliefs were Puritan of the day, which taught monotheistic religion and emphasized family and education values, as did the original Benjamin Tribe. This was extremely important for America as it became a primary pillar to her foundation, which is still followed today.

The Boston Tea Party, 1773 (Daniel Benjamin)

Although the actual event remained nameless until recollections and comparisons started showing up in print in the 1830s, the Boston Tea Party, as it has come to be known, sets itself apart as the most prominent description of what America was becoming. This event raised the awareness and gave the fight cry of "no taxation without representation," which once and for all separated the American colonies from European rule.

English Parliament would dictate the rules over the colonies. The events related to the Tea Act of May 10, 1773, simply gave the Whigs, more commonly called the Sons of Liberty, the platform necessary to push a strong message back to England. Tea prices actually went down during this uprising. It forced both the East India Company, which had been given all the tea sales rights to the English colonies under the act, to have to compete with the nontaxed Dutch suppliers and as well as the black market providers. The representation issues went unresolved, and the English Parliament continued to tax and penalize the colonies with English laws without giving the colonies opportunity to insert reasoning.

The Boston Tea Party was more of a political protest against England's Parliamentary procedures, which placed charges and decisions against the American colonies without even giving the colonies a representative to vote their wishes. Many of the protestors were merchants who were being forced to pay taxes on tea sales to make up for the missed taxes from the black market tea sales. The black market Dutch tea sellers were also unhappy with the low-priced sales of tea due to the open-market wars. Finally, the East India Company was given the rights to sell their tea shipments without paying taxes, giving them an unfair monopoly in the English colonies.

When the East India Company ships loaded with tea arrived in November and December 1773, the Sons of Liberty disallowed the tea from being delivered on American soil. Thus, no taxes could be charged by England. Royal Governor Thomas Hutchinson refused to allow the Sons of Liberty to force the tea to be returned to England without paying the port taxes, in effect stranding the ships.

After failed efforts by Samuel Adams and his protest followers to convince the consignees to give up their desires of offloading the tea from their ships and getting Governor Hutchings to forgo the port tax, the protestors took matters into their own hands. This led to the events of the Boston Tea Party.

It must be noted that tea shipments had arrived at several other colonial ports during this time, and those ships were allowed to leave their ports untaxed and return to England still fully loaded with their tea cargo. What made the events in Boston unique was that Governor Hutchinson was loyal to England, and two of the consigners of the *Dartmouth*, *Elanor*, and *Beaver* ships carrying the tea were his sons. English law required ships to unload and pay their duty tax within twenty days, or the cargo could be confiscated.

On the last day of *Dartmouth*'s deadline, everything reached a boiling point. That evening of December 16, 1773, protestors, including several of the young Benjamin boys, poured out of the meeting headed up by Samuel Adams who had lost control of the gathering. Roughly one hundred protestors dressed as Mohawk warriors boarded the *Dartmouth* and dumped all 342 chests of tea into the bay. The first box thrown overboard is believed to have been thrown by a young Daniel Benjamin dressed in disguise as a Mohawk Indian.

Both the London Parliament and many colonial loyalists where shocked at this event. Even Benjamin Franklin felt the cost of the tea should have been fully repaid. The British government felt the actions must not go unpunished and created several Intolerable Acts intended to punish Boston and restore English authority.

The Boston Tea Party marked a significant event and would become a foundational point as the thirteen colonies began to band more and more together and focus their anger against England and the Parliament. They ultimately started to see themselves truly as an independent country.

Following the Tea Party events, Parliament responded with the Coercive and Intolerance Acts in 1774 intended to end local government in the colonies and restore English authority. The colonies viewed the overreach of King George's rule to be tyrannical attacks against their constitutional and human rights. This placed the final nail in the coffin and sealed the idea that the American colonies no longer needed the support of England, leading to the creation of the First Continental Congress. Throughout the colonies, a common theme was quickly growing and gaining support—the theme of independence.

Undeterred, both sides continued to clash until finally escalating, and the American Revolutionary War would begin outside of Boston on April 19, 1775.

The American Revolution, 1775–1783 (Ebenezer and Daniel Benjamin)

Ebenezer was living in Albany, New York, in 1776 when he enlisted in the Seventeenth Regiment at the age of forty-one. He would reenlist several times until he was forty-six. He would go on to serve in Col. Samuel Elmore's regiment in Connecticut for one year from April 1776 to April 1777.

He also had the opportunity to serve as a captain under Marinus Willett, regarded as one of America's greatest leaders of the American Revolution and personal friend of George Washington. Willett was also the leader of the Sons of Liberty, and on April 23, 1775, upon learning about of the battles at Lexington and Concord, he broke into the New York City arsenal with several of the Sons of Liberty and several of his officers and took all of the British weapons. After realizing what had happened, the British tried to escape but were captured by Willetts and his men, including Ebenezer Benjamin, at Turtle Bay. Because of these actions and other similar actions, he and his men were given the title of Rebel Rousers during the war.

Ebenezer also enlisted and served under Duchess County Militia in the Associated Exempts under Col. Zephaniah Platt who would later become a New York Congressman and New York Supreme Court Justice.

The American Revolutionary War, also known as the American War of Independence, was the war that began as a conflict between Great Britain and its thirteen North American colonies, which declared independence as the United States of America. The war itself was a progression of taxes that had taken place over many years, leading to the Boston Tea Party and the thought of no taxation without representation. Freedom from religious persecution and the learned knowledge from all the Indian Wars when the colonies were able to defend themselves without help from the motherland furthered the colonial separation from British authority. All of these thoughts proved to the American colonies that they were indeed independent and should form their own government. After the Sons of Liberty retaliated destroying a shipment of tea in Boston Harbor, Britain responded with punitive measures against the Massachusetts Bay Colony. The colonies formed the Continental Congress to combine their strength and coordinate their resistance.

Daniel Benjamin was a young man living in Preston City, Connecticut. While still in his teens, he signed up to serve aboard the ship the *Castle*. His service lasted thirty-six months and one day. His officers were Captain Bradyle, Colonel Crafts, Captain Warner, and Col. Paul Revere. Daniel was a member of the Sons of Liberty along with his father Ebenezer. Both were men of loyalty and conviction and wanted the British out. Both men also shared similar views with the larger percentage of the colonists, but as a young man and due to his mentorship from Paul Revere, Daniel felt he had to be front and center of all of the action. His actions would collide with the Red Coats while witnessing the first shots of the revolution in Concord, Massachusetts. Through his relations with Revere, he also came to know John Hancock and Patrick Henry and, sadly, even Benedict Arnold.

Daniel Benjamin never had the opportunity to fight directly alongside his father, but his father had had great success previously during the French and Indian War. Daniel's father, Capt. Ebenezer Benjamin, would also fight alongside George Washington as one of his special guards and would be present as Washington crossed the frozen Potomac and tracked the traitor Arnold before he fled back to England. This left Ebenezer to fight throughout the revolutionary stage until age forty-six.

Although Daniel never got to fight alongside his father, Daniel would see battles as he fought for America's cause during the war. The younger Benjamin was gifted with friendships at a young age that would align him during the war with some of America's greatest heroes.

Daniel's relationship with Paul Revere and the mentorship he received along with his friends of the Sons of the Liberty would all serve him throughout his lifetime. Daniel would go on to serve in the famous Eighth Regiment from Albany, New York. Historians agree that Albany was a hotbed of revolutionary activity because of its strategic location to all of the parties involved in the war and key military bases.

Albany was also strategically centered between Canada and New York City. The location was considered a stronghold and a major transportation junction of the 1770s. Because of its reasonable proximity to West Point Military School, the Continental Congress commissioned a large percentage officers from the city. Many were native sons of Albany and would go on to become the legendary heroes of the revolution for their major contributions to winning the war.

These young men fought through the horrors of war, seeing their friends and brothers die by musket shots and sabre stabbings as they marched to Valley Forge in 1778 with George Washington and the Battle of Monmouth.

The British had attempted to disarm the militia at Concord in 1775, which led to a skirmish and ultimately to Congress's appointment of George Washington to lead the Continental Army. On July 2, 1776, the Continental Congress voted for independence, issuing its declaration on July 4.

Battles would continue for several years on American soil, in Europe, and in their respective territories, as there had been quite a lot of pent up anger that needed to be resolved. The American War for Independence was simply the excuse needed. The war would continue until the Treaty of Paris was signed on September 3, 1783, in which Great Britain agreed to recognize the sovereignty of the United States and formally end the war. This date also marked America as an official independent nation.

Patriots followed independence with the Test Laws, requiring residents to swear allegiance to the state in which they lived. Test Laws were designed to root out individuals who were loyalist to Britain or opponents to independence. These laws forced individuals to pick a side and did not allow them to remain neutral. Failure to pick meant possible imprisonment, exile, or even death.

Americans who supported Britain were barred from public office, forbidden from practicing medicine and law, forced to pay increased taxes, or even barred from executing wills or becoming guardians to orphans. Congress enabled states to confiscate British Loyalist property to fund the war. Some Quakers who remained neutral had their property confiscated. States later prevented Loyalists from collecting any debts they were owed.

The aftermath of the war is interesting. The war lasted a little more than eight years. Roughly eighty thousand Continental Army soldiers and volunteers fought for America against fifty-six thousand British soldiers and thirty thousand of their Hessian mercenaries. Twenty-five thousand patriots died, of which eight thousand deaths were in battle, and seventeen thousand were from the smallpox outbreak and other diseases contracted mainly while held as prisoners. Patriot soldier ages ranged from ten to fifty-seven. Of the 20 percent of the colonists loyal to Britain, almost all were Catholic; 6.5 percent of the American population participated in the war. George Washington was never paid for his military service.

The war also led to substantial financial changes throughout America and Europe. Prior to the war, the colonies were experiencing the highest standard of living in the world. However, the American Congress had not yet set up the necessary financial tools to properly finance the costs and efforts both during the war and afterward.

By 1791, the United States had accumulated a national debt of $75 million. The United States finally solved its debt and currency problems by creating a national bank, which enabled the US government to assume all of the state debts and create a funding system based on tariffs and bond issues that paid off the foreign debts.

Britain ended up with a $330 million national debt. France had an unstable tax system, and the cost of the war spiraled them into a terrible financial crisis that led to the French Revolution.

Spain also suffered from military spending, but due to their more stable financial position, which was readily backed by their silver reserves, Spain's economy easily recovered.

As Charlie continued reading story after story about how his ancestors had worked and fought so hard in so many situations to build the foundations of America and continue its progress as a new country—the country he loved so much—he became overly excited. He envisioned himself fighting the battles, tossing tea in the face of repressive authority, riding with Paul Revere, or crossing the Potomac with George Washington.

Charlie had been pacing in circles as this information sank into his mind. Then he sat down, hyperventilating about the thought of George Washington. He knew his mother would yell at him if she could hear his thoughts, but the only words that currently ran through his mind were: *George Washington. Oh my God. My family fought directly with George Washington. George fricking Washington.*

He didn't know if he should call the news station or call for a parade. Once the original shock had passed and Charlie regained his normal composure, he read on.

The War of 1812, 1812–1815 (Ebenezer Benjamin Jr.)

It could be said the War of 1812 was the war that sifted out more of the American boundaries during a time of expansion. Once again, a Benjamin would be recorded fighting as a Loyalist and defending his nation. The war was labeled as being a war of America verses England, but because England and her European counterparts were still trying to control commerce in the new and vastly profitable American economy, many offenses converged.

The Napoleonic Wars were being fought. The French, Dutch, Spanish, and English governments were still reeling from financial losses during the Revolutionary War, and America and Canada were also trying to take account of their actual boundaries. Simply stated, the European and American countries were maturing after America's introduction. As far as wars go, this one was seemingly quiet compared to previous wars but played a significant role in further defining who controlled commerce in North America.

The American Civil War, 1861–1865

Many of the Benjamin family members fought throughout the Civil War, and all would be able to share unique stories of their experiences. One of the things that made the Benjamin narrative so different is they were all wealthy members of society due to large inheritances as well as earnings from their own successes.

Successful people rarely saw their children off to war. The Benjamin descendants, however, have no records showing they resisted the war. In fact, most showed up as volunteers.

They fought for the North and shared a primary belief in keeping the country fully united. History shows their being asked to do things far beyond the ordinary ask on many occasions and their agreement to engage. Family members were shot, stabbed, and starved, and still, they trudged forward. They were tall men of the day, most over six feet at a time when most men were five seven. Prior to the war, most of these men were making their way through life as farmers, merchants, lumber barons, sheriffs, lawyers, and judges.

Records show the Benjamin family members were disgusted that the relations in their young country had deteriorated to the point where it meant more to kill a neighbor, friend, or even brother than it did to work things out, especially when these people were said to follow Christianity. These Benjamins witnessed everything but what they believed Christianity to stand for as they saw the horrors of war firsthand.

What were the two sides really fighting about? Northerners really weren't concerned over the issues of slavery. They were primarily slave-free, and fighting a war with the high likelihood of being maimed or killed in the process was not worth it in most people's minds at the time. The negative impacts feared by the results of the country splitting in half or having some of the states secede and what it would do the new democracy and the country's financial situation created enough of a stir for the North to become involved.

In the Northerners' minds, they were fighting to protect the Union. Pres. Abraham Lincoln constantly reminded everyone that this was his main objective. As the war progressed, he understood the impact of slavery and added the demise of slavery as a secondary objective. By announcing the Emancipation Proclamation in 1863, the Union Army received an immediate increase of roughly two hundred thousand black men and free and escaped slaves to its ranks.

On the other side of the argument, not all Southerners were fighting to preserve slavery. The majority did not own slaves and did not require the economics behind it. Instead, most Southerners fought to preserve their states' freedoms against what they felt was the federal government's overreach.

Antislavery supporters felt opposition to this issue as a form of anarchy and evil and against all Republic and Christian beliefs. Before the Civil War started, both sides had started to create political points prior to the presidential election in 1860. The Northern states were trying to outlaw slavery throughout all states, while the Southern states were postulating that the end of slavery would destroy the Southern economy and any attempts were federal government overreach. The other factor that was driving the fight was the fact that large Southern plantations had already spent the money necessary to purchase the slaves who supported the cotton industry, which was the backbone of the Southern economy at the time. All of this pushed the discussion on splitting the Union and entering a civil war if necessary.

After Abraham Lincoln's election victory over Southern Democrat John Breckenridge, South Carolina called an emergency meeting at the state convention center to declare secession and nullify all federal laws. They voted unanimously to secede on December 20, 1860, before Lincoln ever took office and adopted the Declaration of the Immediate Causes, which justified South Carolina's secession from the Federal Union. This led several of the other Southern states to secede over the next several months.

During Lincoln's inaugural address On March 4, 1861, he made it clear he had no interest in invading the Southern states or ending slavery in the states where it currently existed. However, he preached the power of having the complete Union and that the Constitution overpowered the newly created Southern state articles and legally voided them. He also stated federal lands and buildings would remain as such, and he would use force if necessary to protect them. All federal marshals and judges would be removed from the Southern states. Mail would stop at the state borders. Tariffs would be charged for goods received.

The Benjamin family members were highly conflicted with the issues of the day. On one hand, being Northerners and believers of individual hard work and success, they didn't agree with slavery from a physical or philosophical perspective but also didn't want to fight and kill fellow

Americans. On the other hand, the Benjamins didn't want to see the country they loved so much and that their ancestors had fought so hard for and contributed so much to build torn apart from within. In the end, they agreed to fight for unification.

Lincoln was hoping for sensible resolve, which he felt threats would create. It didn't work, and hostilities began on April 12, 1861, when Confederate forces fired upon Fort Sumter and started the war.

Once the war had started, many, including Lincoln, thought it would end quickly with little bloodshed. From the onset, the war was romanticized and actually sounded similar to camp, except with the addition of guns and an enemy.

As the Benjamins and many other soldiers showed up to report in, they were given wool uniforms and supplies that included a cap; a belt; a blanket roll; a canteen; socks; a shelter kit with a rubber blanket and poncho to protect them against the rain and wet fields; a knapsack gun with a bayonet, scabbard, and cartridge; and cap box supplies. They also received a personal item sack that held their shaving razor, a toothbrush, and a comb. Their final provisions would include some paper, ink, and a pen along with envelopes and stamps, which they could use to write letters to their loved ones, although as they would soon learn, little time would avail itself for these later provisions. When they had time between battles, many of the men would try to write as many letters as possible. These letters would serve history by the descriptions of the war outlined in these field reports. Other free time was enjoyed by playing cards, tossing horseshoes, reading, boxing, cleaning their supplies, fixing their equipment, and playing the new game called baseball, which became popular during the war.

As Charlie studied this information, he became very interested. He was a very visual person and saw in his mind's eye large groups of people enjoying comradery on a nice afternoon. These visions all felt warm and fun to Charlie.

Each day started by five o'clock in the morning with a bugle's revelry call and outlined by drums announcing the daily activities until sunset. Breakfast was always the first call to action followed by roll call and sick call. Guard duties were then announced, and the soldiers were lined up for the daily march. The drummers kept the marches in step as they moved along. Battle calls among the different positions used both drums and bugles to coordinate positions and maneuvers during the fighting. Music was also popular during noncombat times. Many soldiers were musically talented and could play many instruments. They would sign and make up songs for their marches as a way to pass the long days.

During the summers, the camps looked like canvas cities. During the winters, these camps added thick layers of smoke due to the heavy concentration of campfires. More established camps constructed log huts covered by mud and straw to better protect the soldiers from winter's harsh elements.

Orders were many, and the soldiers followed most of them without hesitation with the exception of the rules against having pets. Most soldiers and officers up to the highest ranks allowed pets to join their companies. The pets offered pleasant distractions from the war, which most soldiers appreciated. Troops had cats, raccoons, squirrels, birds, and chickens but preferred the accompaniment of dogs.

Soldiers earned ten to fifteen dollars monthly and sent the money home to their families. Soldiers would receive letters and packages from home. The letters were generally read aloud to their mates to keep morale uplifted. Lucky soldiers would receive packages filled with tobacco, coffee, newspapers, books, Bibles, sewing supplies, fruit, vegetables, rice, new underwear, socks, soap, playing cards toiletries, and other essentials.

As the war progressed, the Benjamin family members witnessed and wrote about war's ugly side. They wrote about stories they heard and things they saw. They described the horror of seeing the blood as it drained from young men's eyes, leaving a bland, dull, dead stare as they died in battle. In their minds, they could hear these boys' mothers and wives cry out in anguish as the boys took their last breaths. In their minds, they could see the boys playing as children just years before. The bloody grass where these boys lay was not soft and cool anymore from the morning dew as it had been just hours before. Instead, it was now warm, hot, and red. It smelled of the devil and the hell he had unearthed.

The war recruited everyone and anyone who would listen. Men were lumped in as one and given one message: fight or die. Many may have been teachers, carpenters, or farmers last week, but this week they were forced killers. Last week they may have been friends with someone they knew in Virginia, but this week they'd kill him and light his family farm on fire, forever destroying their world. A young man may have slept in a warm bed last night; tonight, though, he'll spend it in a soaking tent as a rainstorm washes through the area. If he's lucky enough, he'll survive without falling to pneumonia only to kill his first enemy within a week. After killing his first, he would be forever haunted by the life he took. Curiosity of what it feels like to kill is replaced by the hallow grounds of remorse and the hauntings of the dead.

The young soldier would become consumed with guilt of the event and fail to hear what's happening around him until it's too late. He's been shot multiple times. He lies in his own blood, feeling the warmth separate his back from the cold ground. He thinks to himself, *What happens when the blood is gone?* He gets colder as the blood leaves his body. He's in pain, but he's drifting off to sleep. His last thought is of those young men he killed. He wants to apologize, but they are gone. He thinks to himself, *Thank God I'll be gone too. I'll be a lucky one this time. The pain will all be gone.* His eyes fade out.

Suddenly, he is reawakened. His next feelings are those of confusion. He feels pain again but can't believe it. Heaven was always a happy place in his mind, but this is not happy.

He comes out of his daze and the field doctor says, "You are a lucky man, soldier. We found you and will save you."

The young soldier is handed a wet rag to bite on. Confused still but obedient to the doctor, he complies. Suddenly, he feels the tearing of flesh and muscle, the grinding of bone, and the stinging of nerves on his feet. Then he feels nothing below his knee. He sees a nurse lift his leg up and discard it in a tub with other limbs. He hears the screams, smells the stench that he smelt in the battlefield, and then soils himself. He no longer thinks about the enemy. Life has left him even though he's still alive and is told again that he's lucky.

The stories from the Benjamin family members, like other family members involved, are gruesome. In their minds, the war is not romantic in any way, and they miss their families, their farms, and their ways of life. They just want to go home.

From the beginning of the war until its conclusion, there would roughly six hundred thousand to eight hundred thousand soldier deaths, and that death toll climbs to more than one million when you count citizens. The number varies for several reasons. Poor records were kept at the time by mistake and with purpose. Field records were simply poorly kept during this period. Also, it is assumed that freed blacks fighting for the Union died two to one over their white counterparts, but poor records were kept by them as well. Poor records were also purposely kept by the government. No pension could be obtained by soldiers alive upon release, so many were released just prior to dying and not counted. Tens of thousands of soldiers succumbed to war injuries and disease after being released. Either way, when you understand that there were roughly thirty million people alive in the United States at that time, death came to more than 3 percent of the entire population.

Most scholars agree that the South never had a chance to win this war for several reasons. First, there were more people who didn't own slaves than people who did, which took the heart out of the fight for the Southerners. Imagine sending your child off to war to fight a fight that would not change a thing for you or your family and that you don't believe in. Your child may die while fighting for a neighbor's ownership rights of a slave. If the young man was forced to fight, would his heart be in the battle? Was the young man motivated? Experts have proven time and time again that having heart in a fight is the greatest advantage of all.

Secondly, the Union was somewhat unmotivated to fight as well because most soldiers did not understand what the full impact of keeping the Union intact meant. Their hearts weren't fully engaged either. Even though the union was unmotivated, they crushed the opposition by the sheer size of their army verses the Southern militia. Experts analyze this with the understanding that had the South won too many battles, the unmotivated North would have awakened resulting in the annihilation of the South.

Third, Lincoln produced common sense during the discussion that slowly worked on the political consciousness and changed hardened thoughts about the entire situation. Lastly and most importantly, the war against slavery was a Christian challenge. You can't be both a Christian and a slave owner without being a proven hypocrite. With this, Lincoln truly had God on his side. The global consequences proved this point, as most of the world followed America's lead, forever eliminating slavery.

At the onset of the war, the South tried to bring England and France over to fight against the North. Lincoln and his Secretary of State William Seward threatened that with any country that recognized the existence of the Confederate States of America would be faced with tariffs and war from the North. As a result, Europe stayed away. For payback, the Southern cotton growers stopped cotton shipments to Europe, hoping to create a financial emergency and ultimately return Europe to the negotiations table. Unfortunately for the South, Europe found other superior and cheaper cotton suppliers, which hurt the South during the war and greatly delayed their recovery period following the war.

Lincoln's final Emancipation Proclamation and push for the addition of the Thirteenth Amendment issued on January 1, 1863, offered Democrats who were quietly on the president's side some sensible talk about slavery and involuntary servitude except for matters dealing with criminal punishment. The president's hope was to provide a bridge in order to repair deeply damaged relationships in their states, especially along the border states.

As the South started losing a succession of back-to-back battles that led to a significant number of causalities and deep financial concerns, the South sent delegations to Washington. They offered to pay for the federal properties lost in the early days of the war and enter into a peace treaty with the United States. Lincoln rejected all negotiations with Confederate agents and would not accept the Confederacy as a legitimate government. Any treaties would create a false recognition that the Southern Confederacy was a legitimate sovereign government.

On April 14, 1865, President Lincoln was shot in the head by John Wilkes Booth while watching a play at Ford's Theatre in Washington, DC, with his wife, Mary. He died early the next morning, making Andrew Johnson the president. The war had not yet ended, and Lincoln didn't live to see how his efforts changed slavery in America and around the world.

Meanwhile, Confederate forces across the South started surrendering as news of Gen. Robert E. Lee's surrender reached them. President Johnson officially used a proclamation to declare an end to the war on May 9, 1865.

The Thirteenth Amendment was ratified as law by state vote on December 6, 1865, and Secretary of State Seward proclaimed it in Lincoln's absence on December 18, 1865.

The war changed the country, the states, and men like the Benjamins forever. Men of the time felt the war was probably necessary to solidify the young nation, but it was a sad chapter for all of the families involved.

After reading all of the information, Charlie was in awe at what his ancestors and others went through during this time. As he put away his books to leave, his feelings were somewhat numb. Then the thoughts of George Washington and his ancestor popped back into his head, and he again said to himself, "George fricken Washington … Wow!"

19

Secrets Revealed

Every now and again some families develop oddities that are unexplainable to those around them and, if so, can become quite a challenge in certain circumstances. In the Benjamin lineage, these oddities can be tracked to family members about every fifth or sixth generations. Oddities have been recorded with specific members of the family about every 150 to 200 years, including extreme visual differences, clairvoyance, and clarity of understanding of the world around them, how to clearly lead people during challenging times, and the ability to physically move people without resistance. These things, along with several other minor abilities, give these specific family members small advantages in life.

When some of the rarer gifts are possessed, such as ability to see and sense things unnoticed by others using auras or manipulating nature's energy flow to maximize inner strength well above levels of average individuals, witnesses report almost superhuman qualities. Throughout history, many members of family bloodlines have achieved individual mythical status, high political status, great wealth, or much power. In most cases, these people achieve one or two levels of achievement, but in more rare instances, some of the lineage is able to achieve all of these characteristics in total.

What makes this even more unusual is these traits do not consistently appear with everyone in the lineage, which allows for enough time to pass between those affected and witnesses to profess what they have seen from the family members who possess the abilities. These traits are not only found in men but have also revealed themselves in some of the women. If the traits or gifts as some report show up, they are usually revealed in just one of the children in a particular family and are not shared by all of the siblings.

Because of the distance created by time between generations of people in the family who are gifted with these oddities, many of those who witness these oddities have no idea of past events of similarities experienced by the generations before them. Only a deep study of the lineage and the people in it could reveal its totality.

As one would imagine, Charlie had difficulties getting his arms around everything. All his life was spent waking from wild dreams and seeing unusual things on a regular basis during his waking hours. He had learned to keep his thoughts and visions to himself as best he could, but many times the events manifested themselves beyond just Charlie and extended to being witnessed by his family or friends.

Charlie never had one or two isolated events but rather had constant situations arise. On many occasions, he felt he needed to pass along tips that would help others, but they would simply become startled by what he shared with them. So over time, he would become reserved about sharing the information except if situations truly threatened him or those for whom he truly cared.

For example, if he were driving at night with his family as a young child, he would comment on things he saw off in the darkness that the others could not see. They would ignore Charlie's comments, thinking they were just odd things being said by a young child. As his family drove along the country's highways and back roads, he would constantly chatter about seeing animals along the way. Nothing ever seemed too odd. He wasn't reporting spotting herds of elk or packs of wolves; instead, he would generally make everyone aware of deer, raccoons, skunks, etc.

One night as the family was driving through the desert en route to a family reunion everything changed for Charlie's family. Charlie would never again be allowed to simply ride in the back seat of the car again. Charlie's father had been driving late into the night in the family station wagon, and only he and Charlie remained awake while his mother, sister, and brother were fast asleep. Charlie told his father to slow down because they were approaching a group of deer ahead off to the right side of the road. Charlie's father saw nothing, so he ignored his son's banter and kept up the speed. As the car approached the deer, Charlie recognized the obvious peril that was about to happen and screamed, "*Stop!*" at the top of his lungs. With that, his father jammed on the brakes, throwing everyone violently forward and scaring Charlie's mother, sister, and brother half out of their minds at the same time.

Once the car stopped, the family immediately became unhinged at Charlie, yelling and screaming at him as their adrenalin pulsed rapidly through their veins. They still saw nothing except for the small bit of empty road in front of them where the headlights illuminated. Suddenly, his father sat silently looking forward, mesmerized by what he was seeing. A large grouping of deer was now crossing the road in the direct path the family was traveling. They would have undoubtedly hit the animals if not for Charlie's actions. Soon Charlie's siblings and mother were also completely silent. Charlie, on the other hand, knowing the danger had passed, sat silently, turned on his overhead car light, and proceeded to play spot the hidden picture in his *Highlights* magazine. From that point on, the family elevated him to always sitting up front during nighttime drives.

After many similar close calls involving almost hitting occasional deer or other critters, the family stopped taking his observations as general mumblings of a kid and not really paying too much attention to his remarks. Instead, they began listening to his remarks as a congregation concentrates on every word of the preacher.

Over the years, Charlie's ability to spot things others could not see continued to improve. Whenever any neighbors lost their pets, young children, wallets, car keys, etc., they would ask for Charlie's assistance to help locate their missing things. Living in a rural area, their pets and children never strayed too far away, so finding them was generally an easy task, but the car keys and wallets were always a challenge. He was never able to figure out why people thought someone would be able to locate wallets and keys when those things did not present auras.

Bud, Charlie's father, never really sorted things out completely, and his response to anyone who asked about the boy was to chuckle quietly and pass it off as if the stories were simply the results of a prank or a joke. Bud seemed somewhat embarrassed by the attention that was placed on him when others asked about his son. Never really coming to terms with Charlie's abilities, even after his son's visual differences had saved his life on multiple occasions, he always struggled with how to explain everything to others.

Bud's response at first was that of excitement. During different times of his life, he would attempt to use Charlie's abilities for personal gain, although not in a bad way. Bud was simply trying to deal with Charlie's differences on his own terms. Charlie believed his dad struggled with everything and felt he was always being pulled between his father's personal conflict: "Should I share my son's abilities with the world?"

Much later in life, after being married, Charlie watched his wife deal with similar challenges as his family. She also had to learn how to deal with Charlie's differences. He watched his wife, Sheila, and noticed she handled his differences exactly opposite of how Bud managed things. Sheila was a very inquisitive person who loved science and looked for oddities and questions in life that need to be answered. She was a very well-read person with the simple desire to not only find the answers to life's mysteries but also present the answers to others with the hope that the answers could change the world for the better.

After they were married, Sheila soon realized something was very different with Charlie's sight along with other obvious oddities. As in the case with his family, he would often tell her to look at one animal or another in the distance as they drove down a dark road. Sheila would tell him that she didn't see anything at first and would blurt out, "What are you pointing at? I don't see anything!" Finally, something would appear. Over time, she stopped thinking he was making up stories and acting like a big shot because she would eventually see whatever he saw.

Charlie was happy because he realized she had heard many others describe events they had witnessed over the years. He knew Sheila's curiosity would eventually drive her to find answers. During the early years of their marriage, Sheila heard story after story along with great details about events that had happened. She had even witnessed minor events herself. However, one major startling event she witnessed firsthand happened during an afternoon hike on the edge of town with Charlie. This experience would immediately motivate Sheila to find the answers to her curiosity.

Charlie had noticed a camouflaged makeshift homeless camp hidden off in a remote part of the trail. He pointed the camp out to his wife; however, she was not able to easily spot the camp. Charlie wanted to go into this camp and roust the squatters out of the area, but Sheila felt it was too dangerous to go it alone. Because he was a good husband, he listened to his wife's every word and didn't investigate any further.

The following day, Charlie had to leave their house early in the morning to catch a plane for an out-of-town meeting. Whenever Charlie traveled, Sheila would save the local newspapers for him to read upon his return so he could stay up to date on all of the current events. After returning a couple of days later, Charlie was reading the papers and noticed a story about witnesses who swore they had heard what they thought was a woman's scream. At the time of the event, the townspeople were only able to locate an unconscious and injured homeless man, ending any further searches.

Still, a stir continued in town, and there were many reports of hearing an occasional whimper from a woman that seemed to come from the area where they had located the injured homeless man. However, the man wasn't able to speak, and no woman was located. Because only the man had been located after an extensive search that had included a search-and-rescue helicopter, it was assumed only the man had been injured. As the man still lay in the hospital unconscious and unable to talk for a few days, no one was able to figure the mystery out. The cries eventually stopped, and after several days of additional searches turned up nothing, they ended without answers.

What was interesting to Charlie was two days after he had spotted the encampment the homeless injured squatter was found alone. Thinking back, though, Charlie remembered seeing multiple auras when he was with his wife, so he returned to the area to investigate things further. His wife was reluctant to go with him because she knew the other people who reported hearing the screams had found nothing. While Charlie had been out of town, local and neighboring police, along with forty-some search-and-rescue members, were led through the area by a well-known psychic. They hoped to discover where the voices had originated but found nothing and concluded the investigation.

Because Charlie remembered that he had seen multiple auras, he had to investigate the encampment for himself. Remembering that the auras had revealed a couple of larger people and one smaller person, he believed a child was also involved. Charlie convinced a small group from the search-and-rescue team to do one more sweep of the area. The team was also able to convince the helicopter unit armed with heat-seeking capabilities to make one quick pass over in the area where Charlie had seen the auras.

The helicopter immediately located a second homeless man who had been hiding a woman and a young child. The second homeless man had been in an obvious altercation, and further investigation would prove he had assaulted the man who lay unconscious in the hospital and taken the woman and child captive. The man in the hospital eventually recovered from his injuries and later testified as to what had happened.

After this incident and other stories from past events gained traction, more and more people started to pay attention to Charlie's abilities and began looking for answers, including his wife. Strangers started asking for autographs, and newspapers started publishing stories. Most were true, while others teetered on fiction. Charlie couldn't buy groceries, eat out, or even get a cup of coffee without being mauled. He hated the attention but didn't know what to do.

Charlie's wife decided enough was enough and started calling around to find a specialist who could work with Charlie and give him some reasons for his differences. After many calls, Sheila got some traction with the UCLA medical school who agreed to a meeting.

The morning of Charlie's meeting with UCLA was colder than usual in Southern California. The air was damp and heavy, which created a gray skyline that filled the air. Charlie was extremely nervous of the unknown as he ventured into the waiting room. He sat and quietly waited his turn, looking around at the other people in the room. His mind ran wildly, wondering what the doctors would be looking for and what tests they would want to perform. He wondered if all the people in the waiting room were like him. Were they also weird by comparative standards? Would the tests be painful? Would he be locked up in a nuthouse where he would spend the rest of his life being poked and prodded?

Finally, Charlie's name was called, and he was led back into a dimly lit office. The walls were all paneled in dark mahogany wood. The only light was an old-fashioned chandelier with small lightshades that threw off a dull pink color. There was a large desk for the doctor and a couple of leather sofa chairs circled around a low, round wood table covered in magazines and puzzles.

He figured the So Cal docs were about to start checking his sight differences, measuring his webbed toes, and tugging on his elastic skin. What they wouldn't be able to measure was his telepathic capabilities that enabled him to get people to do pretty much anything he thought about within reason. He could easily play with their minds on this day, but he truly just wanted to know what was happening to him that made him odd. Charlie simply wanted to be like everyone else.

He knew his abilities were now going to be medically reported and would soon be in the hands of many people around the world, but it would be okay because at least he could finally let his guard down and accept whatever was waiting for him.

The medical world went to work, giving their best answers and theories regarding his sight abilities. Everyone would be giving their answers and prognoses to his condition, and they would have the answers Charlie and his wife were both seeking—well, the answers *she* was really seeking. Charlie learned later from his own life experiences that it is usually much better to traverse through life without saying too much. Miranda had always been correct that whatever you say and do can and will be used against you.

The day dragged on. Normally, Charlie couldn't care less about the freaky goings on about doctors or their so-called unusual findings. He still didn't much care about So Cal's medical findings, but he did start to become more and more apprehensive, as logic told him as the day stretched on that these doctors and whatever findings they wrote in their journals could forever change his life. These same doctors would be examining his differences for the world to see. More importantly, he would have to live with their reports and summarizations, good or bad.

Because of his apprehension, he hadn't slept well the night before the doctor's visit. As a result of his lack of sleep, he was grumpy and initially impatient during the visit.

He didn't mind doctors as a general rule as long as they were working on someone else. He giggled to himself as he was thinking these goofy thoughts. Doctors were a very peculiar breed. They felt empowered to ask you thousands of questions, but as soon as you ask them just one question, their attitudes change from calm in nature to combative. Because doctors are highly trained with years of medical experience, they feel you should simply trust their findings as correct. Asking a doctor a simple question is translated by them as though you are asking them to prove their answers. They do not appreciate this in anyway. Asking too many questions could cause you to wake up three days later with your frontal lobe removed.

The more Charlie thought about everything, the more he knew he had everything to lose and little or nothing to gain by going through their process. But in life, you sometimes have to acquiesce with others, or the community around you can create a living hell for you.

The same people who exist under the group mentality exist everywhere around us. Even though we may not realize it to be true or hope that it's not true, people in the medical field are no different than others. They largely share the same prejudices in life that state if it's different, it's weird.

If the findings reported were odder than even he realized, his family would probably be fine dealing with it. His friends could also probably deal with it okay because they were used to dealing with his weirdness. What he wasn't sure about was what would happen if his unusual features got out into the world beyond his immediate friends and family.

What would be the result of strangers knowing about his different visual senses? Would the world be okay with this? Would he be placed in the freak category? Would his family and friends suffer the same fate? Many questions circled through Charlie's head during these processes, but once his life had become part of an examination by others, there was no turning back. So, he went through the tests and would react accordingly to the tester's results.

For the first time in Charlie's life, he felt scared and cornered with no way out. At the same time, he felt relieved from having to secretly wear the burden of hiding his differences from the world.

The day of testing on Charlie seemed to drag on forever. The university had booked an early morning appointment for his vision test. He had no idea what the university had prepared for him with these tests, and he entered the facility ready to have a quick eye exam and get the hell out of there. Did he mention how much he hated visiting doctors' offices? He hated them *a lot*.

He always wondered why some doctors' offices had "No Soliciting" signs on their front doors. Charlie thought, *Do they really have to work at keeping people away?* That's like posting a sign in the viewing area of a mortuary that says "No Loitering." Does it really need to be said?

When Charlie stepped into the office, he quickly learned that what was to follow would be more than just another day. After walking into the testing center, they sat Charlie down in a large office with a drop-top table filled with disassembled puzzle games and asked him to wait for the doctor.

His mind hated clutter, and this table was nothing but a bunch of clutter. He took it upon himself to relax his mind by organizing everything as he waited for the doctor. As he waited, he quickly organized everything by reassembling the puzzles. Unannounced to him, these puzzles were left purposely to see his response and were designed as a measurement to test his intellect. Charlie's speed at reassembling the puzzles was secretly being filmed and reviewed by the doctors who would be testing him throughout the day.

It's important to note that by his standards, Charlie thought that he had acted with great restraint by waiting a full minute before becoming a bit bored. Anyway, these puzzles were very easy for him to work to reassemble, and he had completed what he thought of as simply an opportunity to organize and straighten up a bunch of clutter. Upon completion, the doctor and a few assistants immediately entered the room and revealed that the task was actually a measured study of time. They further described to Charlie that his time of both starting the project and completing the project were both new record times. Also, upon completing the reassembly work, the doctors divulged to Charlie that his progress had been viewed though a two-way window. Charlie's was angry about being manipulated and spied on and told the doctors they shouldn't leave a mess of toys strewn all over the table and then spy on people. Now he really disliked doctors.

After calming Charlie down, the head doctor gave him a standard IQ test to complete. Obviously, he was very quizzical as to what this had to do with the sight test he was scheduled to complete. He was told that the IQ test was a standard procedure for someone about to be tested on the Kirlean camera and that the university would be performing multiple tests on him to identify whether there was a correlation between intelligence and the ability to see things differently than most people.

Charlie had suspected more deviant behavior from the medical group because they lied to him the first time, but like a good student, Charlie completed the IQ test as just another thing that needed to be completed as a standard operation. Thinking nothing further about the test and not really caring too much about it or the results, he went to work on it. It should be noted that he did not believe in tests of this nature because he felt any test could be manipulated by the test taker. Regardless, he finished the test quickly and without fuss and gave it to the doctor. Apparently, the doctor thought Charlie had finished the exam too quickly and reviewed it for completion.

"Charlie, did you really take the test, or did you just randomly skim and fill in the *A*, *B*, *C*, or *D* bubbles so you could get out of here quicker?"

"Yes, I read and answered everything," responded a surprised Charlie.

With that, the doctor asked Charlie some random questions from the test to confirm he had actually read the materials. Charlie's answers matched what he had turned in on the test, so the doctor concluded that Charlie had indeed read the exam.

Upon checking his answers against the master, the doctor concluded that Charlie must have taken the exam properly because most of his answers were correct, and there would have been no way he could have gotten so many questions correct by simply guessing. The results pointed out that Charlie's IQ was much higher than average. Charlie also pointed out that the questions from the test that had recorded Charlie's answers as incorrect were actual correct, and Charlie proved this to the doctor and his team. It should be pointed out that Charlie was not egotistical, self-centered, or overconfident. He was simply correct about the test answers just as he was correct about most other things.

One last test Charlie had to endure prior to the Kirlean camera tests being performed was the electroencephalograph (EEG), which measures electrical activity in the brain. Charlie had to admit this was pretty interesting and started to feel that these doctors may know what they were doing. These doctors had studied enough brains to know what normal brain activity looked like, so anytime something wacky or unusual was going on, the doctors would know how to make the necessary adjustments to their technology. Then, of course, just to remind anyone who was being tested that they were doctors, they would start sticking a bunch of electrodes to their test subject's head that led to a bunch of computers. These types of tests are usually performed on people suffering from seizures or when they want to see if a drug addict has fried his brain. In Charlie's case, they probably were leaning toward a hypothesis assuming he some kind drug use in combination with a hard hit to the head.

In any case, Charlie figured the EEG points out detectable abnormalities in the brain. If the findings were bad and they found a person's melon has suffered too much damage, Charlie believed the docs would just crank up the juice to finish frying the person's brain and stick him in a rubber room where he couldn't cause any trouble.

So, after the doctors greased Charlie up and connected all of the diodes, he told them to hit the juice. They all kind of looked at Charlie a little sideways and then started their tests. Charlie guessed he had been incorrect about his earlier assumptions as he received no shocks or jolts of electricity and never even blacked out. After a long, boring morning, he was somewhat disappointed that these tests were not very traumatic. He had emotionally prepared for the worst.

At the conclusion, all findings were negative. At first, Charlie thought a negative result was bad—really bad. The doctors must have found something positive in his head, but nope, their findings were 100 percent negative. How could this be? There had to be something in his skull, he thought. After all, he had driven himself to the appointment, talked on his cell phone while driving to the appointment, dressed himself, and fed himself. *Wow, 100 percent negative!* He was sure there had to be a mistake with the findings, so he finally broke his own rule and asked the doctors a question. His questions were quickly answered with the affirmation that negative findings were good and meant there were no problems. *Phew.* That was a relief.

Finally, after all the tests were finished, the science team brought in the Kirlean camera, which was connected to an aura biofeedback imaging machine, and prepared the tests. This was new to Charlie. He had read about these cameras but never seen one. It looked simple enough. It had a flat TV-type screen about two feet square and was attached to something called a high-voltage regulator, which was connected to a box that recorded and stored the images while then transferring them to the flat-screen. When they revealed what the camera and tests could do, Charlie was very excited. He had been telling everyone his whole life things that he could see, but this would be the first time in his life when he could prove it.

Charlie asked excitedly, "Will the photos you take be able to be printed? I want to show them to my friends and family."

The scientists smiled. They appreciated Charlie's excitement and told him they could. They even joked about giving him an order form so he could pick out his favorites so they could send him five-by-eight glossies.

Charlie enjoyed their humor and was in high spirits as he was about to be proven correct and vindicated against all of his life's doubters. He was very surprised the doctors had started with these tests instead of trying to prove whether he was nuts first.

The lead scientist and head doctor now stated, "Okay, it's time for all of you to leave, so we can run these final tests."

The people performing the test allowed only three of the people to stay in the room to monitor the results. Charlie could tell these people were highly skilled. Before they performed the test, they spent quite a lot of time telling Charlie about what they were about to do and also warning him about the risks of disclosing the possible findings. Not of their accord, all three had been interviewed by the CIA and would be obtaining information from these tests, which would be stored as classified documents under CIA control. These three individuals had also been informed of Charlie's bloodline oddities and their connections and interwoven details relating to many important events throughout world history.

The doctors were actually scared for Charlie. They feared great harm could come to him if the tests they were about to perform confirmed everything and ended up in the wrong hands. Even if Charlie truly knew the dangers of compromise that could come to him by nefarious individuals if they got their hands on this data, he wouldn't have cared. He was tired of hiding and thought the world would believe what it wanted to and react just the same.

The doctors proceeded to perform their tests flawlessly. They showed Charlie photos of live people with diseases and asked Charlie to point out where these people had low energy associated with reductions of proper circulation. They showed Charlie photos of plants, one of which had been recently poisoned but was not showing any signs of deterioration. They asked Charlie to point to the sick flower. He correctly answered because he could see the low aura associated with the coming death. They also showed Charlie people interviewing others and asked him to point out the liars. Again, he answered without flaw. Charlie amazed the team. He was able to answer the one hundred-plus visual questions perfectly without any mistakes.

Everything was going very well with the tests until they got closer to the conclusion. Charlie told one of the doctors who he had witnessed all day as having a weak aura on his left side to go get tested. The doctor laughed off Charlie's comments. But one of the other doctors heard Charlie's advice and pointed out the aura camera had also clicked off a couple of photos showing the same weak aura. These photos confirmed Charlie's observations, so the doctor stepped out quickly to get further medical tests. That doctor would contact Charlie several days later to report that he had undergone an emergency stint procedure, which very well may have saved his life.

Charlie was quite exhausted after a *long* day and was more than ready to get out of there. He couldn't help feeling relieved about how the test results were finally going to squelch all of the naysayers who had doubted him his entire lifetime for one reason or another. He could only smile to himself because he would be able to rub these results in their faces once and for all. What a great time this would be.

At the close of the testing and to his surprise, in walked Charlie's old friend from the CIA who now introduced to both Charlie and his wife what they could and could not do with the information they possessed. Charlie was now and would always be considered classified and owned by the US government. Charlie was disappointed as he realized there could never be any discussion of these or other similar events or he would be considered a security risk. Charlie would then most likely be taken away without trace to protect the United States. The agent also stated the two should always understand that wherever they traveled, whether in the

United States or abroad, they should always understand they were being tracked. The information he shared was not given as a threat and was, in fact, conveyed to help them both better understand that agents would always be there to protect US security as well as the young couple.

Shocked is the best word to describe Charlie's and his wife's emotions at that point. Charlie had dealt with the CIA years ago and was afraid of them but failed to ever mention any of his past dealings with them to his wife. In a million years, he never would have thought that the tests his wife had set up for him on this day would lead to this. Not only was he implicated in this mess with the government, but now his wife was too. He felt like hell to say the least.

With that not-so-fun news, Charlie and Sheila felt maybe a little vacation would be good. They could simply disappear as best as possible for a while and let everything die down and then return. So, the couple booked a flight to Europe without telling anyone. They knew they would surely be tracked but didn't much care at that point. They simply needed some peace and quiet.

They would stay away for a couple of months, travel around, and just have some fun and see some of the sights. After all, they had both wanted to see some of the places they had learned about with Charlie's Benjamin lineage over the past few months. So what the hell. This seemed like the best excuse. Plus, no one in Europe would know who they were. Things would be very uneventful for a change.

Final Chapter

Reclaiming the Throne

U pon their arrival in London, Charlie and his wife set down their bags while getting their rental car. As soon as their bags were out of their hands, two men grabbed them and ran to a waiting car where the men and the bags were gone in a flash. A second car immediately sped away from the curb, following them as a man ran behind them yelling something they couldn't make out. The couple was speechless.

With all of the travel situations Charlie had been through in the past he thought, *Here we go again. Why do they always have to come after my bags? If they have questions, then why not just talk with me directly?* He thought about his poor suitcase being held against its will, tied down by ropes, its little roller wheels duct taped so no one could hear the squeaking, all alone somewhere having the belongings removed from its inner cavities as it lay their helplessly.

As a child, Charlie had never viewed the world through paranoid eyes, but after being faced with such things happening so many times, Charlie started to view the world differently. He and his wife made their way to the car rental office and stood in line, trying to ignore the chaos that had just taken place outside.

Everyone in the car rental office stared at Charlie and his wife until the *bang, bang* of obvious gunshots broke everyone's concentration for a brief moment, causing them to lurch forward. Charlie looked out the window but couldn't see anything. Everyone in the rental car facility would again fasten their focus on the couple. Charlie, thankfully, still had his wallet and gave all the necessary identification to get their rental car. They were not happy about losing their luggage but knew they could simply replace the stolen clothing and toiletries.

Instinct is to respond nervously to a very confusing situation. As time goes on and events continue to progress, confusion and nervousness is replaced with anger due to the pain in the ass and inconveniences that came out of the government's actions.

After entering a new country with no luggage, no clean clothes, no toothpaste, and no shaving kit but well stocked with hunger from being trapped in a plane for the past fourteen hours, the couple decided the best thing would be for them to find a nice place to get some dinner. Charlie guessed that once they got to their hotel, their luggage would be waiting for them as though nothing had ever happened. That was what had always happened to him in the past.

The gunshots were very different this time, however, so he couldn't be 100 percent positive his luggage would make it. Still, he felt there were good odds. Having dealt with the effects of paranoia over the years, Charlie learned that even paranoid government agencies and their processes are very orderly and have normalized systems. Charlie learned to just allow the government process to take its normal course of action instead of fighting it or even spending time trying to figure things out.

In the beginning, he used to go to the airline's missing luggage claim desks and let them know his luggage had not arrived. They would look in their computers to locate the missing bags only to find absolutely nothing listed. They could never find a relationship between his baggage claim tickets and any records in their computer locator system. Within minutes, TSA officials would arrive, escort Charlie away from the ticket counter, and assure him they had located his luggage and it would arrive at his hotel room shortly. They were correct. The luggage always did arrive as promised.

The standard shipment process included a hotel bellhop who had been tipped by someone to actually deliver his bags. The funny thing about his conversations with the TSA was they always assured him his luggage would arrive at the hotel. Charlie purposely made a point to never tell them where he was staying during his travels. Yet, his bags always knew where to go. The only thing he felt bad about this time was he feared someone was just shot stealing bags that truly only contained clothes and bathroom supplies.

Well, here they were, in the inner circle of London, which is unarguably one of the most active cities in the world. Life without ever having the pleasure of visiting London's city center and walking the streets, visiting stores, dining in restaurants, and drinking in pubs is a life not lived. London is one of the greatest cultural cities in the world. The city has always celebrated its rich royal history and their cultural significance. Their royal families have always promoted enchanting symphonies, theatrical excellence, educational superiority, ornate architecture, religious dynamics, and, of course, world expansion of these positive traits by creating cultural dominance.

London's inner-city circle captures this dominance by tying everything together with its great parks, glowing buildings, warm inner shops, and cobblestone streets. Bustling crowds converge throughout the city as though they were all electrically connected like a live performance acting in perfect harmony as though written and performed by Beethoven or Mozart himself.

So here they were in the crossroads of the world's finest cultural city, and within ten minutes of their arrival, their bags were stolen. Someone, or multiple people, had possibly been shot, and obviously someone from the CIA or some other agency or agencies were following them. Yup, this would be a peaceful vacation.

With all that had happened since their arrival to the city, they tried to put all of the issues out of their minds and settle in for a nice meal to get better adjusted to their new surroundings. During dinner, the couple started talking about all of the times Charlie's differences had created interest in him, leading to havoc and disruptions by others. They discussed the pressure of years of harassment and all the times he and his family had to fear harassment or even worry about whether they would be bothered even when nothing transpired at all. It was this thought of constantly looking over their shoulders that worried the couple the most. They knew it would never end. Their lives would never be the same again … unless they took control.

Charlie asked Sheila to not talk openly about ideas because he had now had a healthy paranoia about being listened to by their followers and didn't want to tip them off. Also, because Charlie had many dealings with these people in the past, he had an idea how they worked. He wanted the chance to think quietly about some ideas that were already floating around his mind about how the two could get out from under the grips of these circumstances.

Reflecting on all of the harassment his family had endured over the years and wanting it to stop, Charlie couldn't get it out of his head how London would make a great cover for him to trick the government into finally leaving him and his wife alone once and for all.

Charlie and Sheila were staying at the Ritz Hotel London, which gave them great proximity to Buckingham Palace, Hyde Park, the inner-city area, the subway, and the US Embassy, which would all prove helpful for his plan to work. All they needed was some extra time, which Charlie hoped his plan would give them. With that, they ordered dinner and quietly enjoyed their meals. When they went back to their room, they discovered their luggage had magically reappeared. And so, the couple went to bed.

Charlie whispered to his wife that he had a plan and needed her to trust him. He told her to sleep with her clothes on, leave the television on, and not take anything out of their luggage or even touch their bags. He walked to their outer window and opened it enough to crawl out. He then quietly picked the inner room door separating their room from the next room over. Luckily for them, the room was rented. It had clothes in the closet and was currently unoccupied. Charlie figured the people were surely out enjoying this great city.

Charlie then dialed London's MI6 and pretended to be a CIA agent. He reported the couple had escaped out the window and were en route to Scotland Yard for unknown reasons. He then pulled the SIM cards from their phones and flushed them down the toilet. He suspected the agencies were both very well aware of their presence in London. He knew if he was correct, they would be smashing in their hotel door at any minute. He also knew they probably had tracked their phones, and flushing the SIM cards down the toilet would cause their followers to believe they somehow escaped through the building's sewer system.

Charlie and his wife then closed the door in the neighboring room and waited quietly. Within mere seconds, they heard a forceful knock at the door, and when no one responded, the sound of the door being forced made a loud crash. The couple heard American voices shout out that the couple was gone.

The plan had worked so far. To prepare a news event to clear up the secrets once and for all and ensure the world would meet Charlie and hear his story, Charlie had called several news agencies and scheduled a news event prior to flushing the SIM cards. To guarantee the news teams showed up, Charlie had also sent out his lineage records via his smartphone to the four top London news agencies, as well as to the three top news agencies back home in New York City.

The lineage records confirmed his bloodline back to the Benjamin Tribe and outlined everyone along the way. He also let the news agencies know he would arrive at Buckingham Palace at exactly midnight to reveal an incredible historical secret that could and would be proven. The current monarchy, he added, thought the secret had been forever hidden since the War of the Roses. On this night, the secret would finally be told.

Charlie knew they only had minutes and would have to move fast. The next facet of Charlie's plan had already moved into action. It would be a diversion. Knowing they didn't have much time to work, he immediately used the phone in the unoccupied room to call several other secret intelligence agencies that had harassed him through the years. He explained that an important announcement would be made at midnight at Scotland Yard. He actually enjoyed calling the teams that had tracked him, threatened him, tried to trick him, or attempted to kill him over the years to set up a meeting he knew they would attend while he would not. He called France's Directorate General for External Security; Russia's Federal Security Bureau, which is the main successor agency of the Soviet-era Cheka, NKVD; and the KGB. He also called Germany's Bundesnachrichtendienst, the foreign intelligence agency of the German government, the UK's MI6 group, and, of course, the mother of all intelligence organizations: the CIA.

If this plan failed, no one would ever hear from Charlie and his wife again, and the couple would simply disappear into obscurity along with all of the knowledge, secrets of Charlie's lineage, and odd powers he possessed. If there really was a covenant between the Benjamin Tribe and God, surely tonight would prove it was real as Charlie and his wife knew this night would require intense holy intervention if it were to work out.

The couple had all of the intelligence organizations going to a wrong address, and when they arrived to attend a nonevent, they would be less than happy. They would also most likely figure out the real meeting would be taking place at Buckingham Palace after hearing chatter from the news teams heading there. Surely, they would conclude the intent of that meeting. Because of these facts, the couple would have to find a way to sneak into the news event, hopefully as millions of people watched on television, and they would have to do this completely undetected.

Everyone would be attending one party or another. They just had to figure out how to get to the right one. Knowing the stakes were high, the couple joked with each other, repeating a line they had heard from an old cartoon where the main character said, "It's a good day to die!" and off they went ready to play the game.

The couple secretly listened to the agents on the other side of the wall as they commented about the open window and discussed how the couple was on their way to the Scotland Yard meeting that clogged their radios. The agents then quickly scurried out the door. The couple forever borrowed some of the clothing from the room they currently occupied along with some perfect necessities, such as scarfs, hats, and gloves, and casually left the hotel. As they walked out of their hotel into the darkness, they knew this night would be like no other they had ever experienced.

The distance from the Ritz to the palace was only a half mile; however, on this evening, the journey would take a couple of extra turns. They only had two hours if they were going to make their scheduled visit on the news in time and hopefully alive.

As they scuttled out the door, they saw the intense glow of flashing lights as though the whole city was suddenly ablaze with police in search of the couple. They guessed their route to the palace would be watched as information became available about the released news of Charlie's lineage and the assumed threat it posed against the royal monarchy.

The couple decided the best way to get out of the immediate line of danger would be to hop on the underground going away from the palace, as no one would suspect that. They could think of a solution to their desperate situation once there.

They knew Charlie's smart-ass escaping game would really initiate the authorities and the city would be alive and bustling in search of the couple. Luckily for them, they had carried enough cash to avoid using their credit cards and having their movement tracked.

Once out of the inner circle of London, Charlie and Sheila found a person willing to let them use his cell phone to call the US Embassy. They convinced the person on the other end of the phone to meet them at the north end of Hyde Park. From there, they would climb into the trunk of a borrowed police car that the embassy person would ask his police buddies to provide. The car would then take them to the entrance of the palace to make their appearance. They just had to make it to the meeting place without being discovered.

The stranger from whom they borrowed the phone had a brother who was a cab driver, and after hearing the couple's story, he agreed to help. He called his brother, who agreed to pick them up and drop them off at the rendezvous. On the way to the park, the couple sat quietly as they made their way through the night. Police were everywhere looking for the unknown suspects.

The couple and their driver remained quiet. Their hearts raced. With so many strangers involved, they weren't sure if everyone could be trusted or if they would make it to their destination unscathed. The couple sat low in their seats and simply prayed for a peaceful outcome.

Once at their destination, they found the awaiting police car and hoped it was the right one as they approached it. Upon finding that the car was indeed the one they had hoped for, the driver popped open the trunk, and they quickly climbed in. The ride from the park to the palace was only several blocks, but it felt like hours as the two lay paralyzed in fear they would be captured. They had let go of all control and hoped the driver would be honest and get them to their destination alive.

Charlie knew that in times of great duress, people's minds quickly shop through all the different scenarios but will generally point them to the right conclusion if they are able to listen to themselves. This time, though, their minds kept trying to fill them with doubt and kept telling them only one thing: "You're done for."

Suddenly, the car stopped and stood motionless for several minutes. Finally, the trunk opened, letting in the coolest breeze of fresh air the couple had ever experienced.

"Come on, guys. Hurry up before you are spotted," said the driver.

With that, the couple quickly and quietly escaped the trunk's confines to an awaiting news audience. The driver had performed his mission, and the rest was up to Charlie and Sheila.

Charlie grabbed Sheila's hand and said, "Come on—over there." He pointed toward the direction they needed to go.

They made their way to the awaiting steps of the palace. As they stood there waiting for the barrage of reporters to get into position, Charlie recognized many of the secret authorities who started to make their way to their positions. Just as the authorities were about to reach them, the news cameras instantly lit up the night to that of high noon, and the authorities instinctively faded back into the crowd and out of sight.

It seemed like a thousand questions came in all at once. Charlie's contacts had done a great job getting enough of the story out to the news agencies so that it created a huge media buzz. The couple immediately presented their story. Armed with the lineage information Charlie had sent them earlier, the couple's story presented itself to the awaiting world equipped with all the necessary facts to confirm everything. From that point, the audience was able to make up their own minds.

Charlie and Sheila were now famous, and their story had reached the world. Their story would no longer be a secret, successfully ending the danger that had dogged Charlie his entire life and that had threatened him and Sheila and Charlie's whole family only moments ago.

Visions of Charlie's forefathers flashed through his mind. He heard William the Conqueror himself encourage him along to tell his story. When they finally made it to their destination, Charlie stood in awe. He didn't have any prepared words or a speech ready for the moment and wasn't at all sure what he was going to say, but the words flowed out of his body as though what he was saying had been written and rehearsed for a thousand years.

As the couple stood with microphones in their faces, they knew their lives would be different forever. The world would have a million questions, as history would now be corrected. The couple who moments before had been obscure figures would now be forever infamous. But most importantly, they would now be safe and free from the games. Thinking about this made them both very happy. With reporters' questions, camera lights, and flashing bulbs going off all around them, they glanced at each other and sneaked loving, happy smiles.

Charlie's information and presentation placed factual evidence describing how the Jewish Tribe of Benjamin swept across Europe guided by God's covenant and opened this covenant to all people with the introduction and ultimate spread of Christianity from individuals rooted in the same tribe. The Jewish-Christian covenant from God would continue across the ocean and reach the shores of what would become America. These same values that changed the world an ocean apart would go on to guide one of the greatest nations the world had ever witnessed.

Charlie went on to explain how his bloodline was shared by many people around the world. In fact, this bloodline could become connected to others not because of a list of relatives but because of who they were inside and how they acted in life. The bloodline was created and opened as a result of God's covenant with man, not man's covenant with God. Any man-made bloodline claims or ruling claims resulting from fear or greed did not give true direction. Those claims were man-made, corrupt, and devoid of independent fairness. Leadership from man could only come from open appointments elected by the people. All dictatorial leadership without approval and appointment through open voting was false and couldn't be trusted or followed.

As Charlie finished his speech, the crowd stood silent, in shock from what they had just heard and witnessed. Charlie thought this was surely the end for him, but the crowd, knowing what had just transpired, realized the real king had just returned home. Almost like watching dominos fall, the crowd quietly started to take a knee and bow in respect.

Instead of being the end for Charlie, it was just the beginning. In tow with several embassy members and a consortium of police and other officials, Charlie and Sheila turned toward the palace to take their final steps to the grand entry.

Before being shuffled toward the palace gate, Charlie caught a glimpse of his old buddy from the CIA. He gave Charlie a respectful wink and nod before stepping back into the crowd. At that moment, the cathedral chimed: *bong, bong, bong, bong, bong, bong, bong, bong, bong, bong, bong, bong.*

Their hour had arrived as the two made their way to their final destination. Their legs seemed to weigh a ton, and they moved slowly, almost frozen in place as they made their way over the last several feet of walkway.

Armed with his confirmed pedigree and confirmation from the US,

English, French, and Israeli governments and further authenticated by the Catholic Church under an oath of secrecy, Charlie approached the house that his heir had built more than a thousand years before—his rightful home.

What would he say to them? The current royal occupants, knowing Charlie's facts to be true and knowing their usurped lineage originated out of a false line with a history of manipulation and cover-ups through periods of dissolution, had spent the past few decades trying to disperse themselves back into acceptance with average citizens through means of marriages and bloodlines from offspring. The citizens would soon come to also know the truth.